TERRI BLACKSTOCK

"Justice may be blind but that doesn't keep it from facing mortal danger. In *Aftermath*, expert storyteller Terri Blackstock ratchets up the suspense in a novel that delivers on every level. Conflicts rage and loyalties are tested to the ultimate limit. Set aside plenty of time when you pick up this book—you'll not to want to take a break."

—Robert Whitlow, bestselling author of *Trial and Error*

"In *Aftermath*, Terri Blackstock plumbs the depth of human emotion in the face of devastating tragedy, grief, and loss. Yet, she still manages to give readers her trademark suspenseful story, sweet romance, and hope for the future. From gut-wrenching scenes in a cancer patient's hospital room to seeing the world through the eyes of a young woman with a debilitating mental health disorder, Blackstock pulls no punches about human frailties. Does the end justify the means? Romantic suspense lovers won't want to miss *Aftermath*."

—Kelly Irvin, bestselling author of *Closer Than She Knows*

"Plot twists and likable characters light up this latest romantic suspense from bestselling author Blackstock. Themes of redemption and grace mark this love story that will be a hit among fans of Christian fiction and clean romantic suspense."

—*Library Journal* for *Smoke Screen*

"Blackstock's intense and twisty story will please fans of her faith-grounded crime dramas."

—*Publishers Weekly* for *Smoke Screen*

"Wow   y favorite
author   ne sitting
simply   iver a plot

"*If I Live* is a grabber from page one, delivering an exhilarating mix of chase, mystery, and spiritual truth. Longtime Blackstock fans will be delighted, and new Blackstock fans will be made."

—James Scott Bell, bestselling author
of the Mike Romeo thrillers

"Emotions, tensions, and suspense all run high in this fast-paced, edge-of-your-seat thriller."

—RT Book Reviews, 4¹/2 stars, TOP PICK! for *If I'm Found*

"Crisp dialogue and unexpected twists make this compulsive reading, and a final chapter cliffhanger leaves things poised for a sequel."

—*Publishers Weekly* for *If I Run*

"A fast-paced, thoroughly mesmerizing thriller . . . An enthralling read with an entirely unexpected conclusion makes the reader question if a sequel could be in the works."

—NY Journal of Books for *If I Run*

"Few writers do mystery/suspense better than Terri Blackstock, so I leaped at the opportunity to read her latest . . . Needless to say, when Book Two comes out, there will be no 'if' about it. I'll run to get in line."

—Love & Faith in Fiction for *If I Run*

"*If I Run* is a gripping suspense novel. Both of the central characters are very appealing, engaging the reader . . . The tension is palpable throughout and doesn't let up until the very end . . . Highly recommended."

—Mysterious Reviews

"A story rich with texture and suspense, this family murder mystery unfolds with fast pacing, a creepy clown murder suspect, and threatening blog visitor to boot."

—*Publishers Weekly* for *Truth Stained Lies*

Books by Terri Blackstock

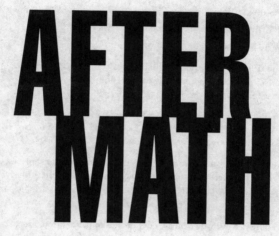

TERRI
BLACKSTOCK

THOMAS NELSON
Since 1798

Published in Nashville, Tennessee, by Thomas Nelson. Thomas Nelson is a registered trademark of HarperCollins Christian Publishing, Inc.

Interior design by Emily Ghattas

Thomas Nelson titles may be purchased in bulk for educational, business, fundraising, or sales promotional use. For information, please email SpecialMarkets@ThomasNelson.com.

Library of Congress Cataloging-in-Publication Data

Names: Blackstock, Terri, 1957- author.
Title: Aftermath / Terri Blackstock.
Description: Nashville, Tennessee : Thomas Nelson, 2021. | Summary: "A childhood friend and the faith she taught him got Dustin through his childhood. But friendship might be what destroys him now, and his faith is slipping away"-- Provided by publisher.
Identifiers: LCCN 2020051061 (print) | LCCN 2020051062 (ebook) | ISBN 9780310345978 (paperback) | ISBN 9780310348580 (library binding) | ISBN 9780310348566 (epub) | ISBN 9780785237501
Subjects: GSAFD: Christian fiction.
Classification: LCC PS3552.L34285 A69 2021 (print) | LCC PS3552.L34285 (ebook) | DDC 813/.54--dc23
LC record available at https://lccn.loc.gov/2020051061
LC ebook record available at https://lccn.loc.gov/2020051062

This book is lovingly dedicated
to the Nazarene.

Taylor Reid's phone flashed as she snapped the selfie with her two friends, their heads touching and their backs to the stage. The shot from the third row, with the lead singer in the background and the three of them in the foreground, was perfect. No one would believe their seats were so close.

They turned around to face the band, dancing to the beat of the song they'd been listening to in the car on the way to Trudeau Hall.

Taylor quickly posted the pic, typing, "Ed Loran targets nonpoliticals for his rally with band Blue Fire. Worked on us!"

She put her phone on videotape and zoomed onto the stage.

"I don't want it to end!" Desiree said in her ear.

"Me either!" Taylor yelled over the music.

"Maybe they'll play again after his speech," Mara shouted.

The song came to an end, and the crowd went crazy, begging for one more song before the band left the stage.

But an amplified voice filled the auditorium, cutting off the adulation. "Ladies and gentlemen, please welcome the next president of the United States, Ed Loran!"

The crowd sounded less enthusiastic as the band left the stage and Ed Loran, the Libertarian celebrity magnet, made his entrance. Taylor kept cheering and clapping, letting her enthusiasm for the band segue to him.

It happened just as the candidate took the stage. The deafening sound, like some confusing combination of gunshot and lightning bolt, a blast that blacked out the lights and knocked her to the ground. Smoke mushroomed. Screams crescendoed—shrieks of terror, wailing pain, shocking anguish . . . then sudden, gentle silence, as if she were underwater. A loud ringing in her ears filled the void.

She peered under the seats, choking for breath as dimmer lights flickered through the smoke. Even from here, she could see the fallout of whatever had happened. Blood pooling on the ground, people hunkering down as she was, feet running . . . What was happening? An explosion? A crash? She looked around and couldn't see her friends.

She clawed her way up and looked over the seat. Smoke and fire billowed from the stage into the crowd, and heat wafted over her like some living force invading the room. Muffled, muted sounds competed with the ringing.

Get out! Now! She dropped back down and crawled under two rows of seats until she came to someone limp on the floor. She felt herself scream but couldn't hear her own voice. Scrambling to her feet, she went to her left to get to the aisle, but her foot slipped on something wet. She grabbed the seat next to her to steady herself, then launched into the frantic crowd in the aisle. The room seemed to spin, people whizzing by, people under her, people above her, people broken and ripped and still . . . She stepped and fell, crawled and ran, tripped and kicked her way to the bottlenecked doorway, then fought her way through it.

The ringing in her ears faded as she tumbled downstairs, almost falling into the lobby below. The sound of crying, coughing, wretching, and the roaring sound of pounding feet turned up as if some divine finger had fiddled with the volume.

She set her sights on the glass doors to the outside and pushed forward, moving through people and past the security stations they'd stopped at on the way in. She made it to the door and burst out into the sunlight.

Fresh, cool air hit her like freedom, but at first her lungs rejected it like some poison meant to stop her. At the bottom of the steps, on the sidewalk, she bent over and coughed until she could breathe.

After a moment, the crowd pushed her along toward the parking garage until she remembered that her car wasn't there. She had parked on the street, blocks away. She forced her way out of the flow of people and ran a block south. Where was it?

She turned the corner. Her car was here, on this block. Near the Atlanta Trust Bank. Wasn't it? Or was it the next block?

Sweat slicked her skin until she found her silver Accord. There!

She ran to it and pulled her keys out of her pocket, wishing she hadn't lost the key fob. Her hands trembled as she stuck the key into the passenger side lock and got the door open. She slipped inside on the driver's side, locked it behind her. Instinctively, she slid down, her head hidden as if someone were coming after her.

What just happened?

One minute they'd been taking selfies and videotaping the band, and the next they were on the floor . . .

Where were Mara and Desiree? She hadn't even looked for them! Should she go back for them?

No, that would be insane. She could smell the smoke and fire from here. They would know to come to the car when they got out.

Call the police!

She tried to steady her hands as she swiped her phone on.

"911, what is your—"

"An explosion!" she cut in, her voice hoarse. "At the Ed Loran rally at Trudeau Hall!"

"Where are you now?" the woman asked in a voice that was robotically calm.

"I got out. There's fire . . . People are still in there. Please send ambulances!"

"Ma'am, did you see what exploded?"

"No . . . the stage area, I think. I don't know where my friends are. Please . . . hurry!"

"We've already dispatched the fire department and police, ma'am."

She heard sirens from a few blocks away and cut off the call. She raised up, looking over the dashboard for the flashing lights. She couldn't see any, but the sirens grew louder.

She knelt on the floorboard, her knees on her floormat and her elbows on her seat, and texted Desiree.

I'm at the car. Where are you?

No answer. She switched to a recent thread with Mara and texted again.

Got out. At car waiting. Where are you?

Nothing.

She dictated a group text to both of them.

Are you all right?

They were probably running or deaf, fighting their way out like she had. She tried calling them, but Mara's phone rang to voicemail. When Desiree's phone did the same, she yelled, "Call me! I'm waiting at the car and I'm scared. Where are you?" She was sobbing when she ended the call.

Hunkering on the floor was irrational. She knew that, but it didn't change her fear. Some enemy lurked just out of sight, an airplane dropping bombs, an army shooting missiles, anarchists just getting started. What if there was more?

She peeked over the dash again. A few more people ran past to their cars parked on the curb near her. She slid back up onto the seat, still slumped down so she wasn't visible, and started videotaping with her phone. She would want to process this later, document it, post it to social media, compare notes. She would want to have video of that moment when Mara and Desiree made it to the car.

But they didn't.

She stayed hunched in the car as two guys in Ed Loran T-shirts came up the block from behind her, got into the car in front of her, and pulled out. A car across the street pulled away from the curb and did a U-turn.

Maybe she should move her car, but what if her friends expected it to be at the landmark in front of that bank? She should wait.

As time passed without another incident, she sat up more fully, jittering as she waited for them to come. She called them a dozen times each, at least, sent multiple texts.

Finally she stopped as certainty crushed her like a lead blanket. They were still in there. She hadn't seen them because they were probably on the floor. Why hadn't she looked for them? How could she have left them?

She had only thought of herself, only followed the instinct to survive. She hadn't given one thought to helping her friends.

Eventually her impatience gave way to boldness. She got out of the car, leaving it unlocked in case they came back, and on legs that felt too weak and tired to hold her up, she trod up the block the way she had come.

She had to find them. It wasn't too late to do the right thing.

02

The wail of the siren behind him drew Dustin Webb's eyes to his rearview mirror, and in the setting sunlight he could see that the car urging him to pull over was not a squad car, but an unmarked Ford with a flashing light on the dash.

He was driving the speed limit on the interstate—why was he being pulled over? He moved to the right lane and negotiated an exit from I-20, onto an Atlanta street that was almost as busy. The car followed him, its siren still blaring.

"I wasn't speeding!" he yelled to his rearview mirror. He found a parking lot about a mile from the interstate and pulled off the road. The Ford followed him to a halt. Not disguising his irritation, Dustin opened his door to get out.

"Sir, stay in the car and put your hands on the wheel."

Dustin looked back. There were two of them in plain clothes, and both had weapons drawn. Was this a robbery?

"I need some identification," Dustin called through the door as they moved closer.

"Hands on the steering wheel!" one of the men yelled again. In his rearview mirror, Dustin saw that a police cruiser had pulled in behind them. Two uniformed cops joined the other two men, their weapons drawn, too.

Four weapons pointed at his head? "What's going on?" he yelled. "What did I do?"

Two more police cars approached, one pulling in front of him, another stopping next to him, blocking him in. The cops inside joined the others, all with guns drawn.

"This has got to be a mistake!" Dustin shouted.

"Slowly exit the car with your hands above your head!"

Dustin slid out, keeping his hands in the air.

"On the ground, facedown!"

He lowered to his knees, then to his hands and his stomach.

They descended on him, zip tying his hands behind him, frisking him and taking out his wallet and his phone. When they seemed satisfied that he wasn't armed, they yanked him to his feet.

The one who'd pulled him over showed Dustin his badge. He was a special agent with Alcohol, Tobacco, and Firearms. "Mr. Webb, I'm Special Agent Halsey. We had an anonymous tip this morning about what's in your trunk."

"Anonymous tip?" Dustin repeated, incredulous. "Wait a minute." He took a step backward as a familiar sense of injustice he hadn't felt in years constricted his lungs, and he swallowed to combat the sudden dryness in his throat. "There's nothing in my trunk. My gym bag, some tools . . ." They had the wrong guy. Any minute now they would realize it. Any second . . .

"We need to search your vehicle," Halsey said.

"Do you have a warrant?" Dustin asked.

"We have one on the way."

"On the way? What is this?" This would drag out longer if they waited for it, and Dustin didn't want that. He had nothing to hide. "Just go ahead. Search it. There's nothing."

He stood near the rear of the car, watching as they took his key fob out of his pocket and unlocked his trunk.

The trunk came open, and there was his gym bag with his sweaty clothes from when he had worked out days ago.

But something wasn't right. There were other things in the trunk, things he hadn't put there. Boxes he'd never seen before. "What is that?" he asked.

"Back away, everybody," Halsey yelled. "Get the render-safe team here."

Dustin knew what that meant. In the army, he'd served in the Ordnance Corps and had been on a bomb diagnostic team himself, whenever there was a bomb or mine threat. Halsey grabbed him and walked him to the squad car in front of his car and opened the back door. Dustin knew better than to resist, so he bent and got in. They closed him in, and officers stood guard at his door. He turned around and strained to see through the rear window. What were those boxes?

There were more cops showing up now. He looked at their T-shirts and the markings on their uniforms. This was a multi-agency effort. What was going on? They had closed off the road, with police cars blocking all lanes on both sides. A German shepherd on a leash barked and lunged at Dustin's car as someone in an ATF shirt walked the dog closer.

This was the Twilight Zone. He couldn't have been more confused if he'd been on a three-day bender, but he hadn't had a drink since he got out of the army.

He started to sweat, and his heartbeat sped up to a fight-or-flight tempo. He needed help. He laid his head back on the seat, closed his eyes, and prayed that whatever this was, they'd realize he wasn't to blame. The last time he'd looked in his trunk, he'd only had that gym bag, a set of jumper cables, maybe a flashlight. Someone had planted something in his trunk, something that required the ordnance people to identify or detonate, then they'd called and tipped off the police.

Reality hit him now with full force. His stomach roiled and his head began to ache. Someone had set him up. He was in a lot of trouble, and he didn't even know why.

03

Jamie Powell stepped up to the microphones attached to the makeshift dais on the courthouse steps. Wind whipped her hair, blonde strands slashing across her face, making her wish she had worn it up today. She tried not to touch it during her statement, but now she swept it back so it at least wouldn't stick to her lips.

Her client, Martin Ash—clad in a pinstriped suit that made him look like a caricature of himself—stood behind her, beaming like a lottery winner. His charges would have given him a maximum of twenty-five years in prison, but the acquittal just announced would allow him to walk free.

"Ms. Powell, did you expect the acquittal from the jury?" a reporter from the *Atlanta Journal Constitution* yelled.

Jamie leaned toward the microphones. "Whenever a jury is out for three days, you don't know exactly what they're going to bring back, but we did have some early indications based on the questions they sent to the judge."

"What was your strategy going into this trial?" a CBS network correspondent asked.

Jamie looked back over her shoulder to John Brackton, the partner in her firm who was spearheading this case. He hadn't had much to do with it day to day—it had been Jamie's show. But she still had to defer to him since he was the lead attorney. He was already stepping forward.

Just as he began to speak about the strategy that she had implemented in the courtroom, Jamie felt her phone vibrating in her pocket. She ignored it and kept her eyes on her boss, tracking everything he said, in case she needed to clarify anything.

All at once, phones chimed, buzzed, and chirped. One by one, the reporters turned their attention from John to their phones. One reporter turned and whispered to his cameraman, then pushed back through the crowd to leave. The cameraman lowered his camera, shoved his way up front, unclasped his microphone from the cluster on the dais while John was still talking, and ran down the steps. Briefly distracted, John stumbled on his words but tried to go on. "So we were able to show the jury exactly what the truth was . . ."

Other members of the media pushed forward and unclipped their mikes as John droned on. "The plaintiff complained of irregularities, but . . ."

A siren blared as a police car sped by on the road in front of them, followed by fire trucks. It was as if there was a conspiracy to keep this press conference from happening.

Jamie watched one cameraman run to the curb. His network van pulled up, and he jumped in. It screeched off.

John paused in his bluster as the rest of the media began to abandon them. He looked at her. "What's happening?"

"No idea." She grabbed the last person removing his mike. "Tell me what happened. What text did you all get?"

"An explosion or something over at Trudeau Hall."

Only then did it register—the smell of smoke wafting on the air. The sirens got louder again as ambulances tore past.

Trudeau Hall was downtown, just a few blocks north of here. She looked in that direction and saw a foggy drift of smoke hovering in the air.

"I thought I was going to get to speak," her client whined.

"I thought you were, too," she said, "but the press was already breaking up. A bigger story to cover."

"I want my name cleared," he said. "I need to get on TV to prove my innocence."

"We'll see if we can get you an interview tonight," she said. "It'll be even better than an impromptu press conference. For now, just go home and enjoy your freedom. It's all over."

Martin reluctantly went back to where his wife was waiting with his family. Jamie swiped through her phone, looking for more news about what was happening less than a mile away.

"Let's get to the office before they start blockading the streets," John said, and she followed him down the steps and out to the parking lot.

From here, they could see more smoke up the street and people running from the direction of the concert hall.

"I'll see if I can find out more about what happened," John said as he got into her passenger seat.

She put her briefcase in the back seat of her Lexus and slid in behind the wheel. "Couldn't have been too long ago, but I didn't hear anything, did you?"

He didn't look up from his phone. "No, nothing. Maybe it was while we were still inside."

She turned on the radio and switched it to a local FM station. An announcer was talking rapid-fire.

". . . Trudeau Hall, where Ed Loran was holding a political rally. The place was full, and people have been calling in and telling us that they heard an explosion from the front of the room. We're told there were many fatalities. First responders are on the scene. We're trying to get information right now about where family members can get word about their loved ones. Stay tuned, and we'll keep you updated as we learn more."

Her stomach sank as she thought about the mayhem that must be happening in that building right now. *Please, God, take care of those who are still alive . . .*

John cursed. "You can't go that way. Turn right here."

She whipped into the right lane and barely made the turn that took them farther from the concert hall. But traffic was nearly at a standstill there, too, as more ambulances sirened through.

John's phone rang, and he put it to his ear. "John Brackton."

As he talked, Jamie's mind raced. An explosion in a crowded concert hall? Loran was popular, but the band who played at his rally today was even more popular. The crowd was probably young. How many of them had died? What must their families be going through? Were there people still trapped, in need of rescue?

Suddenly she wanted to get to her mother's house, pick up Avery, and hold the seven-year-old tight until she complained. She wanted to smell her daughter's hair and savor her safety.

It took twenty minutes to get five miles back to her office. They were almost to the firm's parking garage when Jamie's phone rang. She checked it. It was a line at the city jail.

"I have to take this," she told John, who was still on the phone. "I can let you out here if you want."

He nodded and got out, still talking on the phone, and disappeared through the front door.

Jamie swiped the phone on as she pulled into the parking garage. "Jamie Powell."

"Hey, kiddo."

She couldn't quite place the voice, but it had the warm, nostalgic sound of familiarity. "Who's this?"

"Dustin Webb."

She caught her breath. Of course. That deep, raspy voice, and he was the only one who'd consistently called her kiddo. "Dustin? Why are you calling from the jail?"

"I'm in trouble. I need a lawyer."

She shook her head, as if trying to adjust her brain. "What happened?"

"I was pulled over, and I let them search my car. I had nothing to hide . . . that I knew of."

Her heart jolted. "That you knew of? What did they find?"

"Explosives, apparently."

She drew in a breath and tried to think. Explosives? After a local bombing? This wasn't good. "Dustin, listen to me very carefully. Do not talk to them. Don't say a single word until I get there."

"When can you come?"

"I'm in my car now. I'll be there in a few minutes. But I'm serious, Dustin. No sarcasm, no smart-aleck comebacks, no jokes. Nothing. Tell them you're waiting for your attorney, then don't say another word."

"Got it."

Still holding her phone, she almost ran into a post as she

pulled into a wheelchair space, then backed out of it and turned around. She headed for the exit signs. "Why did they pull you over in the first place?"

"They said they'd gotten a tip. They had a search warrant on the way. I didn't put those boxes in my car. I didn't even know they were there, so I told them to go ahead and search."

She frowned, her mind racing. "Do you know who could have put them there?"

"No idea. I don't know what's going on."

"Okay, not a word, Dustin. I'm on my way."

She navigated her way down the twisting ramp of the parking garage and pulled into traffic, heading toward downtown. This morning when she'd gotten out of bed, she had believed anything could happen today. Martin Ash could be found guilty and be dragged out of the courtroom, providing all the drama that the media had come for. Or he could be found not guilty and set free. But she had never once thought that Dustin Webb might come back into her life.

They hadn't been in touch in the past fifteen years, through no fault of her own. He had ignored all of her letters, her phone calls, and her texts in those first couple of years after he left for boot camp. She had tried to find him on social media, but he wasn't the type to put himself out there like that. Even when her husband died of a drug overdose, he hadn't come to the funeral. He had sent flowers and a card that said he was praying for her. She hadn't even known he prayed. That was the last she had heard from him.

But the end of their relationship didn't negate the beginning, no matter how improbable their friendship had been when it began, when she was nine.

She would never forget the thirteen-year-old boy who'd

moved in with the family next door to her and sat on the porch or bounced a basketball in the driveway for hours a day. She'd heard neighbors talking to her mom about his four foster homes and the fact that his aunt and uncle had finally moved him in with them. She didn't know what a foster home was, or why he wasn't with his parents, but she knew he was lonely. She left him alone since he never looked up at her when she was out playing.

But one day her black Lab puppy dug under the fence and got into his aunt's yard. Dustin captured him and brought the squirming dog back. He found her sitting in the tree in her front yard. "Hey, kiddo, you missing someone?"

"Coco, what are you doing out?" she asked, climbing down. "Thanks for catching him."

"It wasn't easy. He's fast. You know he dug a hole under the fence?"

She dropped to the ground and reached for the dog. He licked Dustin's face. "He likes you. Do you have a dog?"

"Nope. Never have. Aunt Pat is allergic."

"She had one before her son went to college. He took him with him."

"Figures." His face changed. "Anyway, if he comes over again, I'll bring him back."

As he started to walk away, she called out, "Is your name Dustin?"

"Yeah," he said, turning around.

"Mine's Jamie."

"Good to know."

"Do you like it here?"

He gave her a half-amused smile, then said, "It's okay."

"What's a foster home?" she asked.

He looked around, as if to see if anyone could hear, then came back closer to her. "How did you know that?"

"I don't know. I guess I heard somebody say it."

"Look it up."

"I did. Is it like when you live with strangers?"

He grinned again. "Something like that."

"How come you lived with them?"

"Because my parents died."

"I'm sorry," she said. "I didn't know that. I didn't mean to—"

"It's okay," he cut in. "Car wreck, a long time ago."

"Do you like living with your aunt?"

"She doesn't like living with me."

"How do you know?"

"You ask a lot of questions, you know that?"

"Yeah, I've been told."

"So how do you get on her good side?"

"Whose?"

"My aunt Pat. If you saw her with her kids, maybe you know better than I do."

"She was nice to them," Jamie said. "She probably just needs some time to get used to you."

"Nobody ever gets used to me," he said.

"I'm going to, now that we're friends."

He smiled fully now, but she knew he was just amused. "Keep thinking that, kiddo. We'll see how you feel in a few months."

She watched him go back to his yard and wondered if he'd ever talk to her again.

But the next day, when he was in the backyard, she yelled at him over the fence. "Hey, Dustin!"

"Hey, kiddo," he said.

She climbed up on a bench beside the fence and looked down at him. "Do you feel better today?"

"I didn't feel bad yesterday."

"You weren't too happy. Did I hurt your feelings?"

"No. I don't get hurt feelings that easy."

"My questions didn't make you mad?"

"Of course not."

"Then can I ask some more?"

He sighed and sat down on a chair at a patio table. "Go for it."

"Do you have a grandma?"

"Both of them died."

She got that feeling again that she was making him mad. "Do you like art?"

He laughed. "Do I like what?"

"Art. Or music? You look like a musician."

"What does a musician look like?"

"I don't know. Kind of cool."

"I look cool."

"I didn't say you did. Just . . . musicians."

"It's okay. I like art and music, I guess."

"Do you play checkers?"

"I have."

"Want to play?"

"Not right now," he said.

"Tomorrow?"

"You're pushy, aren't you?"

"It's not like you have anything to do. It's summer and you just got here, and you don't know anybody."

"Maybe tomorrow," he said.

The memory made her smile now, because they had played

checkers often after that, even though he preferred video games. But her mom wouldn't let her go in his aunt Pat's house, because she liked to keep it just so, and besides, her mother thought he was too old for them to hang out inside each other's houses. So they wound up sitting in the driveway and playing.

Their friendship started out grudgingly on his part, but over the months, he stopped acting like he was just walking by when he happened on her, and he seemed to grow less embarrassed to be caught playing with someone so much younger. He tolerated her questions more and more, and even started questioning her.

They'd remained friends into her teen years and through his college era, through all their dating experiences and relationships. She had relied on him as more than a friend, and he seemed to rely on her as a trusted confidante. That was why his cool departure had been so disruptive, and why his silence since had been so painful.

She hadn't even been aware that he had moved back to Atlanta. Her mother still lived next door to his aunt Pat, and she had never mentioned it.

None of that mattered now, she thought as she zigzagged her way up the outermost streets of downtown Atlanta, trying to avoid the emergency traffic and roadblocks. He needed her now, and she wasn't going to hold those years against him. She had to put all that aside and lean on the professionalism she had fostered over the last years. None of her history with Dustin—finished or unfinished—should affect what she did now.

04

Dustin sat alone in the interview room at the police station, knowing he was being watched via the camera in the corner of the room across from him and through the two-way glass window next to him.

Who would enjoy seeing him pulled over like a criminal and detained for having explosives in his trunk? Who would benefit from that? He couldn't think of anyone in his life right now who would do such a thing, unless it was a prank that had gone wrong. But if it was, the prankster would have called it off long before this.

He shouldn't have called Jamie. Of all people, why had he thought of her? He hadn't even known her phone number, so he'd had to call her mother at her childhood home to get in touch with her. She had given it to him with no apparent reluctance, then tried to strike up a conversation until he'd told her he had to go.

He stood up just because he was tired of sitting and paced the few steps across the small room, trying to imagine how this would play out. Jamie had always thought the best of him when no one else had. As a kid, she'd been one of the only people who was ever glad to see him. Aunt Pat only yelled and complained, and Uncle Joe sat quietly, pretending Dustin wasn't there.

Dustin had gone about his teenaged life wearing boredom like a costume and feigning apathy as a buffer against the accusations that came each day at suppertime. He hadn't picked up his towel after his bath. He hadn't done his Tuesday chores right. He hadn't said "yes, ma'am." After accusing him, Aunt Pat would launch into a monologue about how her own children had never done such things, how they had shown pride in their surroundings and taken responsibility for their actions. Always she mentioned how he'd been thrown out of four other homes. He had learned to zone out somewhere within the first ten words. When he'd started playing the bad boy role for real—skipping school, sneaking out at night, and drinking in the parking lot of the sub shop that stayed open all night—her vitriol had gone to the next level.

He thought back on that kid he had been and wondered why the little girl next door had been able to see through the subterfuge. How would it go now? Had she outgrown that skill to see past his actions and into his soul? Would she look at him now and see only the train wreck of the past couple of hours, as if that represented who he'd been for the past fifteen years?

How could she know that her influence in his life had been more than just friendship at a vulnerable time? There was so much she didn't know—that he'd excelled in the army and that he'd had his own successful business for years. She had no way of knowing about that day when he'd been discharged from the army, and he'd found himself feeling the way he'd felt when he was thirteen, suddenly thrust into a world that didn't fit him. His mind had drifted back to her and he'd longed to talk to her, but she was married to her high school boyfriend, Joe, someone Dustin had tried more than once to warn her against.

His homesickness for Jamie had led him to a church one Sunday night, and he'd found comfort there. The one he chose belonged to her denomination, and the people seemed like her, and he heard familiar words that she had quoted to him often. He'd found himself going back again and again until finally he had his own Bible and had prayed his own prayers, and the words became his, and his faith was owned instead of borrowed.

How ironic that he found himself in jail after all that. How tragic that the first time she would see him in years was when he was in life-altering trouble.

He sat back down and closed his eyes. *God, I know you see me. I know you've got this. I just don't know what's happening.*

He heard voices outside the door and looked at the two-way glass, wishing he could see what was going on out there. Then he heard Jamie's voice, a little deeper than it had been at eighteen, but it still had the same timbre and that satin sound that comforted him.

He got up and waited to see her face.

05

From the corner near her car, Taylor walked slowly toward the concert hall. There it was, strobed by the blue lights flashing on police cars parked haphazardly around it. Ambulances still idled, doors open, their lights punctuating the emergency that had changed so many lives in less than a moment.

Why weren't they hurrying? Surely they hadn't yet loaded and transported all of the injured.

The answer squeezed her heart and stung her eyes. Maybe there was no hurry. The dead couldn't be moved.

Several media people stood on the corner, the microphone-clutching talent glammed and styled. Camera crews pushed as close to the barricades as possible, zooming in on drama they could use on the eleven o'clock news.

Taylor walked past them, her eyes fixed on the doors she and her friends had gone in. Had Mara and Desiree come out and been herded to some other location? Were they wandering in shock, looking for her car? Had they gotten an Uber?

"Excuse me," a reporter said, motioning for her cameraman to follow her. "Are you one of the victims?"

Taylor didn't want to be on TV. "No."

"But you have blood on your pants."

She looked down, stricken at the sight of the blood spatters on her right side. When had that happened? Whose blood was it? Desiree had been sitting to her right . . .

She stumbled off toward the perimeter, wiping her nose as she ran. She ducked under the tape, and a cop the size of a linebacker grabbed her arm. "Ma'am, you can't go any farther. We need you to stay back."

"I have to find my friends! I don't know where they are. They may still be in there."

"Ma'am, were you in the building when it happened?"

She felt her lips twisting as she tried to hold back her sobs. "Yes . . . I got out . . . but my friends . . ."

"What's your name?"

"Taylor," she said, sniffing. "Taylor Reid. I have to find them. I've been waiting at my car, but they never came. I'm worried about them."

"Taylor, where were you sitting at the rally?"

She hugged herself to stop her shivering. She was so cold, but it must be ninety-five degrees here in August. "On the third row, near the front."

"Can you describe what you saw?"

"The stage just . . . exploded. I was on the floor. Is Ed Loran dead? The band? I don't know how they could have survived."

The cop's interest level changed, and he stopped trying to usher her back to the barricade. "Okay, Taylor? I need you to come with me, okay? A detective is going to need to interview you."

She followed him blindly between police cars and ambulances. Maybe her friends were sitting in the ambulances getting bandaged for scraped knees. Maybe they had forgotten where she'd parked the car. She looked inside each vehicle as they passed, but none of the victims inside with sooty faces and shocked stares were her friends.

The officer led her to a group of police who were standing in front of a black van, talking on radios to the officers inside the concert hall, chattering in urgent voices.

"I have a witness here," he called to one of the men in regular clothes. "Detective, this is Taylor Reid. She was sitting on the third row but managed to get out."

The detective looked down at her bloody pants leg. "Taylor, can you come talk to me for a few minutes?"

"Yeah, okay." She followed him to the van. He stepped inside, and she got in and slid across the bench seat.

He sat next to her. "I'm Detective Borden," he said. "Can I get you some water?"

She suddenly realized how thirsty she was. "Yes. Thank you."

He reached into an ice chest and pulled out a bottled water. She wondered if, on their way to answer the 911 call, they'd stopped to fill up the ice chest.

"You're shaking," he said. "Are you cold?"

She shook her head. "I'm fine."

"Is any of that blood on you yours?"

She looked down at it again. "No. I don't know whose it is." She looked up at him through her tears. "Do you have a list or something of the people who were hurt? Maybe they're at the hospital."

"We don't yet. It's still too early. If you'll tell us what you saw, maybe it'll help us find who did this."

She wiped her nose and took another resolute sniff. "It was . . . just as Ed Loran was coming onto the stage. The band had left the stage, and everybody was on their feet applauding. Then I heard this huge, deafening *bang*. I don't know if it knocked me down or if I just dropped. There were people on the floor all around me. I don't know if they were dead. I should have checked and helped them, but I didn't. All I could think about was getting out of the building."

"Did you see anyone who looked suspicious before the blast? Someone on the stage or in the front rows?"

"No."

"Anyone in the audience with a backpack or a big bag?"

"No. We had to go through those metal detectors when we came in. We could have purses, but nothing bigger, and they searched those." She thought of the band she had come to see. "The band . . . Did they get hurt, too?" She realized the question was ridiculous, since no one in the stage area could have survived an explosion of that size. She covered her eyes and her face twisted again. "They're all dead, aren't they?"

"Tell me how you got out."

She could see that he was trying to refocus her thoughts, so she did the best she could. "I just felt panicked until I could get to the aisle. There was this crush of people all running toward the door."

"When you got outside, did anyone catch your eye?"

"There were others running. People with soot on their faces . . . panicked people."

"Was anyone doing anything that seemed odd? Walking

when others were running, looking calm instead of panicked, going the wrong way?"

"I don't know. I didn't notice anything like that."

"Do you have pictures from the concert?"

"Yes." She pulled out her phone and found the photos, then handed the phone to him.

He took her phone and said, "Can you just wait here for a minute? I'll bring your phone right back."

"Okay, but if someone calls will you pick up? I really need to hear from them."

He agreed, so she let him take it outside the van. She sat there alone, feeling oddly cut off without her phone and wishing she hadn't agreed to let him take it. What if they wound up keeping it for evidence?

When Detective Borden got back in, she reached for her phone. "I can email or text you the pictures."

"I've taken care of it. I air-dropped them to myself, but we'll need to talk to you again later."

"Okay, but my friends. Seriously, I need to know . . . Can you find out if they were taken to the hospital?"

Detective Borden said he would check and see what he could find out. He seemed to vanish into the frantic activity around the van. She waited for fifteen or twenty minutes, then realized he wasn't coming back. She looked out the tinted van window. SWAT snipers stood inside the glass doors of the building, their weapons readied. They must suspect there were more threats.

She stepped out of the van, and one of the cops standing there asked her for her contact information. She gave it to him, and he promised to get it to Detective Borden.

"He was checking the hospital list for my friends. Please . . ."

"We don't have a list yet. Some of those who got out of the building were injured, and they were taken to the hospitals, but we haven't been able to rescue anyone still in there."

Her jaw fell open. "Are you serious? Why not? They could die!"

"Ma'am, we need for you to get out of this area. The whole place is an active crime scene. In the meantime, you could call University Hospital. That's where the injured are being transported."

"Okay," she said. "Can I just . . . stay here until I see them or hear from them?"

"No, ma'am. We'll need you to go back outside the perimeter. But please call the detective if you think of anything else we need to know. Did he give you his card?"

She shook her head no, so he reached into the van. He handed her a card, and she stuffed it into her pants pocket.

Looking back the way she had come, she realized she would be surrounded by media as soon as she stepped under the tape. The blood on her pants was like a waving flag. She wanted to change clothes so she wouldn't have to dwell on whose blood it was. But she didn't have any more clothes in her car, and she couldn't imagine driving home to get some until she knew where Mara and Desiree were.

It was getting dark. She hovered in the shadows until a group of other victims appeared near the reporters, eager to share their stories. The press descended on them, and she took the opportunity to escape. She walked a block down the road, where no media lurked, and sat down on a bus stop bench. She could see the lights of the police cars from here, and anyone who might spill down the steps of the building.

She tried calling Desiree again but got another voicemail. Mara didn't pick up, either. She knew their phones were on, because they'd been Snapchatting the whole time.

Snapchat! She opened the Snapchat app on her phone and went to her feed. The last thing she'd gotten from Desiree was a video of Blue Fire singing her favorite song. Mara's last post was a Snap of the three of them before the lights went off in the auditorium. Taylor remembered that Mara had still been recording video as the band left the stage and Loran was coming out. Which meant that she might have been recording when the explosion happened. But she hadn't posted it.

If Mara was conscious, she would have posted. Mara never missed an opportunity for a dramatic Snap.

Taylor scrolled down her feed and saw that the news was already out. People were already posting about what had happened.

Her ringtone played, and her heart lurched. But instead of Mara's or Desiree's face, she saw that it was Mara's fiancé. Maybe Mara was calling from his phone! She swiped it on. "Mara?"

"It's Lucas," he said. "She isn't with you?"

She started to cry again as she told him what she knew. He quickly got off the phone, intent on finding Mara. She hoped he would remember to call back if he found her.

Minutes later, it rang again. This time it was her older sister. She clicked the phone icon and said, "Harper!"

"Taylor! Thank God you're alive!"

Those sobs rushed up again, overtaking her.

"Are you all right?"

She twisted her lips, trying to control her voice, but when she spoke, it was a jumble of words that she knew her sister couldn't decipher.

"What? Where are you?"

She sucked in a breath and tried to calm down. "I'm a block down from Trudeau Hall. I can't find Desiree and Mara! They could have been injured. There's blood on my clothes and I didn't even look to see if they were hurt. I was just trying to get out and I didn't think—"

"I'm coming to get you, Taylor."

"No, I have my car. I just can't leave."

"What street are you on?"

She looked up, trying to see a street sign. "Government Street, I think. I'm on a bench, but I'm going to go back to my car on President Street." She got up and started walking. "How will they get home if I leave?"

"They can call Uber. Honey, listen to me. You're in shock. You're not thinking clearly. The news said they haven't found the people who did this yet. Whoever did it is still out there, probably nearby. Just go to your car and wait for me. I'm almost there already."

Harper's call cut off, and Taylor continued walking. She wiped her nose on her sleeve. She hadn't done that since she was four. To reach her car, she had to pass the concert hall again. As she approached the barricade where media were crowded, she slipped past and headed around the block to her car. Still no Mara or Desiree.

She moved her car up to the spot closest to the corner, where she had a better view of the distance to the building where her friends might still be. She called Emory University Hospital, where the police officer said the injured were being taken, but they didn't have a record yet of the people who had been brought in.

She needed the news. She turned on her ignition, and the

radio paired with her phone and started blaring Blue Fire's latest album. She and her friends had been listening to it in anticipation all the way here. The band had been the draw that got them to the rally. Where else could you see them for free, when crazy-expensive tickets for their concerts sold out in minutes?

She clicked on her radio mode and found a station that was reporting the news.

"Police say they're canvassing the building for other bombs. Family members are being told to assemble at St. Mary's Lutheran Church several blocks from the conference hall to await word on the condition of their loved ones."

She wasn't a family member. Would they let her in?

She sat there for several more minutes, listening and watching up the street. She jumped when she heard a horn and looked to see her sister's car idling beside her. Harper's passenger window was down.

Taylor let her window down. "Hey."

"Get in."

"I can't! I have to stay."

Her sister left her car in the road, engine running, and came around to Taylor's door. Harper opened it and bent down to hug her. She had been crying, too, and for a moment Taylor let her cling to her.

When Harper could speak, she said, "Leave them a note. If they come to your car, they'll see it. But you're coming with me. You have got to change clothes, and you're shivering. Are you cold?"

"No, I'm sweating."

Harper took over and leaned into the back seat. She dug through Taylor's bag until she found a notepad and pen. "Desiree and Mara, please call me immediately!" she wrote in big letters that covered the whole page.

She left the pad on the passenger seat and pulled out Taylor's car keys and her bag. "Come on. This is not negotiable."

"There's another location for family to wait for news. I want to go there."

"I heard that, too. At St. Mary's. Come on, that's where we'll go."

As Taylor slid into Harper's car, she tried calling her friends again. This time, the screen went black. "Oh no, no, no! My phone died."

"It's okay."

"No, it's not! Do you have a charger in here?"

Harper pulled one from her console. "Here. But you know, it probably wouldn't be a bad thing for you to stay off social media. At least until you hear what's going on with them, anyway."

"Are you serious? I want to know what's going on, and I have to keep my phone on so they can call me."

"Okay," Harper said. "Just sayin'."

Fatigue hit Taylor as she leaned back on the headrest. While her phone charged, she felt cut off again, unnatural, out of touch. It seemed like an eternity before her phone came on after a few minutes of charging.

As they approached St. Mary's parking lot, she saw others pulling in. Family members got out of their cars wearing looks of anguish.

Taylor wasn't ready for this. She looked at her phone. It was only 3 percent charged. "I need to sit here for a few minutes until I can get enough of a charge, unless you have a charger I can plug into the wall in there."

Harper dug through her console and came up with a power adapter. She unplugged the car charger and plugged the cord into the adapter. "Here you go."

Taylor checked her phone. It was only at 4 percent now. She hadn't missed any calls while it was off. "Okay, let's go."

More people were arriving now, all of them distraught. She and Harper followed a group of new arrivals into the church's gym.

Police officers had set up a table at the entrance and were checking each family into the gym. Three people ahead of her, a reporter with a camera was being turned away.

When she got to the front, the officer asked, "Are you family?"

"I . . . I'm looking for my friends . . ."

"I'm sorry. We're trying to keep this limited to family members—"

Harper jumped in front of her. "Excuse me, do you see the blood on her clothes? She was there, in that building, and she escaped—but she hasn't found the friends she came with. Are you seriously going to turn her away while she's still in shock and can't think about anything else until she knows if they're okay?"

The reporter turned around and lifted his camera.

The cop cleared his throat. "No . . . you can go in. Just give me the names of the people you're waiting to hear about. We'll let you know as soon as we get the lists."

The lists . . . the wounded and the dead. Which list would her friends be on? She gave him their names.

"The bathrooms are around that corner. We're going to have food and drinks brought in soon. For now, we're trying to keep everyone in here, but we may have to move to the sanctuary if there's overflow."

As they started to go inside, the reporter stopped her. "Excuse me. Were you at Trudeau Hall when the bomb went off?"

"Yes," she said.

"Could you tell me what you saw?"

The camera lens lowered to the blood on her pants, then moved back up to her face.

"She can't talk to you right now," Harper said. "Please just let us get by."

He backed out of their way when a cop turned around to intervene.

Taylor shot inside the gym and found the bathroom. She pushed inside before Harper had caught up to her, and went to the mirror for her first look at herself. Her brown hair was speckled with gray ash, and her face was covered with soot. Her eyes were red and swollen. "I look awful."

"We really need to get you changed. I have my gym bag in my car."

"I don't want to wear your dirty gym clothes."

"They're not dirty. I never go. I just carry it in case the urge hits me, which it never does. It's yoga pants and a long T-shirt. You'll look better in it than I do."

Taylor soaped up her hands and washed her face. "I don't care about changing."

"But the families shouldn't see you with bloodstains on your clothes. Trust me, honey. Would you want Desiree's or Mara's family to see that if they wind up here?"

Taylor started to cry again and shook her head. Harper held her for a long moment. Then Harper led her into a stall and made her sit on the toilet to wait for her. In minutes, Harper was back, a little out of breath. She shoved the gym bag under the door.

Others came in. The sounds of sniffing and nose blowing silenced Harper and Taylor. Taylor pulled off her jeans and her blouse and rolled them up. She slipped into Harper's clothes. Her sister was a size bigger, so the clothes were loose. But she yearned for comfort, so they would work. She wished she could shower.

When she came out, her sister hugged her and led her to the sink to splash water on her face again. Then she took her hand and led her out to the growing, grieving crowd.

06

Jamie had dressed for TV interviews today in case the verdict came in, not for butting heads with police officers on behalf of a criminal defendant. She looked in her console for a hair tie and pulled her hair back in a more severe ponytail. But it did nothing to make her look more intimidating.

She gave up and let it fall to her shoulders. It was all about attitude, anyway. She simply had to convey that she was a bulwark for her client, a wall that couldn't be breached. She grabbed her briefcase and walked quickly into the building, then shot through the room to the person at the desk.

"I'm Jamie Powell," she said. "I'm here to see my client, Dustin Webb."

The uniformed officer pointed to the back. "He's in an interview room."

"Who's the lead officer on his case?"

"Detective Borden is our lead detective working with the

feds. He just got back from Trudeau Hall. He's very busy. Do you need to see him?"

"Only if he expects to interview my client."

Jamie ran through what the officer had said as she waited for him to call upstairs. If Borden was the lead detective on the explosion, then the charges against Dustin must be connected to the bombing.

Borden approached her a few minutes later with two others.

"I'm about to meet with my client before you interview him," Jamie said before they greeted her. "But I'll need to see an inventory of what you took from my client's car."

"We're still logging things, and the car is at the lab."

"Okay, just the contents of his trunk, then. What, exactly, did you find?"

"Four boxes of RDX, taken from the ChemEx ammunition plant that was robbed about ten days ago."

The picture wasn't coming into focus yet. "So how much RDX was stolen from the ammunition plant?"

"A lot more than the four boxes we found, plus some TNT. But it looks like the rest were at Trudeau Hall."

There it was. The line connecting the dots. "Any evidence that my client was near the concert hall before the rally?"

"The case is still fluid," Borden said.

"And you had a warrant to search his car?"

"Yes, I had sent someone to get it from the DA's office, but before it got to us, Webb gave us permission to search the car."

"Not something a guy would do if he knew his trunk was full of stolen RDX. I want to see the warrant, anyway."

"We'll get it to you after the interview."

"And what prompted you to pull him over?"

"We had a tip."

She frowned. "A tip that Dustin Webb had explosives in his trunk?"

"Yes. And that he was involved in the bombing."

"Who gave you that tip?"

"It was anonymous, but obviously it played out. We have a building with a lot of dead people just a few minutes away."

She couldn't let them keep making that connection. "Is he being charged with terrorism?"

"Not yet."

"I don't think I have to tell you that there's a huge leap from finding four boxes of plastic explosives in his car to connecting him to a horrific bombing in a crowded concert hall."

"It's not my job to make his crimes make sense to you."

She sighed. "Where is he?"

"I'll get him for you. Wait here."

At first Jamie paced anxiously across the small floor. Then she resolved not to let her emotions betray her. She sat down on one of the chairs in the waiting area and pulled her computer out of her briefcase. She paired it with her phone's hotspot and pulled up Dustin's rap sheet. She scanned it quickly. No arrests since the misdemeanors in his teen years—one for disturbing the peace on graduation night, and the other for possession of half a marijuana joint when he'd been pulled over for speeding. She remembered both of those times.

He had attended two years of community college and a year at a state university, living at home to save money, until there was a snafu with his financial aid. He'd worked odd jobs, trying to save enough to return to college. It was an uphill battle, so he'd finally joined the army, thinking that would get him back on track. According to the databases she accessed, nothing illegal had happened since. He'd had two deployments to Afghanistan in the Ordnance Corps of the army, and he'd eventually finished school after an honorable discharge.

He'd started a business here five years ago installing commercial security systems. It was called GreyWebb Securities.

"Ms. Powell?"

She looked up and saw Borden coming back. She closed her computer, slipped it into her case, and stood.

"He's in Interview Room 3."

She went back to the interview rooms she had visited a few times before and found Room 3. She saw him through the small vertical window in the door and hesitated a moment.

He hadn't changed much in fifteen years, though today he had a light stubble beard. He hadn't been processed yet, so he still wore his own clothes—jeans, a Nike T-shirt, and scuffed sneakers.

She couldn't help her faint smile as she opened the door. "Dustin."

He looked at her, and she saw a flash of who he used to be in his eyes. "Hey, kiddo."

She quenched the urge to hug him as she stepped inside. No doubt, they were being watched. Dustin sat on one of the chairs at the metal table, and she wondered if they'd given him the chair with two of the legs shorter than the others. They loved throwing their subjects off balance to distract them.

A bruise from his eyebrow to the crest of his cheekbone caught her eye. "Are you all right?"

"Yeah," he said. "I'm fine."

Her professional instincts told her to rein in her feelings, to sit down at the table and start asking questions. But there were instincts that had been there before adulthood. Following those instead, she went to sit in the chair beside him, on the side where she could see the bruise more clearly.

He met her eyes as she sat down. "I'm in deep, huh?"

The tension of her emotions drove all rational thought from her mind. "Yeah, you are. What did they do to you?"

"Nothing," Dustin said. "They were just in a real big hurry to put those zip ties on. I might have gotten a little concrete burn."

"Did you resist arrest?"

"No," he said. "I did what they told me."

"Good." She got up and set her briefcase on the table that was bolted to the floor, then turned back to him. "I was mad at you for years for not calling me, but I never thought your first phone call would happen like this."

He shrugged. "I always did have great timing."

They stared at each other for a long moment, then finally he said, "You look great, kiddo."

"So do you." Her throat closed for a second, and she swallowed hard. "Dustin, what happened?"

"They pulled me over—"

"No. What really happened? Why you?"

"Jamie, if I knew, I'd tell you. I installed the security system at ChemEx. It was complicated and elaborate and took months. Then there was that theft. My partner and I were questioned after it because we had access, but we told them the truth. I have never taken anything from them and never would."

"Do you know about the bombing?"

He frowned. "There was a TV on the wall when they brought

me into the station tonight, and I could see that something had happened, but I didn't see much. A bombing?"

"It was at the Ed Loran rally at Trudeau Hall."

The stricken look on his face revealed his amazement. "Jamie, they don't think I . . ."

"People are dead. Lots of them. They're still at the scene. It happened a little before they stopped you."

"Wait a minute . . . I didn't do anything . . . I don't know who . . ."

"Dustin, this is really serious. You never should have let them search your vehicle."

"They had a warrant there shortly after I said okay, anyway. It was inevitable. I didn't have any idea there was something in my trunk . . . God help me. They think I made the bomb."

"It doesn't matter what they think. It matters what they can prove." But she knew better than that. The concept of innocent until proven guilty was growing more antiquated by the day. "Tell me everything you did today, starting with waking up."

He described a routine day, getting up, drinking coffee, walking his dog, inspecting a business and writing a quote, getting a hamburger for lunch, going back to the office.

She jotted it all down, then looked at him. "You have a dog?"

"Yeah," he said. "I have to find somebody to feed him and walk him. Maybe he needs to be boarded until I get out of here."

"I can take care of boarding him. You'll want to get him out of there before they get a warrant to search your house."

He told her where she could find a key and gave her the name of the vet who could board him. "Okay, now let's go over everything you told them before I got here."

"I told them those explosives weren't mine. That I didn't know how they got there. After I talked to you, I shut up. But four boxes full of RDX? Come on! They're not mine! And someone planted them in my car for a reason."

Jamie leaned forward. "Have you had any experience with RDX?"

"Yes, in the army. When you mix it with certain plasticizers and waxes, it's stable enough to handle pretty roughly and withstand heat and cold. I got pretty familiar with it so I could detonate bombs we needed to neutralize." He shook his head and looked up at the stained ceiling. "I'm the perfect scapegoat. So convenient."

"Did the security system at the plant have video?"

"Yes, but after the theft, we looked through it all and didn't find anything. There was a blip in the footage for about forty-five minutes the night of the theft, so whoever it was knew how to disable the cameras."

"Someone walked out of that plant with RDX that wound up in your car. And if the bomb at the concert hall was made with RDX . . ." Her voice trailed off. "Dustin, there are going to be other charges. They think you made and planted the bomb. They'll want to grill you about who else was involved. We're talking terrorism."

"If they blame me, they'll probably pull Travis in, too."

"Who's Travis?"

"My business partner and best friend. But this comes at the worst possible time for him. His wife is dying of cancer."

Jamie wouldn't let her mind linger on that. "How long have you been in business with him?"

"We worked together at a security tech company after we

were honorably discharged, and a couple of years ago, we started our own business."

"So you were in the Ordnance Corps together?"

"That's right. The government taught us how to assemble a bomb so we could protect our soldiers from them, then they turn that knowledge against us for reasons that have nothing to do with us. Travis has been in the hospital with his wife since she went in two weeks ago, and I can account for every minute of my time today. Trust me, Travis didn't sneak out of the hospital to pull a heist at the ammunition plant. This whole thing is ludicrous."

"The bombs could have been planted yesterday or last night."

"Then I'll account for that time, too! I didn't do it."

She locked into his eyes for a long moment, trying to see any deception he might be harboring there. But Dustin had never been a liar. "I know you didn't."

He raked his hand through his hair. "How could you know? For all you know—"

"I do know," she said. "But we have to fight this. Can you afford to hire me?"

He frowned. "Yes. You don't have to worry about getting paid."

"I need to know because I work for a firm. Personally I'd be happy to do it pro bono, but if you're paying, then I'll have all the resources of my firm behind me."

"I can mortgage my house if I have to, and I have some savings and investments. But if you don't want any part of this, I understand," he said. "I don't expect you to put your career and reputation on the line. This is going to get ugly."

She blinked back tears. "I want so much to get you out of this," she said. "But this is big. You may need someone more experienced. Someone who's handled cases like this before. I take criminal cases, but usually they're white-collar crimes. This is bigger than anything I've done."

"I want you," Dustin whispered. "I couldn't go through this with anyone else."

That was all she needed to hear.

"Jamie, I swear. I've never hurt anybody intentionally, and as much trouble as I was in my teens, I cleaned up my act in the army. I've never made anybody mad enough to want me put away. I don't know anyone who would blow up a building with people in it."

"Did you follow Ed Loran's campaign?"

"No, but I wasn't against him, either. I never gave him a thought. I didn't even know he was having a rally."

"Have you ever posted about him on social media? Anything at all?"

"This may shock you," he said, "but I don't do social media."

She didn't tell him she had checked social media for any trace of him many times. "Good. That'll help."

"Everybody is going to think I did it. Killed those people . . . The ones lying in the hospital with burns and injuries . . . their families . . . Everybody will think I did it."

She blinked back the mist in her eyes. "Not if we get you out of here fast. Your bond hearing's tomorrow. The media may not hear about your arrest before then. If we can get proof of your innocence before they even know you've been arrested, then maybe we can head off the worst of the publicity."

He rubbed his face. "It's still going to be ugly. It could destroy you, too, by association. If you want out, just tell me. I wouldn't blame you."

"You always had my back," she said. "I'm going to have yours. Be careful what you say during the interview. They're not just looking for information. They're looking for things to use against you. If I need to stop you, I will. I'll stop them, too, if I don't like where they're going. But you have to follow my lead and listen when I tell you to stop talking."

He nodded. "I will."

She got up and opened the door. The two detectives who had been sitting a few yards away ambled in and took their seats at the table. She hoped Dustin was ready for this.

07

On her way home from the jail, after Dustin had been interviewed for hours, Jamie called Zeke, one of the private investigators who contracted with her firm.

The phone rang four times before Zeke picked up. "Jamie Powell, you better tell me something good, because I don't like trouble when I ain't even got my shoes on."

"Then put them on now," she said. "I'm sorry to call you when you're home, but I need you to drop everything and do some work for me."

"I don't know," the gruff ex-cop said over the bluetooth speaker in her car. "I got some other cases going. I'm short on manpower."

"It's an emergency," she said. "I'd consider it a personal favor, and it may only take a day or two."

"A personal favor? You trying to catch your boyfriend with another woman?"

"No," she said. "I have a close friend and client who's getting framed for the bombing."

"Whoa!" Zeke said. "You want me to help him?"

"No, I want you to help me. I need for you to go everywhere he's been and pull security video. I'm trying to establish his alibis for the last few days, and also see if we can catch anyone planting evidence in his car."

"You got a list?"

"Yes. I'll email it to you. His arraignment is tomorrow, and I'm going to try to meet with the prosecutor in the morning. I'd like to have this info before that."

"So an all-nighter?"

"You know I'm good for it."

"Okay, Jamie," he said. "I'll pull some of my people off of other cases. But you're gonna owe me one."

She pulled into her mother's driveway as he cut off the phone call. She sat there for a moment, sending Zeke the list she had taken from Dustin after his interview today. She whispered a prayer that Zeke would come up with something she could use with the prosecutor tomorrow. She couldn't present evidence at the arraignment, but she knew this prosecutor, Louis Dole. She had worked for him for two years right out of law school. If she could show him compelling evidence before they went to court, he might agree not to contest Dustin's bond.

She sat in her car for another long moment and took a deep breath before she saw her daughter. She should have gone by Dustin's house first to feed and walk his dog, but Avery would be getting ready for bed by now. She could go afterward, feed him and take him outside, then leave him there until the kennel opened in the morning.

Her gaze strayed through the darkness to the house next door, where Dustin's aunt Pat still lived. She thought back to when she was thirteen and he was seventeen, and they'd sat between the yards as the moon came up, talking like equals.

He had been like a big brother to her, schooling her in the dangers of dating, teaching her about types of boys to avoid. There had always been a cautious affection in his time with her, though he'd never touched her.

Now it was her turn to help him.

She turned off her car and went into the house. The living room was dimly lit with one lamp, and a TV played quietly over the fireplace. She heard her mother's and daughter's voices in the back.

She went down the hallway to the room her mother had fixed up for Avery even before she was born. "Good, you're still up."

"Mommy!" Avery sat up in bed, reaching for her.

"I've been trying to get her to bed for an hour," her mother said, sliding off Avery's bed. She was wearing a Bon Jovi T-shirt and faded jeans, and her hair was tousled. "First we read a chapter of *Diary of a Wimpy Kid*, then some of *Charlotte's Web*, and now she wants me to sing."

"I'll take over, Mom."

"Is Dustin all right?"

"He will be, I hope."

"Are you staying the night?"

"No, I have to keep working. His arraignment's tomorrow, and I need to go over a bunch of things. Avery can sleep here."

"I want you to be here, Mommy."

"I know, but I can't tonight. You love sleepovers here. Maybe Mimi will make you pancakes in the morning before school."

"Only if she gets to sleep soon," Jamie's mother said, then left the room.

Jamie stepped out of her shoes, climbed into bed with Avery, and slipped under the covers.

"What's wrong with your friend?"

"Dustin? Did Mimi tell you about him?"

"She said he used to live next door."

"Yes, and he's in trouble. Someone's blaming him for something he didn't do. I have to help him."

"She said you had a crush on him."

Jamie frowned. "My mother said that? It's not true. He was a very close friend. Like a brother."

"He sounds nice."

Jamie kissed her. "Go to sleep now. Close your eyes, and I'll sing. But only one verse."

"Three verses," Avery said.

"One."

"Two, please!"

"None."

"Okay, one."

Jamie grinned and stroked Avery's forehead until her eyes closed. She started to sing softly, an old song her mother used to sing to her. By the time she got to the end, Avery was sound asleep.

She lay there for another few minutes before slipping out of bed. She got her shoes and walked barefoot up the hall. Her mother sat watching the local news about the bombing, her own bare feet propped on the coffee table.

"How is he really?" her mom asked.

"He's in jail. Unless I can figure out something, he may be there for a long time."

"You have to get him out!"

"I know." Jamie sat on the arm of a chair. "Did you tell Pat?"

"She called me. She said the police came by to question her about him. Of course she didn't know anything about it."

"How was she?"

"Upset, of course."

"Upset about how it might make her look when the press finds out? Or upset about what Dustin's going through?"

"I don't know. I can't speculate on that."

"I know. She's your friend." Jamie got her bag and kissed her mother on the cheek. "Guess I have to go. I'll try to pick her up after school tomorrow."

"Stay in touch."

Jamie went back out to her car and checked her watch. It was ten o'clock. She still had to take care of Dustin's dog, and then she had a ton of research to do on his case. She was going to be up all night.

08

Jamie turned onto the gravel driveway next to the mailbox with Dustin's number on it, put her headlights on bright, and made her way toward the house. It was set in a cluster of trees. That was good, she thought. It was hard to see it from the street. Maybe that would keep the press at bay when they started hearing about Dustin.

She got a flashlight out of her glove box and slipped out of her car. She could hear barking inside the house. She shone her flashlight beam along a small ledge over the garage door and found the key exactly where Dustin had told her it would be. As she tried to unlock the front door, she could hear the dog going nuts on the other side. She hoped he was friendly and that he wouldn't attack her the moment she opened the door. She hadn't even asked Dustin what kind of dog it was, or even his name.

When she got the deadbolt unlocked, she decided to give the

dog a little heads-up before she opened the door. "Good doggie," she said, and the barking only intensified. "I'm Dustin's friend and I'm gonna feed you. Are you hungry?"

She took a deep breath and opened the door. She heard his panting and his claws sliding on the hardwood floor as he backed away. She turned on the light and slowly moved inside. The dog lunged at her and she let out a choked scream as he took a running start and jumped up on her, his front paws pushing her shoulders. The force knocked her back, and she landed on the floor.

She didn't know whether to run or play with him, but when he started licking her face, she couldn't help laughing. "You're very enthusiastic! And huge. How old are you?"

He moved off her, picked up a ball, and brought it to her.

"Wow, okay," she said. "We can play ball a little later." She scratched him behind his ear, and his eyes squinted in obvious enjoyment. "Look at you," she said. "A black Lab. I used to have a black Lab. His name was Coco."

The dog had a collar with a little silver nameplate. His name was Dude. She laughed. That sounded like something Dustin would name his dog. "Hey, Dude," she said. "I bet you need to go outside, don't you?"

He bounded away from her now, toward a room at the back of the house. She followed him through the living room, which surprised her with its clean decor in masculine earth tones and expensive accessories that indicated success and pride. Dustin had come a long way. And now he even had the dog he had longed for as a kid.

She followed the dog into the great room that was combined with the kitchen. He was panting near his leash, which hung on a hook by the back door. "Thanks, Dude," she said, and she got the leash and hooked it to his collar, then stepped out the door. There wasn't a fence, so she couldn't let him go free. She turned her flashlight back on and trailed him through the yard and let him do his business.

She shone the light around the yard and admired Dustin's manicured lawn, trees, and shrubbery. Her beam hit a doghouse on the side of the yard, and she led the dog there to see where Dude hung out. It looked like a little oasis with a pergola-type porch in miniature. Had Dustin built it himself? The thought that he could have done that made her chuckle. Not just any ordinary doghouse for Dustin's dog. Nope. Dustin had too much empathy not to put extra into it.

When Dude was finished, she asked him, "Want to eat? Are you hungry?"

He ran back to the door, his tail wagging and tongue hanging out. She let him in, freed him from the leash, and looked around for dog food.

She had never really seen Dustin in his own environment before. He was always at Pat's house, following her rules and molding to her expectations as much as he could. The homey look of his house filled her with warmth, and she felt a surge of emotion and homesickness for him that she hadn't let herself feel in years.

She looked in his pantry and saw a big bag of dog food on the bottom shelf. Dude's bowl was on the floor in the kitchen, so she filled it up and gave him water, and the dog went right to it, gulping the food down as if he was starving to death. While he ate, she sat down on Dustin's plush couch, kicked off her shoes, and pulled up her feet. The dog would have to go out again after he ate and drank. She should probably stay here until then.

When the dog finished eating, he jumped up on the couch and cuddled up next to her, urging her to scratch his head. "You are a sweet boy," she said. "Your daddy's not gonna be home tonight, but he'll be back tomorrow, I hope. I'm trying my best." She stopped scratching, and the dog nuzzled her hand again.

"I'm gonna have to leave you here tonight. But you'll be okay until morning. I'll take you out one more time, okay? And then tomorrow I'll come and take you to your babysitter for a few days." She felt terrible even saying that. The dog was so hungry for human touch. She could tell he was still a puppy, even as big as he was. He probably wasn't yet full grown. And he probably sat near the door all day waiting for Dustin to come home. She hated the thought that he would do that again when she left.

Finally she got up. "You know what? I don't think I can make myself leave you here." She sighed. "Come on. We're taking you to my house. You can hang with me tonight."

She went to get the dog food and popped the leash on his collar. "Come on, Dude. We're going to have a sleepover." He bumped around and slid across the floor as she took him to the front. She kept the key in case she would have to get back in. She took Dude out to her car and put him in the back seat, but before she even started the car he was in the front seat, riding shotgun.

"All righty, then," she said. He licked her face. "Hey, none of that while I'm driving. Listen to me. You stay, okay? You can't ride in my lap. Stay."

He looked as if he was smiling as he panted. She started the car and pulled out of the driveway.

It had been a heavy day and it was destined to get heavier before she slept, but somehow the dog had lightened it and made it a little easier to bear. Yes, she would still be up all night. But knowing she had Dustin's dog with her somehow made her feel better about that.

09

Word about the dead came to St. Mary's rec room around four in the morning. A preliminary list was brought in. At first there was a profound silence as the names were spread out on a table, then some went to look. Others who stood back, afraid to go, began sobbing as though they already knew the worst. Then almost at once, clusters of loved ones rushed forward, pushing and fighting their way through the crowded hedge around the list.

"I can't do it," Taylor muttered to Harper. "I can't look."

"Let's just wait," Harper said. "Their parents will find out."

Taylor was cold. She'd been shivering all night, freezing as if she were having chills, and now that got even more intense. She sat with tears pooled in her eyes, her mouth shaking, as she watched the crowd and tried to find Mara's and Desiree's parents, all of whom had come in during the night.

People screamed and collapsed as they saw their loved ones' names. Taylor felt dizzy as dread washed over her.

Finally she saw Desiree's parents come out of the glut of people. Her friend's father was holding her mother, whose knees seemed unable to hold her up. A look of agony seemed frozen on her face.

Taylor bent forward, her hands over her head, unable to face what she knew. Her sister put her arms around her as if trying to hold her together.

"I left them," Taylor said in a guttural whisper. "I didn't even think about them."

"Shhh," her sister said. "Stop that. You did exactly what you had to do. You didn't make the decision to leave them. You just followed your instincts. Mara and Desiree aren't gone because of you."

"But what if they just needed help? What if I could have helped them?"

"You could barely help yourself."

Taylor looked up and saw Mara's parents, divorced but together tonight, walking with looks of shock on their pale faces as they came out of the crowd. Mara's mother met Taylor's eyes and shook her head, then covered her mouth and buried her face in Mara's dad's chest.

Taylor pulled her feet up on her folding chair and pressed her face against her knees, in the tightest fetal position she could manage while still sitting. "I have to get out of here," she said.

"Okay. Come on. Get up."

Taylor unfolded and managed to get to her feet. Her legs were shaking as badly as her hands. She was suddenly so tired.

She let her sister walk her out, through the grieving crowd and into the parking lot illuminated only by streetlamps. Moths flew around the halo cast by the light, as if life were normal and nothing had changed.

Life went on. She just didn't know how she could.

10

Jamie hadn't slept well for days before her jury came back in the Ash case yesterday, but tonight she fueled herself with coffee and carbs to focus on the databases where she culled information about Dustin.

Dude had made himself at home on her couch, and every time she ate, he came to sit by her. Apparently Dustin had trained him not to beg, because he sat still, staring at her as she ate, until she tossed him something. Then he would attack it and swallow it in a gulp.

When he fell asleep on her couch, she dug into her work. She had to know everything about Dustin—more than the prosecutor would. But she found very little. Dustin hadn't had more than a speeding ticket since leaving home. The army had served him well in the area of discipline and self-control. People like his aunt had probably placed odds that he would be in and out of jail all his life, since she believed his acting out was the sign of a character flaw. But Jamie knew his trouble in his teens had much more to do with his sense of belonging than it did with some dark spot in his heart.

When she finally turned out the light, Dude awoke and got up, wagging his tail. She opened the back door and let him into her yard, which was fenced in. Dude stopped when he realized it wasn't his yard. Slowly he went out into the grass and sniffed around the swing set, explored the edges of the fence, then found a bush.

When he was finished, she took him back inside. "It's bedtime now," she said. "You stay right here. You can sleep on the couch."

She started to go to her bedroom, but the dog followed her. She turned around. "Stay."

He stayed, and she left him there and went to her bedroom. She pulled the covers back on her bed, then went into the bathroom to brush her teeth. When she came out, Dude was sprawled out on her bed.

"Come on, Dude," she said. "Really?"

He lifted his head, then put it back down. Sighing, she crawled into bed, pulled up her covers, and felt his warmth next to her. He squirmed closer and she stroked his head. "You're sweet, you know that? It's hard to be mad at you."

She had the sense that he knew.

She'd been asleep for only an hour or so when her phone vibrated at four o'clock. It was Zeke. She swiped it on. "Zeke, tell me you've got something."

"You know I do," he said with a chuckle.

"Really?"

"Yeah, several things, actually. I put five of my people on

it, and we were able to confirm most of his alibi from CCTV footage. I'm sending the reports over right now. The security cameras at his home show his car was there when he said he was, and there's no sign of his leaving with anyone else."

"Perfect. What else?"

"The trunk of his car."

"Yeah?"

"He spent about three hours at the hospital the night before last when his friend was admitted, and I was able to get their security video of the parking lot where his car sat. At one a.m., you can see two people pulling behind his car in a white van, and they opened his trunk and loaded something in."

"Did you get their tag?"

"No, it wasn't clear. But it was interesting that they didn't have to break into the trunk. They opened it easily."

"Did they have a key?"

"I wish I could tell, but the picture is grainy and it was dark except for the lights in the parking lot. But it looked like they did have one, yeah."

"How many things did they load?"

"It looks like four."

"Okay, send me a report with any details. I owe you big."

"Oh, my bill will show you how big."

"That's fair."

She got off the phone, found Zeke's email, and quickly printed it out. He had also sent all the video footage he'd collected. She opened a computer folder, inserted all the files he'd sent, and watched them one after another, carefully logging the exact times Dustin came and went, how long he was at each place, whose cameras videotaped each file, and who signed off on turning it over to Zeke. The prosecutor would want to confirm all of it himself.

She spent the next couple of hours preparing what she would say to the prosecutor. It was critical that she make him doubt his case against Dustin and that she give him good reason not to recommend against bond.

Dustin had a few things going for him. They couldn't yet charge him with terrorism, so the prosecutor couldn't connect the dots in court between his having the explosives and the terrorist bombing. The media hadn't yet gotten wind of his arrest for possession of the explosives. It was possible the judge wouldn't yet know of the connection, though Jamie doubted it.

They would worry that he was a flight risk, or that, if he was involved in terrorism, he would proceed with other plots. Or they might think that, if he was out, they could put surveillance on him, hoping he'd lead them to others involved.

She would have to be ready for whatever came up in court.

Dude went to the door and sat down, letting her know he needed to go out. She pulled her robe tighter and stepped outside with him. As he ran around the yard, she went to the front gate and looked out toward the street, cast in a yellow glow from the streetlight near her driveway. Clutching her mug of coffee, she tried to anticipate what would happen when the media found out that an arrest had been made in connection with the bombing. There was no doubt they'd cluster in front of Dustin's house, demonizing him and creating damaging narratives. But she and other attorneys in her firm had been through high-profile cases before, and in the last year or two there had been times when crowds of people with bullhorns had gathered with the media, threatening more than a negative story about the subject. They were there to intimidate the attorney into dropping the client.

She sipped her coffee and tried to imagine how it would be if they thought Dustin was responsible for all those deaths and injuries. He wouldn't be able to go home when he got out of jail.

She finished off her coffee and went out to the garage and up the steps to the apartment she had been using for storage. She went inside and turned on the light. It was dusty in here, and the living area was filled with boxes of Christmas decorations and memories—Avery's toys and baby clothes, her husband's belongings that she was keeping for Avery, and other items she couldn't part with. It wouldn't take long to get it cleaned up. The apartment had a bathroom and a kitchenette, and it was air-conditioned.

Maybe she could get Dustin released by promising he would live on her premises, under her supervision.

But was that wise? Maybe they would need more security. When this story broke in the media, it might be dangerous for even her and Avery to live here, whether Dustin was here or not.

She turned off the light and went back into her house. She dragged herself into the shower to get ready to meet the prosecutor. She couldn't drop the ball. It would be daylight soon.

She just hoped Dustin would go along with her plan to get him out of jail today. He wouldn't like her making a promise that he had to keep.

11

Please don't wake her up." Travis blocked the nurse's aide from getting past the hospital room door with her rolling blood-pressure monitor. "She really needs to sleep," he whispered.

"I have to log her blood pressure and temp."

"Could you give her a little more time? Make her last on your rounds? Please. She went for days without sleeping."

She sighed heavily, as if this was a huge imposition, but she left the room.

Travis turned back to his wife. She lay on the bed so still, her eyes sunken and her skin gray, as if she'd already surrendered. But the new medication they had started her on two days ago would turn things around. It had to. He went back to the recliner he had slept in and drank the coffee they'd brought her with her breakfast. She hadn't been awake to eat it, but he'd refused to let them take her tray. The coffee was cold now, but he guzzled anyway. He had to stay alert.

He turned the TV on with the volume low and read the closed captioning on the screen.

"The bomber at Trudeau Hall is still at large, and federal officers are running down leads . . ." He sat up straighter. A bombing? He turned it up a notch so he could hear the voices.

"Police sources say that a bomb threat preceded the explosion at Trudeau Hall, but the threat wasn't taken seriously."

Travis's attention perked to life as the screen revealed the building he recognized, burned and gutted, and young people with soot-covered faces crying on camera.

"The bomb struck the stage and killed Ed Loran, who was running for president as a third-party candidate. We're told dozens of others were killed, though the final number hasn't been released yet."

Travis stood and walked closer to the TV, as if that could provide some perspective on the news story, even though the speaker was on the remote attached to Crystal's bed.

"But police have confirmed that a person of interest is in custody. We haven't been able to get a name yet, but we will have more later."

His phone vibrated in his pocket, and he pulled it out and looked at the screen. He didn't recognize the number, but he'd been waiting for the doctor to call with the results of Crystal's latest tests. He stepped out into the hallway and answered. "Hello?"

The robot voice told him it was from the local jail. "An inmate named . . ." There was a slight pause, then Dustin's voice said, "Dustin Webb."

"Dustin?" Travis cut in.

The robot cut him off, ". . . would like to call you."

"Dustin!" Travis said, but the robot continued, telling him

he had to set up a prepaid account with his credit card before he could accept the call. He got out his credit card and punched in the numbers. He followed the prompts, put twenty dollars on the account, then waited for Dustin.

"Travis?"

It was a bad connection, not very loud, so Travis turned his phone up. "What's going on, man?"

"I got arrested yesterday. Somebody planted four boxes of RDX in my trunk, then told the police. They're trying to connect me to the bombing at Trudeau Hall."

Travis couldn't catch his breath. He rubbed his fingers through his hair. "Why didn't you tell me? I would have bailed you out yesterday!"

"I was being interviewed for hours. I tried calling you a couple of times during the night."

"I had it on Do Not Disturb from ten to seven. I'm so sorry."

"It's fine. Is she okay?"

"She's sleeping," Travis said. "What can I do, Dustin?"

"Nothing until my bond hearing this afternoon."

"Dustin, who did this?"

"I don't know. I'm racking my brain. But somebody hates my guts."

"Nobody hates you," Travis said. "This is ridiculous."

"I just wanted to let you know. You might get interviewed again. And check your trunk."

"You think this is related to the break-in at ChemEx?"

"Has to be. They stole RDX and TNT. They set me up."

"Let me know what I can do. Anything, Dustin. Seriously, just call."

"Okay, man. Talk to you soon."

Travis hung up and stared into the air as the news sank in. Dustin in jail? A bombing at Trudeau Hall? This didn't make sense. The sad ache of tears welled in his eyes. His heart pounded in triple rhythm, threatening to overcome him completely. But he didn't have time to be overwhelmed.

One crisis at a time.

12

Jamie couldn't make herself take Dude to the kennel that morning, so she put his food and water in her backyard and left him there.

The county prosecutor's office was open at seven thirty in the morning, but the secretaries and receptionists weren't in yet. Jamie stepped inside the small lobby and texted her old colleague.

Louis, it's Jamie. I'm in the lobby.

Come on back, he texted.

She went up the hall toward the bank of cubicles and offices where she had once worked. Louis met her halfway and gave her a warm handshake and a pat on the back. "Good to see you, Jamie. Sorry I couldn't meet you for breakfast, but I had another commitment."

"I know you have a lot going on," she said, following him into his office.

He went behind his desk and sat down, and she took the seat across from him.

"Look at you, sitting at the helm."

"I know, right? Who would have thought?"

"I figured you'd be in private practice by now," she said.

"Making the big bucks, like you? Congratulations on the Ash case, by the way. That's a real feather in your cap."

"Yeah, it was a big relief."

"So you're representing Dustin Webb?"

"Yes. You're the lead prosecutor, right? Since ATF is involved, I wasn't sure."

"There might be federal charges, but right now I'm the lead."

She pulled her laptop and notes out of her briefcase and gave him a serious look. "The thing is, I know him. I've known him since he was a kid. We grew up next door to each other."

"Really." It wasn't a question, but a statement of surprise.

"He didn't do it. He was framed, and I can prove it."

She didn't wait for his reaction, because he heard that all the time. Instead, she pulled up the video of Dustin parking his car at the hospital, his going in and getting filmed inside the lobby, where his face showed. Then she fast-forwarded to the point where the van drove slowly up the parking lot row where he was parked, and two men loaded boxes into his trunk.

"How do we know that he isn't one of those men?" he asked.

"I'm sure you'll pull the same video. You'll see that he didn't come out. Here's the time stamp," she said, pointing to it on the video. "At the exact same time, we have footage of him sitting in the waiting room on the fourth floor. His business partner had a crisis with his wife that night. She's a cancer patient, and they didn't think she was going to make it through the night. Dustin was there for several hours."

"Okay, but he had everything he needed to break into that ammunition plant the week before."

"So did a lot of people who worked there. The night that happened he was at home from eight thirty to seven the next morning. Home security cameras at his house prove this."

"Video can be doctored. And who's to say he didn't get those people to load that stuff in his car?"

"Evidence still matters, doesn't it, Louis? There isn't any, or your charges would be different. And you don't have any evidence that he was at ChemEx the night it was robbed."

"You know this is about way more than the ChemEx robbery. What is it you want, Jamie?"

"The arraignment's at two. I'm asking you not to stand in the way of his getting bond. It's important that we get him to safety before the press learns about this."

He chuckled. "Do you know how much flack I would get from my constituents if I let a potential terrorist out on bond?"

"He's not a potential terrorist. Terrorist statutes require two acts of violence, and they have to impact public policy. Dustin Webb doesn't have a history of violence or any other criminal behavior, he isn't a political person, and there's no connection between him and the theft or the bombing."

"I don't want him out, Jamie, and I don't want to protect him from the media."

"Do you want riots in your city? Outside your office? In front of the jail? Do you want to deal with the vigilantes who would demand his head?"

He sighed and rubbed his face, as if to say he didn't want those things either.

She drew in a deep breath. "I'd be willing to take full

responsibility for him as his attorney. I'm willing to take him into my recognizance. That's how sure I am that he's innocent. I wouldn't have him around my daughter if I had any doubt."

He sat back in his chair, rubbing his chin. "I don't know. I'll give it a look, but I can't promise anything."

"You know me, Louis. You know I'm a good judge of character."

"Not always," he said with a grin.

She knew what he was referring to. She had told him way too much about her husband's addictions. The comment irritated her. "Well, that's a low blow."

"Sorry," he said. "I shouldn't have said that. I know you're a good attorney."

She knew that was as close as she could get for right now. "A few other things before I go. I need the inventories of what you took during his home and car searches."

"I can get you those sometime today."

She gathered her things and started to leave.

"Jamie," he said as she got to the door.

She turned back.

"You might want to get a short-term rental whether he gets out or not. The press is going to come down hard on you, too."

"Yeah, I've considered that."

Leaving the building, she felt a knot in her stomach. She had no idea what Louis would recommend to the judge. It was likely that he would ask him to withhold bond.

Convincing the judge to set bond without being able to present evidence would not be easy. She had her work cut out for her.

13

"Shouldn't you get off the computer for a while?"

Taylor sat on the floor, her laptop on her coffee table. She turned from her screen and looked up at her sister but didn't answer. She'd been poring through social media, studying pictures of the concert, and reading news articles that came up on her platforms. Much of the news was about the band members, all of whom survived, and Ed Loran's death and his popularity since he'd declared his third-party candidacy. He was being celebrated like a national hero.

The television played on the wall, its volume low. "The forty-eight-year-old Libertarian was the former CEO of Cell Three Therapeutics," a reporter was saying, "a controversial biotech company engaged in a decades-long class-action lawsuit . . ."

"You haven't even slept," Harper said. "This isn't healthy."

"I just need to do this," Taylor said. "I keep going over and over it in my mind, trying to figure out if there is some other direction I could have gone or some way I could have turned back."

Harper sat down on the couch behind her and looked over her shoulder. "They're just pictures of crowds. You can't tell anything from that, can you? "

"Maybe. With all the cameras in the room, somebody could have gotten an image of the bomber."

"You can't relive this and make it come out different. It happened the way it happened, and it wasn't your fault. You couldn't have saved Mara and Desiree, no matter how you wish you could."

"I know."

"Do you?" Harper sighed. "Taylor, have you taken your meds today?"

"I don't know."

"Taylor—"

"I'll take it in a minute."

"Because you're doing it again."

Taylor turned around. "Doing what?"

"Obsessing."

"Excuse me, but I was in a bombing yesterday. My friends are dead. My OCD has nothing to do with that."

"I'm just saying that when you're this stressed, things can get worse. You have to be consistent with your medication."

"All right, I'll go take it." She got up and went into her bathroom, poured the pills into her hand, and swallowed them. She stared at herself in the mirror. She wasn't being OCD, was she? She was just doing what any other survivor was probably doing today.

This wasn't like in her late teens, when her life had begun to revolve around her rituals. When her parents had started noticing her growing anxiety and actions they couldn't explain, they had gotten her into therapy. Only then had she admitted to her anxious, fearful thoughts that were relieved only by her ritual compulsions. *This is what's going to kill me* had been one of those obsessions that she'd repeated to herself hundreds of times a day, and it was always followed by cleaning counters with bleach, wiping light switches and doorknobs, pencils and pens. Those rituals made her late for everything, and even then, she still had to wipe down the steering wheel and console.

Another one was, *They hate me.* She would tell herself that whenever she met someone's eyes or had a conversation. It had flattened her senior year of high school and her first year of college. After that, she'd been put on medication. She'd spent the past three years in exposure and reaction therapy, where she learned to stop responding to her anxious thoughts by doing those rituals. The medication had helped her control those thoughts and actions until eventually her problem was like a distant voice in the background, rather than a constant blaring in her ear.

But yes, yesterday had been a trigger. Maybe Harper was right. She had to be careful.

She went back into the living room. "Consider me medicated. Now I'm going to go back to what I was doing, and I'll pay careful attention to myself so I don't spiral."

Harper's eyes were locked onto the TV. "Have you heard this?"

Taylor looked at the TV. "What?"

Harper turned the sound up and backed up the segment on the DVR so that it would replay the report she'd been watching.

The local news anchor on Fox 5 Atlanta was speaking. "Investigators are now saying that the bombing at Trudeau Hall that killed Ed Loran and at least twenty-four others, and injured fifty-three, could have been planted beneath the building."

Taylor grabbed the remote and turned it up even more. An investigator at a press conference came up on the screen. "We now believe that the bomb was not planted inside the building, which explains why no one saw anything. But to create that kind of explosion would require a much greater volume of explosives than was first believed. For it to have exploded from below and do that much damage to the floor above it in the auditorium, it would have been a bomb similar to that used in the Oklahoma City bombing. And that was achieved with a truckful of explosives, as we know. So they're looking now at the possibility that the explosives may have been strategically parked under the building."

Taylor caught her breath. She started to shake. Her heart began pounding.

Trucks under the building.

"Wait. I saw something!" She went to the photos on her phone and clicked through the pictures that she and Desiree and Mara had taken last night. She scrolled back twenty or thirty pictures to just before they went in.

They had taken some outside the concert hall near the bay where celebrities turned into the driveway to be dropped off under the building. The three of them had hung around there for a few minutes, hoping to get a shot of the guys in Blue Fire when they pulled in. They had taken four or five selfies, then finally gave up on seeing the band and went inside.

She studied each picture. The three of them were in the foreground, smiling for the camera. But what was in the background?

Finally she saw something—a U-Haul truck turning into

the entrance for unloading, where VIPs and talent were known to enter the building.

She sucked in her breath and enlarged it to see if the person behind the wheel was visible. But the truck's interior was too dark.

"Here!" she said.

Harper took her phone and studied the picture.

"That could be the truck," Taylor said. "I didn't think anything about it at the time. I only remembered it just now as I was going through them. But it may be important."

Harper covered her mouth, then let her fingers slide down her chin. "I still can't believe you survived. But this explains some things. Nobody could have seen the bombs if they were hidden underneath, packed in a truck that big."

"I'm going to the police." Taylor got up and headed to her bedroom.

Harper followed her. "Taylor, why?"

"I need to show them this picture."

"You could call them or email it."

"Are you kidding? They're probably getting a million false leads right now."

"And this could be another one. That U-Haul could have been a food vendor or concessions supplies, or even roadies for the band."

"But it might not be. I need to show up in person to make sure they see it. I don't want them to take days to get around to this. It could be significant. You said yourself I should get off the computer and get out of here. I'm doing that now. Come with me if you want, but I have to do this."

Harper gave one more of her classic sighs. "All right, I'll come. But we might be there for hours before you can see anyone."

"I'm willing to wait," Taylor said.

She quickly changed her clothes, brushed her teeth, and grabbed her purse, her computer, and her phone.

Then they hurried out to the car and drove to the police station.

14

The law firm of Lewis, Brackton and Devereux was humming when Jamie pushed through the glass doors after her meeting with the prosecutor. Assistants rushed down the halls, phones rang and were answered, and messengers popped in and out the front doors, documents in hand. Lawyers and paralegals clustered in the coffee room, around the water cooler, and in the doorways of their colleagues' offices.

Too distracted to interact with the others, Jamie hurried past all of it to her office. She looked around at the plush room that spoke so eloquently of the progress she had made in becoming a respected member of the firm. Last night she had hardly thought about her win in court yesterday, though she was sure her firm had.

She sat down behind her desk, quickly scanned her messages, and decided none were pressing enough to distract her from Dustin's case. She had to concentrate. There was no room for a slipup now. She wanted him out of jail this afternoon.

There was a knock on the door, and Max Devereux, her mentor and a full partner in the firm, stuck his head in. His youthfully styled, gray-sprinkled hair was perfectly groomed, though fatigue lines beneath his eyes revealed his middle age. "Congratulations, Powell," he said. "Great job in court."

Jamie smiled. "Thank you. It was a team effort."

"Yes, it was," he said, sloughing off the gratitude. "Listen, could I see you in my office for a minute? I need your help on the Genpack case."

Jamie gestured to the documentation on her desk. "Could it wait? I took a case last night, and I have to be in court this afternoon. I have a lot of work to do."

"A case?" Max stepped farther into the office, holding his coffee cup as if it were an elder's staff. He wasn't wearing his coat, Jamie noted, and his tie was loose—unusual for a man who valued his professional image more than his law degree. It was obvious he'd been absorbed in his work all night, since he only allowed himself to look the least bit casual when he was pressured for time. "What case?"

"My client was arrested yesterday," Jamie said. "He's becoming the scapegoat for the bombing downtown. They pulled him over, searched his car, and found four boxes of RDX explosives."

"You've got to be kidding."

"I have security video that shows someone planting it in his car when he was parked in a hospital parking lot the other night. He didn't do it."

"How did this fall into your lap?"

Jamie bristled, but reminded herself that he was her superior. "I know him. I've been friends with him for years."

Max shook his head. "Could be great exposure for the firm.

Most of it will be negative, but if you do a good job, it'll be great for you. You'll have to stay off social media, though, and avoid the press, because they'll crucify you."

She sat back and crossed her arms. "I can handle it. I've already taken the case. I'm going to win it. Dustin Webb is not going to prison."

Max frowned, thinking it through. "The prosecutors will have a tight case against him. Be aware of that. They must have had probable cause to search his car."

"I'm way ahead of you. I've got this."

He chuckled as he left the office.

Any minute now the press would get hold of the information about his arrest. It would be a media circus. She knew Dustin wasn't prepared for that.

She had been in front of the cameras plenty of times with her clients, but she'd never taken a case where multiple deaths were being blamed on one. Would he be safe? Would she?

She shook that thought from her head and told herself to tackle one thing at a time. The press hadn't reported it yet, so she had some time. But once they went to court, all bets were off. The media would descend on them like an avalanche. What if he was let out after that and the outraged mob came after him?

The thought was disturbing, but not yet as bad as the alternative. The thought she couldn't live with was disappointing Dustin.

"Don't let me down, okay?" Dustin's voice played over in her mind like a lyric from the past.

He had said those words to her before her first date when she'd just turned fifteen, and she remembered thinking then, as she thought now, that she'd jump across the Grand Canyon to keep from letting him down.

"And let that guy know I'll be watching when he brings you home. He'd better be real careful."

Jamie had laughed. "You're not my dad. Besides, there's no way you'll be home on a Saturday night. The town would have to close down without you, and the broken hearts . . . Well, I can't even stand to think about it."

Dustin's mirthless expression held the foundation of a promise. "I'm not going anywhere tonight," he'd said.

Jamie remembered the exhilarating feeling she'd had just knowing that Dustin was at home . . . waiting . . . on the off chance that she would need him. It had distracted her from the date.

Her assistant came into her office to hand her some mail. "Lila, I think we might have some trouble after word gets out that I'm representing Dustin Webb. It may be best if I don't stay in my house."

"You could do a short-term rental at an Airbnb."

"I'll look for one now, but would you be okay with renting it in your name, with your credit card? I can transfer the money to you through PayPal."

Lila shrugged. "Sure. Sometimes the landlords meet you to show you around the property, so I can meet them and get the key if you're trying to stay anonymous."

"Yeah," she said. "I think the media are going to be looking for Dustin and for me. I don't want anybody to know where we'll be."

"You've never shied away from that before."

"I've never represented someone being connected to a terrorist attack."

She spent the next few minutes looking for a place to live for a month or more—with a dog—until the media frenzy stopped. It had to be a big enough place for Dustin to stay there as well, if that turned out to be necessary. Lila completed the transaction for her and made an appointment to get the key.

Jamie checked her watch and decided to leave early and visit Dustin before the hearing. She gathered up her papers and stacked them in her briefcase. It was up to her, she thought. She had to get him out of jail today.

15

Dustin wished he could change out of the brown jumpsuit and into the clothes he'd been wearing yesterday, but that wasn't happening. They'd called him this morning for court, even though his hearing wasn't until two, then they'd bused him to the courthouse with all the other prisoners seeing the judge today. Most of them had morning hearings, so they waited in a secure room in the courthouse until their names were called. No food, no water, not even a bathroom trip without an Act of Congress.

It was now afternoon and there was only a small group left, so he prayed he'd be called in soon. He paced across the tiny interview room, his orange flip-flops slapping his feet as he did. How did people stand these for months, years, decades?

God, please help me out of this.

Would the press be waiting for him when he went into court today? He thought of friends, acquaintances, and clients—what would their reactions be when they saw the breaking news and read that he'd been arrested in connection to the bombing? Already, he could imagine six months of work vaporizing. Who would hire him and Travis to install a security system when he was being accused of this?

But the knife twisted even deeper when he thought of Aunt Pat's reaction, the I-told-you-sos he knew were probably racing through her mind right about now. "No son of mine would have wound up in a mess like this," she'd told him more than once when he'd committed school infractions. She'd always known he would bring disgrace and embarrassment to her family, ever since the day he'd been thrust upon her like an inheritance no one wanted. For years, he'd felt certain that Aunt Pat had hidden her silver just in case her sister's orphaned son decided to pawn it.

He could envision her now, running around her house pulling down the shades, hiding her car in the garage, screening her calls, lest someone humiliate her with the knowledge of Dustin's arrest. He almost felt sorry for her.

He heard a sound in the hallway and looked through the small window in the door. It was Jamie. She had stopped at a table to confer with one of the guards. She glanced toward the room he was in.

He stepped away from the door as Jamie came toward it. She looked tired, as if she had slept even less than he had. There was no trace of a smile in her eyes. She was anxious. That wasn't a good sign.

The door opened, and Jamie stepped inside. "Hey," she said. "How was your night?"

"Fantastic," he said. "Slept like a baby."

Jamie wasn't fooled. Had she ever been? "You look like you used to look when you were hung over after one of your nights out with the Crawley brothers."

"Those were nasty rumors."

"Right. You don't look like you got much sleep in that cell."

"It wasn't so bad," he said. "Were you able to get my dog to the kennel?"

The way she grinned told him she'd met Dude. "Yeah, about that. I kind of . . . didn't have the heart to take him."

"So he's still at home?"

"Not exactly. I took him home with me last night."

For the first time since he'd been here, he laughed. "Are you serious?"

"He needed social interaction. I didn't want him to be alone all night."

"Did he sleep in your bed?"

She looked down at the floor and sighed. "Yes, he did. And this morning he seemed so comfortable in my yard, and it's fenced and all, and it was a nice morning, so I thought I'd just keep him there."

"He has that effect on people."

"Yes, he does. He's very enthusiastic. It's contagious."

"*Enthusiastic* is a good word for it. Well, hopefully you won't have to keep him for long. As much as I'd like to stay here, are you going to be able to get me out?"

"I talked to the DA and pulled out everything I had. I honestly don't know. I'm going to ask for bond, and he might stand in the way. We won't know until we get there."

"So . . . if the judge says no bond, what does that mean? Do I have to stay here until a trial?"

"They can hold you until an indictment. Then we can try for bond again."

"Is there already a grand jury?"

"Those are secret, so I wouldn't be told. But I don't think so. Not quite yet."

"So it could take months?"

She let out a hard sigh. "Let's not get ahead of ourselves. We can talk about all this after court. For now, let's just think positive. And pray."

He had been praying, all night. If he knew her, she had, too.

"I'll meet you in there," she said. "They'll probably bring you in in a few minutes. Meanwhile, I'm going to try to catch the prosecutor and see if I can gauge his thoughts."

As she went back to the door, he smiled weakly and said, "I'm rooting for you."

"And I'm rooting for you."

Something about knowing that gave him a measure of peace as he waited.

16

The police station was different than Taylor expected. She stepped inside the glass doors, Harper following close behind her, and looked around for an information desk.

A uniformed policeman stood behind a counter, poring over pictures on his computer screen. Taylor stepped toward him and waited for him to look up.

He finally turned to her. "Yeah, can I help you?"

"Yes. I was wondering if Detective Borden is here. I need to talk to him about the bombing."

"Are you a witness?"

"Yes. I talked to him yesterday, and he told me to call if I thought of anything else. He also said he wanted to interview me today. I found something that might interest him."

That seemed to get his attention, and he stood up straighter and looked past her around the room where mostly empty desks were lined up.

"Hey, Klein!" he called across the room.

A uniformed woman stood up. "Yeah?"

He motioned her over, and she came to the desk.

"You need to take a statement from this young lady. She's a witness from yesterday."

Taylor shook her head. "No, I really want to see Detective Borden. I've already talked to him and given him pictures. I just wanted to follow up because I thought of something else that I didn't tell him. I don't want to start all over. No offense," she said, glancing at the woman.

"It'll be okay," Klein said. "Come to my desk." She led them through the room that was probably usually busier. But Taylor guessed most of the police officers were out investigating the terror attack.

Klein pulled up two chairs in front of her desk and motioned for them to sit.

Taylor wasn't sure why this gave her such anxiety. "Can't you call Detective Borden?"

"I will if I need to. He's working the case." She pulled out a form and poised to write. "I don't have a lot of time. If you could just give your info to me, I'll make sure he gets it."

"Okay," Taylor said with a heavy sigh. "I guess it's better than nothing."

"Story of my life," the woman muttered. "First, tell me your name, address, phone number."

Taylor gave her the information. "I gave the detective some of my pictures yesterday from inside the building just before the bombing happened. But today I heard on the news that the explosion was from underneath the building. It rang a bell for me. It made me think of one of my pictures, something I didn't know might be connected."

Taylor picked up her phone and thumbed through the pictures until she found the one with the truck. "Just before we went into the concert hall, my friends and I were hanging out around the VIP entrance, hoping we could see the guys in Blue Fire when they showed up for the concert. We never did. But we took a few selfies out in front of it. And when I looked back at those pictures, I saw this U-Haul box truck pulling in behind us. It may not be important. I know it could be a caterer or a roadie with the band or merchandise or something. But it just strikes me as odd that it was a rental truck."

The officer frowned, took Taylor's phone, zoomed in more with her fingers, and studied the pictures. "Okay, just a minute. I need to take this for a second."

"Sure," Taylor said.

Klein headed back to the front desk and showed the sergeant the picture. Then she got on the phone.

"Maybe she's calling him," Harper said.

Taylor watched the woman talking animatedly on the phone. "Yeah, maybe."

"It could be just what they need," Harper said. "Maybe they can trace the truck."

Taylor didn't get her hopes up, because the numbness that had set in had left her feeling flat and soulless. *She hates me.* The old, ritualistic mantra played through her head.

"Are you okay?" her sister whispered.

"Yeah. I don't really know what's wrong with me."

"Nothing is wrong with you. You're still in shock. You're experiencing grief, confusion—"

"I'm okay," Taylor said again.

Finally Klein came back to her desk. "I just spoke to Detective Borden. He wants to see you. Can you wait for him?"

"Yes, of course."

"It may be an hour or so. He's a little tied up right now."

"At the concert hall?"

"Probably."

"Have you moved the bodies yet?" Taylor asked.

Klein tipped her head. "I'm sorry, I can't talk to you about that."

"Okay, I get it. It's just . . . some of my friends are in there."

"I know," Klein said. "I'm so sorry. But it's a crime scene."

Taylor closed her eyes. It wasn't right. First, they'd been viciously murdered. And now they were left on that floor?

The officer led them back to the waiting area, but before they reached it, Taylor felt dizzy, as if she might faint. She reached for the wall to steady herself.

"You're not okay," Harper said.

Taylor tried to rally. "I am. I just should have eaten."

"I'll go find a vending machine."

Taylor sat down, and the dizziness subsided.

I'm going to die of this. I'm going to die of this.

She knew what she was doing. She was letting her intrusive thoughts invade her mind again. She would call her therapist when she got home and maybe get in to see her today. She couldn't let herself slide into that mode again. She had come too far to slip back now.

Harper returned with a Coke and a bag of potato chips. "Eat these. We might be here for a while."

Taylor ate them even though she could barely taste. What

had happened to her senses? Had they fallen asleep, since *she* wasn't able to? Were they shocked into paralysis?

As she ate, she felt life slowly seeping back into her.

An hour passed. Then two.

Finally Harper went back to the desk. "Excuse me, but my sister was told that the detective would be here an hour ago. He's still not here. Can we go home, or should we stay?"

"The detective asked that you stay," the sergeant said. "Really, it shouldn't take much longer."

Harper came back to Taylor. "Maybe you should call him yourself. Didn't he give you his card?"

"Yeah." Taylor grabbed her bag and looked through it, trying to figure out what she had done with the card. When she didn't find it, she looked up at Harper. "I think I must have put it in my pocket yesterday. What did you do with my bloody clothes?"

"They're still in my gym bag in the trunk of my car. I'll go get it."

Taylor leaned her head against the wall as her sister went out to the parking lot. She was tired, so tired. Sleep had evaded her last night. Terror invaded her dreams every time she nodded off, so she'd tried to keep herself awake.

I'm going to die of this.

Just a little longer, she told herself. Then she would call her therapist.

17

Jamie stepped inside the courthouse and set her briefcase and phone on the metal-detector belt. The person in front of her was wearing pajamas and flip-flops. So much for trying to make a good impression when she stood before the judge. It never ceased to amaze her that people whose lives and freedom depended on the judge's ruling made so little effort.

The pj-clad defendant had to go back outside to return her phone to her car. The guard checked Jamie's bag and handed that and her phone back to her, since attorneys were the only ones allowed to bring anything in.

"Hey, could you tell me something?" she asked the guard. "Have you seen any media in here this afternoon?"

The guard shook his head. "Not any of the ones I'd recognize."

"Great," she said. She went into the courtroom and looked around. The bailiff walked up and down the room, keeping the place quiet, but defendants and their friends or family members still whispered among themselves. She didn't see anyone she recognized to be media. It was too good to be true that they wouldn't have learned of Dustin's arrest yet. That couldn't last much longer.

Louis Dole, the prosecutor she'd spoken to this morning, stood in the gallery, talking to another attorney.

She took her seat on the second row as the door opened and a bailiff escorted the incarcerated defendants in to sit on the front two rows of the gallery. She saw Dustin walk out in that brown jumpsuit. He kept his eyes downcast, as if that could make him disappear.

The very sight of him walking out like that in front of everyone incited outrage that she had to swallow. It wasn't right. He'd done nothing wrong, even though he'd had a tough start in life. He had made something of himself, and he didn't deserve to be treated like a common criminal.

The bailiff walked them to the front row, right in front of her, and the inmates took their seats. As Dustin walked past her, their eyes met. She hoped he didn't see the tears pooling in hers. That was so unprofessional. She told herself the emotion wasn't acceptable, not in front of the judge and prosecutor, not in this courtroom.

They waited through a number of other cases. Finally Dustin's name was called, and Jamie got up and hurried to the front. Dustin came and stood beside her at the lectern where a microphone would pick up their voices for the judge. She pretended to adjust the mike, but turned it off as she did. It would keep people behind them from hearing their conversation.

"In the case of Dustin Webb versus Decatur County, what is the charge?"

Louis, who stood to the side, answered, "Felony possession

of explosives or incendiary devices." He didn't go on to ask that the judge deny bond, so when he said nothing more, she took that as her cue.

"Your Honor," Jamie spoke up. "I'd like to ask you—"

"Is that microphone out again?" the judge cut in. "Never mind, I can hear you."

She went on. "I'd like to ask you to post a low enough bond that my client can get out today. I'll take him into my own custody."

Dustin frowned at her. She kept her eyes on the judge.

"Ms. Powell, why would you do a thing like that?" the judge asked.

"Because I know him," she said. "I've known him for many years, and I'm confident of his character."

"And you're willing to go out on a limb and put your reputation at stake?"

"Absolutely, Your Honor."

The judge studied the paperwork for a few minutes, then finally looked up. "This is a very serious charge," he said to Dustin. "I can't set a low bond. I'll set it at $500,000, but Mr. Webb, if you post it, you need to stay in town."

"Yes, Your Honor," he said.

The judge finished the case, and Jamie led Dustin back to the gallery. "What happens now?" Dustin whispered. "I don't have $500,000."

"You only need 10 percent," she whispered. "Is $50,000 possible?"

He hesitated. "I have a line of credit for my business. I need to talk to my partner, but I think I can get it."

"Give me his number. I'll call him and get the money."

He told her the number. She tapped it into her phone. "Where did the custody thing come from?" he asked. "Was it really necessary?"

"Yes. We'll discuss that later. They're going to take you back to the jail, and when I have the money, I'll call a bail bondsman and get everything started."

"So I'm getting out today?" he asked.

"That's the plan," she said.

The guard took his elbow to escort him back to jail, and Jamie slipped out of the courtroom.

She went out to her car and called the number Dustin had given her for Travis. He didn't answer, so she left a message telling him who she was and that it was urgent that she speak to him. But how long might that take? She couldn't wait. She drove toward the hospital. She would find him there if he didn't call back.

She was halfway there when her phone rang. She picked up on her car's bluetooth. "Jamie Powell."

"Hey, this is Travis. I got your message about Dustin."

She pulled into a parking lot and stopped her car. "Travis, thank you for calling me back."

"Is this *the* Jamie?" he asked. "The one who lived next door?"

Her face flushed warm. "He told you about me?"

"About a thousand times," he said. "I'm glad he called you."

She pushed that aside. "He's in a lot of trouble. I'm not sure if you're aware that he was arrested yesterday and he spent the night in jail."

"I knew," Travis said. "He called from the payphone in the cell. Do you think you'll be able to get him out?"

"That's why I'm calling you," Jamie said. "The judge set $500,000 bond."

"Five hundred thousand?" Travis asked. "That's ridiculous."

"It is what it is. He only has to come up with fifty thousand to get out today."

"*Only* fifty thousand?"

"That's right. He said that you and he had a line of credit at the bank for your business. He needs to use that for his bond. After he appears in court, he gets it back."

"Of course," Travis said. "We can get that money. I just can't leave the hospital right now."

He gave her instructions, and a short time later Jamie pulled up in front of Travis's house. Wendy, Travis's mother-in-law, came to the door trailed by two toddler boys. Jamie followed Wendy into the house and watched as she searched the drawers in Travis's desk for the business checkbook. "He said it's in his desk, that it's camel-colored. Not here." She tried another drawer.

Something crashed in the living room, and Wendy rushed into the hallway. "Come on, guys. You trying to scare me to death?"

Jamie stepped out of the small study and saw that the crash had been the toy box, now turned on its side.

Wendy sighed. "They don't play with one toy. They play with thirty-five, all at the same time. We were just over here getting a few things. It's easier at my house."

She went back into Travis's office. "Here it is! Why didn't he just say the bottom left drawer?"

Jamie took the checkbook. "I'll take this to him and get him to sign it." She studied the frazzled woman. "Are you okay?"

Wendy waved her off. "Twin two-year-olds . . . What do *you* think? But they're good boys. They're just really, really busy."

"It must be hard when your daughter is so sick."

"Yeah," she admitted. "But we're optimistic. They changed her treatment, and we're hoping this does the trick. She's going to get better. She just has to."

Jamie nodded. "Well, I'd better get going."

"Is Dustin going to get out today?" Wendy asked.

"Yes. We just have to pay his bond."

"Good. Of all people . . . literally . . . of *all* people, Dustin Webb shouldn't be locked up. He's salt of the earth, that man. He would never do any of this." Her eyes filled with tears, and she shook her head. "Sometimes it feels like the whole world is going stark raving mad."

"I'm right there with you."

One of the boys started to cry, and Jamie took the opportunity to wave and slip out. She drove back to the hospital and texted up to Travis. A few minutes later, a guy with longish blond hair and a beard came out. She got out of her car and met him. "Travis?"

"The famous Jamie," he said with a smile.

She started to shake his hand, but Travis reached for a hug.

"I feel like I know you."

Jamie didn't touch that. "Thank you for helping out with this. The check needs both of your signatures."

"Yeah, keeps us both accountable. It's his money, too," Travis said. "Are you sure they'll take a check?"

"I have a bondsman who works with my firm. As long as we have a credit card for them to charge if he doesn't show up in court, we'll be fine. I can get that from Dustin."

He wrote the check and signed it, then tore it out. Jamie took it.

"I'm glad he called you, even though he said he never would."

She frowned. "What? You mean as an attorney?"

"No, just in general. When he talked about you, I'd tell him to call you, and he'd just clam up."

"Why, do you think?" she asked. "I mean, I tried to get in touch with him, but he never answered."

"Some noble sense of honor, I'd imagine."

She frowned. "Honor? How?"

"I don't know. I've probably said too much already. Just . . . I'm glad he got over it."

She decided not to take the time to press him more. As she drove to the police station, she couldn't block the thoughts filing through her mind. Why would he have resolved not to call her all these years, even though she was on his mind? How did he attribute that to honor? The thought hurt, but she tried to push it out of her head.

A little later, Jamie stepped into the police department where the bail bondsman was to meet her. The plan was for them to walk over to the jail across the street together. He'd been in a neighboring county when she called him, so it would take him some time to get here.

She sat down in the waiting area and took a moment to catch her breath.

A girl sitting a few seats away was talking on the phone. "Detective Borden, this is Taylor Reid. Yes, I know they did. But we've been waiting for two hours. I was thinking if you couldn't come, maybe I could come back later. Yes, I want to talk to you, too. Yes. The truck was going under the building. The time stamp on the picture? Let me see."

Jamie looked over at the girl as she fumbled around with her phone and found a picture. She clicked on it to find the time. "It was at 5:08. The rally started at six. Another hour? Yes, I guess I can wait."

Detective Borden? That was the lead detective on Dustin's case. She wondered what the picture was. The girl had said something about a truck.

When the girl got off the phone, the woman next to her asked what he'd said.

"He said he got the picture and that they've already sent people to the U-Haul stores around town. They're working on it."

Jamie leaned toward her. "Excuse me. I couldn't help overhearing. Did you say you're a witness to what happened yesterday?"

The girl hugged herself, as if she was cold. "I mean, I was there," she said.

"Who are you?" the other woman asked boldly.

She got up and moved closer to them. "My name's Jamie Powell. I'm an attorney working on the case."

"I'm Taylor," the girl said. "This is my sister, Harper."

"Do you mind if I take you guys for a cup of coffee across the street?"

"I don't think I need an attorney," Taylor said. "I'm not in any kind of trouble. They just want to talk to me about a picture I took yesterday."

"He said he wouldn't be back for an hour, didn't he?"

"Yes."

"And I'm waiting for someone who's probably not going to be here for another half hour or so. Please, it would be so helpful if I could talk to you."

The women looked at each other, then Taylor shrugged. "Okay, I guess I could use some coffee."

Taylor told the sergeant where she was going, then she and

her sister followed Jamie across the street to a coffee shop half a block down from the jail. They ordered their coffee and sat down at a small table.

Jamie leaned forward and locked in on the girl, whose hair looked tousled, as if she hadn't brushed it today. She had dark circles under her puffy eyes and red mottled skin around them, as if she had been crying until her lids were raw. "I know this is hard to talk about over and over, but can you tell me what you were talking about? Something about a truck?"

Taylor swiped to the picture on her phone. She turned the phone around and showed Jamie. "They're saying the bombs came from underneath the building. And I remembered that we had taken these selfies out by the VIP entrance before the concert. And there was this U-Haul truck in the background, pulling under the building."

Jamie caught her breath. "This could help them find the perpetrators. Do you mind if I send this to myself?"

"I guess not."

Jamie forwarded the picture to her own phone and handed the device back to Taylor. "Did you have any other important information for the detective yesterday?"

Her sister spoke up. "I don't think it's good for her to be dragging all this up."

"No," Taylor cut in. "I don't mind. I need to talk about it. It's all I can think about."

Harper seemed hypervigilant as Taylor described how she and her friends had relished the concert. She told how they'd applauded when Ed Loran came onstage for his rally, when suddenly the explosion happened.

Halfway through the story, Jamie pulled a legal pad out of

her briefcase and started taking notes. "So you were in the third row, you said?"

Harper looked suspiciously at her note-taking. "You said you're working on the case? In what way?"

"I'm just gathering facts," Jamie evaded. "So how did you get out?"

Taylor told her of her frenzied exit. "I was in such a panic to get out that I didn't even look back for my friends. They were injured. They needed me and I abandoned them." Tears took over again.

Jamie touched her hand. "You didn't abandon them. You did what you had to do, what anyone else would have done. What hundreds of others did."

"Still, I didn't even—"

"No, you have to believe this," Jamie said. "You didn't make a choice to leave them. You were on autopilot, just trying to get to an exit. Your fight-or-flight instinct kicked in. God put that in you for a reason."

Taylor looked up at her through wet eyes.

"She's right," Harper told Taylor, then she looked back at Jamie. "I've been telling her that all day." But Jamie could see that Taylor wasn't buying it.

When Taylor finished her coffee, Jamie got up. "Can I get your phone number, in case I need to talk to you again?"

Taylor texted it to her after Jamie gave her own number.

"So, you said you were fact-gathering," Harper said. "What are you doing in the case?"

Jamie knew that Harper was only protecting her sister. She didn't want to lie to her. "I'm actually representing a client. I can't really go into it right now, but I'm trying as hard as the police are to find the killer or killers. The information you've provided could turn the case. I know it's taking a long time, but I hope you'll wait at the station long enough to talk to the detective. He might be able to jog your memory for other details. This could change everything about the case."

"Yeah, so I'd better get back," Taylor said.

Jamie walked her and Harper across the street. When they stepped inside, Jamie saw the bondsman already there, standing at the sergeant's desk, probably getting the information he needed for the paperwork.

She thanked Taylor and Harper, then went to do what needed to be done to get Dustin out of jail.

18

Jamie was finishing the paperwork with Jack, the bondsman, when Dustin was brought to the desk at the jail. He was back in the clothes he'd been wearing yesterday, and he looked more like himself than he had this morning. She got up from the bench where'd she'd been sitting with Jack. "You ready to bust out of here?"

"Yeah, the institution no longer has anything to offer me."

Jamie couldn't help the grin stealing across her face at his reference to the movie *Raising Arizona*, which had been one of his favorites when they were younger. For a second, it was as if they'd picked up where they left off. He gave her a knowing wink.

Jack handed him the paperwork to sign, breaking the moment. As Dustin scanned the paperwork on the counter, Jack shot the breeze with the officer in charge.

"What address is this?" Dustin asked her. "It says this is where I'll be residing."

"It's an Airbnb," she whispered. "Avery and I will be staying there, too."

His eyebrows came together. "Why?"

"Because," she said, keeping her voice low, "I said I'd take you into my custody, but it's easy for the media to find my house. So I rented this. I gave my word to the judge and to the DA, and now to the bondsman, that you'd be with me. So you're stuck."

Dustin's eyebrows knitted together as he stared at her. Finally he turned back to the paper in front of him. "Sounds to me like you're the one who got stuck," he muttered.

Hesitating one last time, Dustin sighed loudly, then finally scrawled his name. He thrust the paper at Jack, then cosigned the check next to Travis's name. "So we get this back after we go to court?"

"That's right," Jack said. "If you don't see the credit to your account, just get in touch with me after you appear."

"All right." He shook Jack's hand and thanked him. Jamie led him to the exit door. They waited as the officer unlocked it. Jamie pushed through the heavy metal door, and Dustin followed her.

The air was humid and heavy with the smell of rain. "What now?"

"We get to work," Jamie said.

Dustin didn't argue with that. As they walked out to her car, she could see the weight of the accusations against him crushing him. She prayed as they got into her Lexus that she would be able to get the charges dropped before the whirlwind of public rage blew him to pieces.

19

I have to help her . . . help her . . . help her . . ." The words twisted over and over in the depths of Travis Grey's dream, turning like a knife lodged in his heart. He jumped, shaking himself from his shallow, stolen sleep. Opening his eyes, he saw the dusty streaks of sunlight cutting between the blinds in the sterile hospital room. *Oh no*, he thought, sitting straight up in the vinyl recliner he'd slept in more than his own bed lately. *I fell asleep again.*

His bloodshot gaze flashed to his wife on the bed, a small, limp figure buried in sheets and tubes beneath a light as dim and fading as her life. *She's still breathing*, he noted with relief.

Travis got out of his chair, stiff muscles rebelling against the effort, and went to Crystal's side. Her hair had almost completely fallen out, but what was still there, he stroked gently. Her skin was grayer than it had been when they'd admitted her the other day, and she was much weaker. He could feel her drifting away, pulling into herself, preparing to surrender to death, but he wasn't ready to let her go.

She's going to bounce back. She always has before. This treatment is going to work.

He turned away from her bed and ran both hands through his hair. It was badly in need of a cut. Quietly, he stepped to the window, peered out between the blinds. People were parking and walking in and out, reminding him that life existed outside this room.

Images of his twin sons flashed through his mind, and he wondered how they were doing with Wendy today.

"They keep asking for Daddy," Wendy had told him on the phone earlier. "I guess they're getting used to Crystal not being here, but it's hard to explain why they can't see you."

Travis had bitterly mumbled that she should just tell them the truth, that they couldn't always have what they wanted in life. But the moment he uttered the words, he'd hated himself and apologized. The situation was too complicated for their young minds to understand. It was too complicated for him.

His phone vibrated, and he pulled it out and saw the text from Dustin. He was out of jail.

Travis breathed a long sigh of relief. He had barely thought about his partner since seeing Jamie Powell this afternoon. What kind of friend was he?

Crystal moved beneath the sheets, and Travis turned toward her. Her eyes fluttered open, their pale glaze blurring the clarity he always hoped for. But behind that glaze, she was still there. She glanced around the room, met his eyes, and the slightest smile lifted the corners of dry, cracking lips. "Perk up, Grey. You look awful."

He tried to smile, but he knew that waking up meant she would have to face another battle with pain. And that was something he couldn't joke his way around. At least, not without effort.

He took her hand. She was cold. She was always cold lately. He pulled up her covers and tried to warm her hand in the heat of his.

"Did I dream about Dustin being in jail?" she asked in a voice barely stronger than a whisper. "Or did you tell me that?"

Travis wished he hadn't told her, but it was hard to be selective about facts when she yearned to know everything that went on and never stopped asking Travis to fill her in. News about friends and family was a lifeline for her. It kept her fighting. "Yep, it's true, but don't worry. It's all a mistake. He just texted me that he's out."

"But it's serious, isn't it?"

"He'll get it straightened out," Travis said with a reassuring smile.

"You have to help him."

"He's using our line of credit for the bond. I'll do whatever else I can. All he has to do is say the word."

But he knew he wasn't going to leave Crystal's side, even if Dustin asked him to. Travis knew Dustin would understand. That was what friends were for.

20

Dustin looked uncomfortable in Jamie's passenger seat, his arm propped on the door beneath the window. "You look like you're bracing yourself," she said. "Don't worry, I've gotten better since you taught me how to drive."

He grinned. "Yeah, I was just having a flashback. Garbage cans and mailboxes flying in all directions."

She laughed for the first time since he'd come back into her life. "You haven't changed," Jamie said.

He glanced at her. "And you still look eighteen."

"I'd say the same thing, but you were never eighteen, were you, Dustin?"

"No, I guess I never was." He glanced off into the distance. His eyes held a trace of amusement, the way they always had when she hit a nerve.

"So tell me about this house you rented."

"We put it in my assistant's name, so no one should be able to trace us there. It's a big house. You can have the bedroom on the first floor, and Avery and I will sleep upstairs. They allow pets, so . . . Dude . . . can stay with you."

He chuckled. "You like that name?"

"It sounded just like you."

His smile faded. "I really doubt all this is necessary. Saying you'd take responsibility for me."

"Trust me, it is. The press don't know about this yet, but they will today. It's not going to look good. The DA and judge could have refused bond. I had to give it everything I had. It was either stay with me or stay in jail."

He sighed. "Well, I appreciate it. I'll pay for the rental, unless you're putting it on my tab."

"We'll work it out," she evaded.

"It's a lot of trouble for you and Avery. How old is she now?"

She smiled. "She's seven. You've never seen her, have you?"

"No, but I bet you have pictures on your phone."

She clicked on her phone and showed him the photo she used as her wallpaper.

He took the phone and studied it with a smile. "That's incredible. She looks just like you. Almost the same as when I met you." He laughed. "Glad she doesn't take after Joe."

The comment surprised her, but he quickly spoke up again.

"I'm sorry I brought that up. It must still be painful for you, what happened with him."

"Yeah, it is. But it's been four years. It's all right, though. I know you never liked him. Turns out you were right about . . . you know. The drugs."

"I didn't want to be right."

"I know." She could have gone deeper, but she decided it was best to let it go at that.

"This rental is actually to protect us as much as you. You've never been on the receiving end of a media frenzy. We have to be ready."

He looked out the window. The gravity of the situation seemed to settle over him like the rain clouds gathering. "Maybe I should get a different lawyer."

She glanced over at him. "Why would you say that?"

"Because you're putting yourself in danger, representing some guy being blamed for killing a bunch of innocent people."

"You're not some guy. You're my friend."

He kept his face diverted, and his hand came up to his mouth.

"Do you remember the day you left to join the army, Dustin? When we were all at the bus station saying goodbye?"

Dustin didn't look at her. "Yeah, I remember. Aunt Pat smiled more that day than the whole time I lived with her."

"But I didn't." Her eyes clouded, and suddenly she felt like that eighteen-year-old standing at the station, realizing for the final time that Dustin Webb was fading from her life. "I was proud of you, though. You sent Pat some pictures of you in your uniform, and she gave one to me. I thought you looked so handsome. You had so much purpose, so much pride. But . . . I really missed you."

He still didn't look at her.

She paused, then found her voice again. "I thought I'd hear from you. That you'd write. Something."

"I got busy."

"Yeah." Jamie swallowed the old emotion that had never let go of her. After a moment she found her voice again. "Well, now is what really matters, isn't it?" She cleared her throat, took a deep breath, and told herself she wouldn't let the hurtful memories get in the way of the good ones. "I know you're tired, but I feel like we need to work fast while we can do it unimpeded. Could you get Travis to meet us somewhere so I can interview him?"

"I doubt it. If you want to talk to him, you'll have to go to the hospital. His wife is really sick. He can't leave her."

"If I go, can you come with me? I need to go over things with both of you."

"I was hoping to go rent a car this afternoon, since they took mine for evidence."

"I'll take you there right now," she said. "Then you can meet me at the hospital. I know you're tired after being in jail, but we have a lot of work to do."

"Yeah, I figured that."

Jamie drove him to an Enterprise shop. In front, cars were lined up, waiting to be rented. "Text me if you have any problems. I can come back and get you."

"Will do."

"See you at the hospital. Listen, if anybody with the press calls, don't talk to them. Just hang up. In fact, don't answer calls unless it's me."

"Don't worry." He got out of the car and leaned back in. "Listen, about Travis. Don't expect him to be too social. Crystal's having a real bad time right now."

"Is she dying?"

"No." He said it as if the mere act of denial could stop the inevitable. "I mean . . . I hope not. They started her on a new treatment a couple of days ago, and we're optimistic. But he's really under a lot of stress."

As she pulled away, she thought about Dustin's words and realized he must be close to Crystal, too. The emotion had been clear on his face, and his denial had sounded like the words of a family member who couldn't cope with the loss.

She hated to storm into the hospital demanding an interview, but time was important to Dustin as well. The media attention was about to slam into them like the bomb that had started this whole cascade of events. She had to be ready.

21

The area around Trudeau Hall was cordoned off with yellow crime scene tape and barricades, but outside the perimeter, at the sign near the street, a little sympathy area had formed, where mourners had laid flowers and pictures of loved ones who had died.

Taylor approached the makeshift shrine and knelt in front of it, the terror and heart-pumping memory of yesterday overcoming her. She pulled out the pictures she'd printed of her friends and placed in clear plastic report covers. Later she would have better copies of these pictures laminated and replace this set. But for now, she wanted everyone who came to see her friends' faces—faces of actual human beings who hadn't seen the explosion coming, the explosion that had snatched away their lives when they were in their prime. She forced herself to look at the pictures already there. There were some she recognized. They'd been sitting in front of her or down the row. Who would have thought they'd all be dead now, mourned by strangers touched more by their deaths than by anything these victims had time to do in their lives.

Harper hugged her when she got up, and as they walked back to the car, a reporter and camera crew confronted her. She was too emotional to talk to them, so she waved them off and locked herself in the car.

Raindrops hit the windshield as they started to pull away. "It can't rain," Taylor said. "Everything will get wet. All the pictures . . ."

"I know," Harper said. "But we can take fresh ones tomorrow. They'll bring more flowers. More posters."

They could rebuild the shrine, Taylor thought as the rain started to come down harder. They couldn't rebuild the lives that had ended with such force.

She cried silently on the way home, wiping her face and her chin, mopping her nose, as Harper drove without talking.

When they got into Taylor's apartment, Harper stayed and made herself busy in the kitchen.

Taylor curled up on the couch, watching TV pundits speculate whether Ed Loran's opponents in the presidential race were possible culprits, while the news anchors suggested it was foreign terrorists who were known to target large crowds. Taylor took in every theory and tried to make sense of it in her head.

Extensive reports on Ed Loran's background waxed poetic about who he was and how he'd become a presidential contender.

"Loran's time as CEO was marked with controversy over the radiation said to be emitted from the Cell Three Therapeutics plant, which allegedly caused the cancer rate in the surrounding community to increase by a multiple of twenty. He navigated the company through that crisis and won the court case that would have cost the company millions in restitution to the town. After he resigned from Cell Three, he took over as CEO of BioTronics, a pharmaceutical company that created a universal flu vaccine . . ."

"I can't decide if he was a good guy or a bad guy," Harper said from the kitchen area.

"Me either."

"Why were you a supporter?"

"I wasn't," Taylor said. "He just had all these relationships in LA, and he had major headline musicians playing at his rallies. I went to see Blue Fire. That's all. I didn't know I was walking into a death trap."

"Politics can be deadly," Harper said. "He was siphoning off votes from both parties. Somebody wanted him out of the way."

"I hope not enough to kill him. Is the world that evil?"

"Yes," Harper said. "It is. Politics has gotten brutal. They'll get to the bottom of it. Just wait a few days."

Taylor hoped it would happen sooner rather than later. She didn't know if she could sleep until she knew whom to hate.

22

Sunlight from the world outside entered the little hospital room like a shy visitor afraid to come inside. Travis plugged the adapter into the hospital TV and started his download of *Duck Soup* onto his computer. He had read an article about laughter being the best medicine and had convinced himself that the Marx Brothers might have just the healing power Crystal needed.

"Wait till you see this," he told her. "It'll crack you up."

Crystal managed to smile. "If you wanted to crack me up, you should have brought those home movies of us in Rio."

Travis sat next to her on the bed as the credits rolled. "The karaoke ones where I sang 'Blue Suede Shoes'? You were mortified."

Crystal laughed for the first time in days. "No, it was when you sang 'I Feel Pretty' from *West Side Story*. It was such a weird choice."

Her words tumbled into laughter again, and Travis laughed, too, savoring every ounce of life he heard in the lilt of her voice.

"Did Dustin videotape all that?" Travis asked.

"Of course he did. Hey, that was the night that waitress hit on him."

"Old Dustin," Travis said. "He's always drawn the women, hasn't he?"

"Out of the woodwork," Crystal said.

The laughter gave him a healing release from his dreads and anxieties. It was enough to make him truly believe that his wife was on her way to recovering yet again.

If only the laughter held such healing power for her, too.

23

Jamie had just stepped into the lobby of the hospital when her phone chimed. She glanced at the screen and saw a Google alert for Dustin Webb, which she had set up earlier. Her heart sank. That meant someone had just mentioned his name in an article posted somewhere on the Internet. She stood in the lobby and clicked on the alert.

There it was, an article on a local TV station's website, posted fifteen minutes ago. Her stomach clenched. Things were about to get ugly.

Dustin walked through the front glass doors, and she showed him her phone. "The media's got it."

He glanced at the headline. "They named me?"

"Yeah. We need to talk to Travis and then get out of here before your picture is all over the news."

"How much did they tell?"

"Just the facts about the arrest." She punched the elevator button. "I'm sure they're digging up more."

"The facts," Dustin muttered. "Crazy how condemning a bunch of facts can look."

The elevator opened, and they stepped on. "They didn't connect you with the bombing yet."

"How long do you think that will take?"

"We can hope it goes over their heads. At least for a while. Sometimes things do. Not that many people will read this. It's a short article."

"No, not many. Just a few hundred potential clients, every friend I have in town, and my dear, sweet aunt Pat."

"Pat knows already," she said quietly. "My mother talked to her last night."

Dustin turned away from her and faced the elevator door. "Terrific. She's probably already called the judge and convinced him to add an extra twenty years."

"I guess she took it the way you'd expect," she said. "Mom said she was upset."

Dustin gave a bitter laugh. "Upset? Don't you think that's an understatement?"

Jamie wished she could tell him that Pat supported and loved him and believed in his innocence. But they both knew that wasn't the case.

The elevator opened. "Let's go see Travis," she said.

They got off on the floor where so many cancer patients were being treated. A family stood in the hallway crying and hugging each other.

Dustin met Jamie's eyes. "Sometimes my own problems seem so small when I compare them to what these people are going through."

"Your problems aren't small, Dustin."

"I know. It's just that Crystal's in here going through God knows what."

"Are you close to her?"

"Yeah," he whispered. "Real close."

She thought he would leave it at that, but after a moment, he went on. "Travis and I met in basic training, and we got assigned together after that. Two tours to Afghanistan. When we got out of the army, we started our security business, and we've been partners ever since. I was with him when he met Crystal. Travis told me right away he was going to marry that girl, bet me a thousand bucks, no less. I lost."

His expression faded into soul-deep sadness as they walked toward Crystal's room. "She's irreplaceable. She has to pull through."

Jamie didn't know Crystal, but she felt Dustin's pain. She set her hand on his shoulder. "She will," she said, wishing she had the power to make it so.

"Yeah, she'll be fine," he said with waning conviction. "Come on, it's this way."

Jamie hesitated. "Maybe I shouldn't go with you," she said, suddenly feeling like an intruder now that she knew just how bad Crystal's condition was.

"It's okay," he assured her. "She can't have visitors, anyway. Travis'll come out to see us."

24

I hate these places."

Dustin's baleful sentiment seemed couched in bitter memory as they waited in the hall near Crystal's room—this hall where she and other leukemia patients spent much of their lives chasing that ever-fleeting reprieve called remission.

"Yeah, me, too," Jamie mumbled. "Hospitals always remind me of when my dad died. It seems like we spent weeks in his room, talking, praying, hoping."

"I remember," he said. "It was rough on you."

"You made it easier," she said.

"Did I?"

"Yeah, you did," she said as she remembered the quiet night they'd shared in his car, driving aimlessly, not exchanging a word. "You took me away from the relatives and condolence calls, and didn't expect me to be strong."

He gave her a faint smile. "You were strong anyway, though."

"Well, it wasn't as if I was the only one who'd ever lost a parent."

He didn't respond to that. She knew he never liked talking about his parents' death when he was six. He looked back up the hall, saw a nurse coming with a tray of medications, and walked toward her. "Excuse me," he said quietly. "Could you please take a message to Travis Grey in 413?"

"Yes," she said, her voice low.

"Tell him Dustin's here."

"Would you mind waiting for him in the waiting room?"

"Sure." Jamie followed Dustin to the small room where a game show blared on a television set, and she saw Travis's kids with Wendy. "Wendy, hi."

Wendy got up to hug both of them. The children giggled as they moved all over the couch, oblivious to the sadness and disease that surrounded them.

Dustin charged toward them and grabbed one of the twin boys. Clearly, he knew the child well. Both boys squealed.

"Dustin, they're too loud!" Wendy said. "All of you boys hold it down."

Dustin put him down carefully. "Shhhh. Let's be vewy vewy quiet," he said.

"Do you really think they appreciate the Elmer Fudd imper-sonation?" Wendy asked. "Because they don't play Bugs Bunny on Nick Junior."

"Well then, we'll have to catch them up."

The boys, too geared up to settle down, bounced around Dustin. "Do me, Uncle Dustin!" Dustin picked up the other child and put him on his shoulders, then dropped him on the couch next to his brother.

"So Jamie sprung you?" Wendy asked. "Dustin, are you all right?"

"Yeah, I'm fine. Jamie wants to ask Travis a few questions."

"Maybe he can come out here and stay with these little rascals so I can go in," Wendy said.

"How's she doing?" Jamie asked.

A shadow fell over Wendy's eyes. "Not very well." She sat down again, and one of the twins crawled into her lap and pressed a surprise kiss on her chin, as if he sensed the sorrow coming over her. Wendy's eyes filled up with tears, and she took his face in both hands and kissed him back. "Mason, you sweet boy. You love Nanna?"

"Nope," he said with a teasing grin.

"Yes, you do. You and Miles take good care of me."

Jamie couldn't help laughing with them, but when she glanced at Dustin, she saw the pensive sadness in his eyes, as if at that very moment he was considering the possibility that the boys were soon to lose their mother, and that Wendy was about to lose her only child.

"Can you guys hold it down?" a man said from the doorway. "There are sick people up in here." It was Travis, smiling down at the twins, who simultaneously abandoned their grandmother and launched themselves into his arms. He stooped and hugged them, then looked over at Dustin.

"Dustin!" He stood up, and the boys resumed rolling on the couch. "Boy, am I glad to see you."

"I'm going back to Crystal now," Wendy said. "You gonna keep them for an hour?"

"Yeah, just call me if . . . anything happens." He turned back to Dustin and Jamie.

"I could watch them if you need to stay with her," Dustin said.

"No, man. You just got out of jail. Let's go somewhere and we can talk while they play."

"Okay," Dustin said. "We'll follow you guys in Jamie's car."

25

The playground Travis led them to was on the lake where he'd fished with Dustin multiple times. The kids loved the area, and they could entertain themselves for a while here—as long as the grown-ups made sure they didn't play too near the water.

As they parked, Dustin realized they were the only ones here. He'd better enjoy it, because this was probably the last time they'd be able to go anywhere without the press mobbing them. As soon as Travis unbuckled the kids from their car seats, the twins bolted out of the car and took off toward the fort on the playground.

Dustin and Jamie walked with Travis to one of the picnic tables near the play area. Jamie noted the pale cast to Travis's skin, as if he hadn't left the hospital in days. Weariness deepened the dry lines of his face.

"You okay, man?" Dustin asked him quietly.

"I'll live." He brought his bloodshot eyes back to Dustin. "How 'bout you? The night couldn't have been easy."

"It wasn't so bad," Dustin said. "Not compared to what you're going through."

"He'll be better when we find out who could have set him up."

Dustin looked at Jamie, sitting across from Travis. She was here for a purpose, and she wanted them to get to the point. He wanted that, too, but the urgency of his case didn't negate the gravity of Travis's situation.

But Travis wasn't bothered. "Yeah, I've been thinking about that," he said. "I might have some ideas."

Jamie pulled a legal pad out of her bag. "Who?"

Travis looked down at the table. "Well, there was that contractor, Jack Roberts. Didn't he have a copy of the blueprint of our security system?"

Dustin shook his head. "When they questioned me about it right after the theft, they told me they'd already talked to him."

"But that doesn't rule him out," Jamie said, writing down his name. "Travis, the explosives were planted in Dustin's car the night before last when he was at the hospital. Is there anyone who came up there that night who might have done that?"

"No, we didn't have any other visitors that night. Just Dustin. Wendy was at home with the kids." He squinted in the breeze as he looked at Jamie. "Are you sure it happened there? How do you know that?"

"It's on the hospital's CCTV. It shows a white van pulling up behind Dustin's car and someone opening his trunk."

"There are security guards out there all the time. If someone was breaking into his car, wouldn't they have seen him?"

"If they had a key, the guards wouldn't have noticed."

"A key? You think they had a key?"

"They got in my trunk without any problem," Dustin said.

"Well, if you could see that, you must have been able to see their faces."

"It was dark, and the cameras weren't that close to them," Jamie said. "They only prove that someone did it that night."

Travis rubbed his face and gazed back at his kids. "I can't believe they would be that brazen. How would they know you'd be there?"

"Followed me?" Dustin said.

"But why?"

"I wish I knew."

Travis shook his head. "It's insane. I can't even get my head around it. But doesn't that video let Dustin off the hook?"

"I would hope so, but we can't count on it. They haven't dropped the charges. I did show the prosecutor, so at least he knows."

Travis rubbed his face and let his fingers slide to his chin. "How did we get here?"

"I don't know, man."

"It's like somebody took the world and turned it upside down."

Mason fell down and cried out, and Travis shot off the bench and snatched him up. The heels of Mason's hands were bleeding, and the sight of the blood sent his wailing into a higher pitch.

"I have water," Jamie said, pulling a bottle out of her bag. She poured it over the little boy's hands, and he screamed as if she was killing him. "I might have a Band-Aid. Do you like Elsa from *Frozen*?"

Mason's crying settled to a whimper. "Do you have Paw Patrol?"

"Sorry, I don't. I have a little girl who makes me buy Elsa." She dug through her bag and found the Band-Aids.

"You like Elsa, bud," Travis said.

"I like Olaf."

"I bet I can find an Olaf in this box." Jamie flipped through the Band-Aids until she found one with the snowman. "Let's dry off these hands."

Miles shouted from the slide, "Daddy! Look!"

Travis looked over his shoulder as Miles came down the slide. Dustin hurried to the foot of the slide to catch him.

"Team effort," Jamie said, putting the two Band-Aids on Mason's hands. "Now. All better."

"I want to slide," Mason said, squirming to get down. Travis set him on the ground and the boy ran off.

"Thanks for that. I shouldn't go anywhere without their supplies. I have a diaper bag in the car, but I wouldn't even know if we have Band-Aids."

"It's a little embarrassing all the mom supplies I carry around in my briefcase," she said.

"Crystal carries things like that around, too. She always has what we need." Travis's eyes welled and reddened, and he looked away. "I probably need to get back, Jamie. I know you wanted to do a real interview, but if we can wait until tomorrow, they'll be at preschool. I can text you the names of people I can think of, but right now I can't think."

Dustin squeezed Travis's shoulder. "Let Wendy have some time with Crystal. You need a break."

"A break?" Travis repeated, as if the words came close to angering him. "I'll have time for a break later. Right now I need every minute." His voice choked off, and he let the thought hang there.

After a moment, Jamie asked, "How bad is she, Travis?"

Travis sat back down. "We started her on a new treatment. It's experimental, supposed to have a lot of promise. I hate that word . . . *promise*. It's not a promise. It's like a weak 'maybe.' Anyway, it's not working yet."

"It still could, man."

"I don't know." He rubbed his eyes. "I don't think she's coming home," he whispered. "We're in her last days. Maybe her last hours."

Jamie touched her heart. "Travis, I'm so sorry."

"The thing is, as long as I'm there with her, reminding her that she has things to live for, I feel like maybe it could change things. Like keeping her engaged with me and our kids, and people who love her, and memories that make her laugh . . . I fantasize that one day she'll wake up and be herself again . . ."

Dustin wanted to tell him he was wrong, that she was still herself, that she would beat this thing. But all the facts pointed in the other direction. "Is there anything I can do?"

"Oh, I wish." Travis took a deep breath, steadied himself, and focused his eyes on a cloud overhead. "Typical Dustin. We came out here to talk about how to keep you out of prison, and you wind up asking me if there's anything you can do for me. Life is not fair, man." He shook his head. "I'm a miserable human being."

"Why? Because you don't have all the answers?"

"Because I should be there for you," Travis said. "I should have been at the jail today bailing you out."

"Come on, dude. You aren't superhuman. You can't do everything at once."

"I've lost control," Travis said. "I can't do a thing about Crystal, and now you."

"Look, don't worry about me. Just take care of yourself and Crystal. I'll be fine. It takes more than a night in jail to get me down."

Travis leaned forward and looked Jamie fully in the eyes, concern sharpening his steady gaze. "Are you going to get him off?"

Jamie inhaled a deep, unsteady breath. "That's my goal. But we might have a long road there. Solving these crimes is the best way we have of proving his innocence. If they impanel a grand jury and indict him, he could be forced to go back to jail. Or if they come up with more serious charges, his bond could be revoked."

"I gave her the names of the managers of the plant," Dustin said, hoping to jog Travis's memory. "A list of employees. The security guards."

Jamie looked at Travis. "Any idea who would have been able to alter the security video at the plant? Who would know how to do that?"

"Again, the security guards," Travis said.

"From what I can tell, I think they were the main suspects until the RDX was found in Dustin's car."

"I never had any kind of run-in with those guys," Dustin said. "I don't know why they would set me up."

"You were an obvious scapegoat," Jamie said. "Whoever did it thought they could get the heat off them if you got blamed. It may not have even been personal."

Miles started crying and Travis stepped toward him. "You're okay, bud." The boy kept crying, so he went to pick him up and look him over. "Nothing broken or bleeding, but I think we're done here," he said. "I've got to get back to Crystal, and these guys need a nap."

"Yeah." Dustin grabbed Mason and they headed to the car. "Let me know when Crystal can handle visitors, okay? I'd really like to see her."

"Yeah, we'll see," Travis said.

They reached the car, and Dustin put Mason into his car seat. "Keep me updated, will you?"

"Of course," Travis said. "Same here."

As Jamie followed Dustin back to her car, she said, "You buckled him in like you've done it before."

"Yeah, we hang out sometimes."

"You mean you babysit?"

"Sure. They're like my nephews. I saw them like fifteen minutes after they were born."

As he got into the car, fatigue settled over him, and he leaned his head back and closed his eyes.

Jamie got into the driver's seat and looked over at him. "I'm sorry, Dustin," she said. "I know it's hard to hear how close Crystal is to passing."

He couldn't answer, just swallowed and nodded. They were quiet as they left the park.

26

The ride back to Dustin's rental car was too quiet, but finally Jamie posed the question that had been plaguing her since they'd left Travis. "Dustin?"

"Yeah."

"Travis told me earlier today that you swore you'd never call me—"

"He just says stuff," Dustin said, shifting in his seat. "It didn't mean anything."

Jamie stared forward as she drove, unconvinced. "Why didn't you want to call me?"

Dustin laid his head on the headrest again and stared up at the roof, not answering. After a moment, Jamie thought he'd discarded the question completely. "Dustin?"

"One time Travis and I were talking about those days when I lived with Aunt Pat, and I told him about you. He asked me why we weren't still in touch. I might have said something like that."

"But why?"

"Because I didn't figure you needed Dustin Webb back in your life, okay?"

Jamie swallowed the knot in her throat and glanced over at him.

He looked out the window to the buildings they passed, his expression hidden from her. "But I did call you, after all, didn't I?"

Jamie didn't answer. There didn't seem to be anything left to say. It had taken an emergency for him to call her. He never would have done it otherwise. She wasn't sure why that disturbed her so much now.

"Hey, you okay?" Dustin asked after a stretch of tense silence.

"Yeah," she muttered. "I'm okay." She pulled into the hospital parking lot. "Where are you going?"

"I thought I'd go by my house and get some things I need."

"I can follow you there," she said. "Then you can load my car, too, if you need to."

"I don't intend to get more than a suitcase. But you can come if that's what you want, since you have to babysit me."

"That's not what's happening here," she said. "You're not on house arrest. I can let you out of my sight."

He sighed. "Sorry. I didn't mean to make you feel guilty for this. None of it is your fault. Just meet me there. You remember how to get there?"

"Yes," she said. "That's a nice area."

"Surprised?"

She stared at him. "What is it you think about me, Dustin? That I expected you to fail?"

"I didn't mean that," he said. "It's just that you know me so well. Probably better than anybody else. Most of the people who really knew me in my past, like Aunt Pat, consider me a loser who's got prison coming to him."

"Pat has never really known you," Jamie said. "But I did."

"I didn't mean anything about you."

"No," Jamie said softly. "You meant it about yourself."

"I don't know," he said. "Maybe I did."

He looked so uncomfortable that she wanted to give him an escape. "Go get the car and I'll meet you there. If the press show up, you'll need help getting away." She watched him get out and walk toward his rental car. She put her car into reverse and pulled away.

The conversation weighed heavily on her mind. How could he think she had such low expectations of him? She'd always been his biggest fan.

She needed sleep, she thought. She shouldn't be so irritated by that exchange. All her clients got testy. They were all on the defensive. But Dustin wasn't just anybody.

She had to shove it out of her mind. There was too much work to do to dwell on her personal feelings. That was a luxury she couldn't afford right now. She had to hurry Dustin up before the press got to his house. They didn't have a moment to waste.

27

Dustin's house looked different in daylight. The yard was well kept, and the landscaping was simple yet well maintained. His land was more beautiful than she had realized last night.

He motioned for her to pull into the garage.

"No press yet," he said.

"Probably because your house is hard to spot. They'll figure it out. We need to hurry."

"I didn't see any news vans."

"That doesn't mean they're not coming."

He closed the garage door, and she followed him into the house. "Dustin, your house is beautiful. Did you do all this yourself?"

"Not really," he said. "Crystal decorated most of it for me. When I bought the house, I only had a threadbare couch and a beanbag for furniture. She literally took me by the hand to the furniture store and made me pick out some things. The next thing I knew, I'd spent a ton of money and she was hiring people to paint."

"So she's a decorator?" Jamie asked, wishing she'd had the chance to get to know Crystal before her health had failed. Maybe she still would.

"No, she's not a decorator," Dustin said. "She just likes to spend other people's money. 'Course, I approved everything as we went along. I really like how it turned out."

He led her into the kitchen, which was clean except for a few breakfast dishes from the morning before. "I'll just grab a few things and we can go."

"Okay." Jamie set her briefcase on the table. While she waited, she checked for any more Google alerts. Two more local TV channels had reported Dustin's arrest. The third had connected the ChemEx theft with the bombing.

He came back with a suitcase and a bucket of what she assumed were Dude's toys. "Ready?"

"Yes," she said. "That's it?"

"I figured there wasn't time for much else."

"You're right," she said. "The address of the Airbnb is on your bond paperwork. I'll get Avery and meet you there. Remember to screen your calls. If anybody calls who's not in your contacts, don't answer. It could be someone from the press, and I don't want you talking to them under any circumstances."

"Right," he said, checking his phone. "Let's get out of here."

28

Avery was over the moon when Jamie took her home to get Dude. She tried to protect her daughter from the dog's overzealous affection, but Avery loved every lick. "Mommy, can we keep him? Please? He's so cute!"

"No, honey. He belongs to somebody already."

"But he likes me!"

"Of course he does. He has exquisite taste buds."

Avery sat in the back seat with the dog as they drove to the Airbnb, and as Jamie drove, she glanced occasionally in the rearview mirror at how happy Avery was with the huge animal. They hadn't had a dog when Joe was alive because of his allergy to them. Then, after he died, she hadn't had the energy to be a single mom, a busy attorney, and a dog owner.

Now she wondered if she'd been depriving her daughter. Maybe she should reconsider that.

She watched for anyone following her as they wound through

town to get to the Airbnb. By the time they arrived, she was satisfied they had made it alone. Avery insisted on holding Dude's leash as they got out of the car, but as he bounded around the new yard like it was an amusement park with delightful new exhibits, Jamie followed them to make sure he didn't pull Avery off her feet.

When Dustin came to the door, Dude burst toward him, pulling the leash out of Avery's hands and leaping up on his owner. Dustin laughed and let the dog push him to the floor, where Dude slurped his face. Dustin hugged him like he was his own child.

Avery was captivated as Jamie introduced Dustin. The dog bonded them instantly as they both explored the backyard and made sure there was nothing Dude could destroy. This would work, Jamie thought. They would be fine here together.

As they ate their dinner of fast food, Avery zeroed in on Dustin.

"Dustin, why are you in trouble?"

"Because . . ." He thought for a minute, as if trying to figure out how to frame it. "Some people think I did something that I didn't do."

"Why don't you tell them you didn't?"

"I have. They don't believe me."

She stared at him with those big eyes, as if she was trying to imagine the whole scenario playing out. "My mom will make them believe you. She's really good at that."

He grinned. "That's what I thought."

"Was Mommy pretty when she was a little girl?"

He sent Jamie an amused glance at the sudden shift in topic. "She looked just like you."

"So . . . pretty?" Avery asked with a smile.

Jamie had to cut in. "Stop fishing for compliments and finish your burger."

Avery took another bite and kept looking at Dustin. "I saw a picture of you at my grandma's house. You were smoking a cigarette."

"Yeah, that was in my decadent days. I quit smoking years ago." Dustin met Jamie's amused eyes. "I had a lot of bad habits back then."

"They'll turn your teeth yellow and make you cough," Avery said.

"Yep. That's exactly why I quit."

Jamie couldn't help grinning at Avery's questioning. When dinner was over and Dustin followed her into the kitchen, he leaned close and said, "She's just like you. All those questions."

"Yeah, she has that curiosity gene."

"Let me do this," he said. "You have mom duties."

Jamie was happy to let him take over loading the dishwasher. She did have to check Avery's homework and get her into the bath. She found herself growing too comfortable with him here, as though he and Dude had stepped into her family and were going to stay.

This was a bad idea. She pushed the thoughts out of her mind and tried to think like a lawyer instead of an old friend.

While Avery was taking a bath, Jamie turned on her bedroom TV to the local news.

The bombing was still the lead story, and the whole first programming block consisted of video and interviews about the tragedy. She flipped to the other two stations. They had the same lead story.

It wasn't until after the commercial that she heard Dustin's name. "Sources at the police department confirm that an arrest was made yesterday in connection with the bombing. Thirty-five-year-old Dustin Webb, an Afghanistan veteran, was detained yesterday after the bombing. He was arrested on charges of possessing explosives stolen from the ChemEx ammunition plant a week and a half ago, and sources tell us that they believe the bomb planted at Trudeau Hall was partially made with the same plastic explosive, RDX, as well as TNT and ammonium citrate."

Jamie felt sick. That tied the bombing even more closely with the theft at ChemEx. Those were the three substances stolen from the ammunition plant.

"Mommy?"

Jamie turned the TV off so Avery wouldn't see. "Yeah?"

"I'm kind of scared to sleep in my room."

"Why?"

"Because it's new, and what if those people come?"

"What people, honey?"

"The news people."

"They wouldn't hurt us. They're just loud, and I didn't want them to bother us."

"But what if they do come?"

"They won't. They don't know we're here."

"It might be okay if Dude could sleep with me."

Jamie smiled. "Dude is downstairs sleeping with Dustin. Maybe another night." She drew in a deep breath. "Tell you what. Go brush your teeth, and you can sleep with me."

"Will you go to bed now?"

"Yeah. I'll work on my computer while you fall asleep."

As Avery brushed her teeth, Jamie walked out of the room

and partially down the stairs. Dustin already had the TV on, and she heard reporters discussing him by name.

So he knew. The thought of what he must be going through brought tears to her eyes. *You're a lawyer, not a friend*, she told herself. Blotting her eyes, she turned and went back to her room.

Really, this wasn't all bad. So the press had learned of his arrest. She and Dustin still had time to prove his innocence to the public as well as the court.

As she got her bed ready for Avery, she prayed silently that the press wouldn't track him down tonight.

Downstairs, Dustin turned off the kitchen TV after the news and went into his room, where Dude had already made himself comfortable on his bed. Jamie had given him the master bedroom with a bathroom so that he could stay in here without bothering her and Avery. He turned on the TV and pulled his laptop out of his suitcase. He crawled onto the bed and typed in the news station that had just shown his picture. He played the clip again.

They'd gotten a photo of him from his army days, dressed in his uniform. How had they gotten that? Had Aunt Pat given them pictures? That was probably a good thing.

He went to each of the other local stations. All of them had posted about him now. One station had dug far enough to find out about the business he owned and its connection to ChemEx. One of his neighbors had been interviewed. "Dustin is a good guy," he said. "I can't believe he would do a thing like this. When I had a tree fall on my house during a storm last spring, he was one of the first ones there with a chain saw to help me. I just keep wondering if they've got the wrong guy."

He breathed a sigh of relief that someone had vouched for him.

"He was kind of quiet, almost brooding," a woman he didn't even know said of him.

"Do you know of any connection he had to Ed Loran?" the reporter asked.

"I have no idea. But obviously he had something against him. It seems like classic political derangement."

He closed his computer and stretched out on the bed, staring at the ceiling. He had no feelings at all toward Ed Loran. He barely knew who the man was. How could he be accused of his death?

Jesus, how could this happen?

He turned onto his stomach and buried his face in his pillow. "I know I was a mess in my past," he told God. "You know all about that. But I never would have done this."

An old passage he remembered from a Bible study he'd done when he'd first found Christ years ago drifted across his mind. It was from Psalm 91. He whispered it as a personal, anguished prayer. "He who dwells in the shelter of the Most High will abide in the shadow of the Almighty. I will say to the LORD, 'My refuge and my fortress, My God, in whom I trust!'"

He pulled himself up and got his Bible out of the pocket in his suitcase. He found the passage and kept reading.

For it is he who delivers you from the snare of the trapper
    and from the deadly pestilence . . .
    His faithfulness is a shield and bulwark.
You will not be afraid of the terror by night,
    Or of the arrow that flies by day.

Tears stung his eyes, and he looked up at the ceiling. From memory of the psalm, he personalized his prayer. "For you will give the angels charge concerning me, to guard me in all my ways . . . Because I have loved you, you've said you will deliver me. You said when I call on you, you will answer me and be with me in trouble. You will rescue me. You are my salvation."

He wiped the tears on his face and lay back on the bed, letting the words seep into his heart. The passage was a prophecy about Jesus, but it applied to God's people, too. The sure knowledge that God had his back filled him with strength laced with calm. He would fight this, but he wouldn't be fighting alone.

"Whatever happens to me, use it for whatever purpose you want. I know you'll help me endure it."

In fact, God already had. God had put an urgency on his heart to call Jamie when he was in trouble. She had come in minutes. She was on top of this. God hadn't left him to the wiles of whatever enemy was out there. He had provided so far. He would keep providing.

Dude woke up and scooted closer to him. Dustin stroked his head until the dog was back asleep. Slowly, God's peace settled over him, and he thought he might actually sleep tonight. There would be time enough to fight tomorrow.

29

Dr. Delaney's office was locked when Harper took Taylor there at seven in the morning.

Taylor had dreaded seeing her psychiatrist since Harper made the appointment, and now she wanted to leave. "She's not here. Let's go," she said.

"We'll wait. The office isn't open yet. She said she'd be here at seven."

"I don't need to see her. I'm fine."

"You haven't slept for the last two nights. I'm seeing things that—"

"I'm not doing rituals," Taylor cut in. "I'm just interested—"

A car pulled up next to theirs in the parking lot, and Taylor cringed as her psychiatrist got out. Would she be mad? Taylor wondered. She probably got calls in the middle of the night from suicidal patients, and Taylor had tried to be low maintenance. But now all that was out the window.

"Good morning, ladies." The wind blew her gray hair as she got out of her car. She came to Taylor and offered her a rare hug.

"I don't know why she called you," Taylor said. "I'm having normal responses to trauma. I don't need to see my shrink about it."

"She isn't sleeping," Harper said. "She was up all night watching social media videos from the concert. She needs some help."

The doctor unlocked the door and led them past the receptionist's lobby and into her office. "It's kind of an unspoken rule that when you suffer severe trauma, you check in with your doctor. There's not a person alive who could skate through a bombing without problems, and you aren't an exception."

"I've been doing really well," Taylor said.

"Let's just talk. Harper, why don't you go get some coffee while we meet?"

Harper hesitated, as if she had more to tell the doctor, but Taylor knew she'd unloaded every concern she had during the phone call that, no doubt, had woken her doctor up this morning.

"Text me when you're finished," Harper said.

When the door closed, Taylor took her seat in one of the plush chairs she'd sat in monthly for the past couple of years. She slipped off one of her sandals, pulled her foot up, and hugged her knee. "She's the one who needs a doctor. All she does is hover over me like I'm going to jump off the balcony or something."

"Have you had thoughts of doing that?"

Taylor rolled her eyes. "I live on the second floor. And no, I haven't even thought of suicide. I'm happy to be alive after what happened." It wasn't true, not exactly, but it was what the doctor needed to hear.

"So tell me about your sleep."

"Okay," Taylor said, "can we get one thing straight first? Being obsessed with something isn't quite the same as having OCD episodes, right? Didn't you tell me that?"

"Yes, I did."

"So I'm obsessed with working the bombing out in my head, looking at pictures, trying to figure out who could have done it, reading all the news that comes out. Wouldn't you do that if you were with two friends who were murdered right next to you?"

"Probably. Every other survivor of that day is probably doing something similar. But your brain chemistry is of concern. PTSD could exacerbate OCD. I think we should adjust your medication. In fact, there's a new drug that might address your issue better than what you're on, and this might be a good time to try it."

"I don't want to be spaced out. Getting adjusted to a new drug is too hard right now. I'll take something to help me sleep."

"Are you having repetitive thoughts?"

"No. Just the usual ones."

"Nothing new since the event? Because Harper mentioned hearing you say some things over and over."

"'We have to find him' is not a repetitive thought. It's a statement. We do have to."

"We?"

"Yes. Them, us, we . . ."

"You?"

"Stop it." Taylor got up and went to the coffeepot against the wall. She got a filter out of the bag next to the pot, put it in, and started scooping the coffee. "I'm not obsessing about myself flying in like Batwoman and saving the day. I don't know who is going to find him, but someone has to."

"How do you know it's a him?"

"They, then. Whoever did this." She filled the coffeepot with water from the sink next to it.

"Taylor, sit down, please. Look at me."

Taylor finished pouring the water in, then turned on the coffeepot. Sighing, she dropped back into her chair and looked at Dr. Delaney.

"You're probably fine," the doctor said. "You have been doing well. You're not going off the deep end. You're just reacting to a deeply disturbing incident. But because of your brain chemistry and some of the issues we've dealt with over the years, I'd like to try this new medication and see if it helps you get through this a little better. If you don't like it, we can change back. I'll also give you something for sleep."

"Okay, but if I feel worse, I'm calling you."

"I want you to." She typed the prescription into the computer, then printed it out and gave it to Taylor. "I need for you to call me if you start to get manic or unusually depressed, if you have thoughts of suicide, if your thoughts get more repetitive or your rituals seem more urgent . . ."

"Sounds like a great medication."

"Those are rare side effects, but I want you to look out for them."

Taylor took the prescription. She was suddenly too tired to fight anymore. She would just take it.

"I want to see you again next week."

"Next week? I can't. I have work."

"Let's make an appointment, and if it isn't possible, we can change it."

"Okay."

"Give yourself a few days. Don't rush back to work. Take some time."

"I am." She got up and texted Harper that she was finished, then she turned back to Dr. Delaney. "I'm sorry you had to be here so early."

"It's fine," she said. "You made coffee. You want some?"

"No, thanks," she said. "Harper probably got me one."

"Call me if you need to. I don't encourage all my patients to do that."

"You've never told me to," Taylor said with a grin.

"Right. But I'm telling you now. Call me. Especially with the new medication. Let me know of any changes."

"Okay, thanks."

Taylor stepped out of the office into the hall and headed to the exit door. Harper was coming into the building carrying two coffees. "You're finished?"

Taylor took hers. "Yes, and she gave me a new medication. She's all over this. So am I. Feel better?"

"Yeah, do you?"

"Never better," Taylor said. "I'm doing great."

They went to Harper's car, and as they drove home, Taylor sipped her coffee. She looked over at her sister. "Did you get me decaf?"

Harper shrugged. "I wanted you to sleep."

Taylor couldn't help the smile stealing across her face. She patted her sister's hand, then leaned her head back on the seat. She was going to be okay. Harper wouldn't have it any other way.

30

The press was onto them. After taking Avery to school this morning, Jamie had driven by her own house to see if anyone waited on her street with cameras and microphones. No one was there yet. She drove over to Dustin's neighborhood and saw two local TV vans parked near his driveway. She kept driving and headed back to the Airbnb.

Dustin was waiting for her when she came in. "You want me to drive us to my office?" he asked.

She set her bag on the kitchen counter. "I don't know. I'm thinking."

He frowned. "What's wrong?"

"It's started. I drove by your house and there were two TV vans there. Nobody at my house yet."

"So you don't want to go?"

"No, I do. I want to see what you guys do and how you accessed ChemEx's security system. But we can't go if they're there."

"So we take my rental car, which no one should be looking for, and if they're at my office, we just keep driving. If they're not there, we go in."

She thought about it for a minute, then agreed. "Okay, let's go."

As he was driving, Dustin adjusted his rearview mirror. "What's the worst that can happen if the press finds me? Can't we get away with saying 'no comment'?"

"Technically, that should work. But then they could follow you and torment you . . . and then there are the angry people out there who lost loved ones and want to settle the score, who show up alongside the press, and—"

"Okay, I get it."

"I'm not trying to make you paranoid. I've just been through this before on a smaller scale. I've watched others in my firm go through it with high-profile cases. It gets really ugly."

"I trust you."

"Have you talked to Travis today?"

"No, not since last night. I called the nurses' desk earlier today and they said Crystal's condition hasn't changed."

She looked out the window, wishing she could get Travis into her office for an interview. She really needed to dig into some things with him. She looked over at Dustin behind the wheel, his Mountain Dew open in the cup holder just as it had been when he was a teen. She felt a little like that younger version of herself, who'd always loved the rare treat of going somewhere with him.

She forced her brain to shift gears. "You never told me. How did you and Travis wind up starting your business?"

"We got a lot of training in the Army Ordnance Corps," Dustin said. "And when we got out, we were offered jobs with a high-tech security installation company in New York. We learned the business and came up through the ranks. About three years in, the company came under new management, and instead of staying, we decided to go into business together. We were both from Atlanta, so we came back here and started it."

Jamie pulled her legal pad out of her bag and wrote some of that down. "So do you have employees? Or do you install things yourselves?"

"What we do is work with architects, contractors, and project managers when a building is being built. We design the security plan along with the architect, and we source the technology and contract the installation. We oversee everything. That's how it usually works. In the case of a building being retrofitted for the security system, we still work with the company and contractors, but things are done in a different order."

"So which was ChemEx? New construction or old?"

"New. Working with chemicals and explosives, you have a lot of regulations and a whole level of security that has nothing to do with breaches or criminal activity but with safety hazards. Our company only deals with keeping the company secure from intruders, which is why we're the ones they look at when there's a breach."

"Do you monitor the equipment after the build?"

"No. The tech companies we source the equipment from offer training to the employees who will work on the security systems, and some of it is outsourced to monitoring companies. Once we finish the build, we're finished, unless they need maintenance or repairs."

"So you haven't been to the ChemEx plant since you finished that build?"

"We went in after the theft to see what was breached. Before that, it had been a year."

"Could you even get into the plant if you wanted to now?"

"Probably. We were included in the biometrics ID systems so we could test the equipment early on. It's possible they removed us after the theft, but companies often keep us on there in case we have to do updates or check glitches."

"So how many companies have you guys done in this area?"

"About ten."

"And there haven't been any breaches in any of the others?"

"No, but ChemEx was the biggest and most significant build we've done. It was a real boost to our business. It brought us a lot of other business. We have contracts for the next three years." He paused and swallowed. "Those companies will probably want to pull out when they find out about this."

He slowed as he came to a building with a business sign near the street—"GreyWebb Securities, Inc." There didn't seem to be any press around yet, so he entered the parking lot.

"GreyWebb," she said. "A combination of your last names?"

"That's right."

Jamie got out of the car and followed Dustin to the door. Dustin unlocked an outer lock, then opened a door into a small foyer with a biometric scanner on the wall. He let it scan his palm, then his eye.

"Because we have to keep blueprints of our security systems secure, we had to install it all on this building, too." He let her in when the interior door opened.

She had expected rooms full of TV monitors being observed by employees, but the big room looked more like a construction office than a tech company. And they were the only ones here.

"Interesting," she said, looking around.

"We're at the end of a job right now. We were supposed to start a build a couple of weeks ago, but the project was delayed by a month. Another one is starting in three weeks. They're big jobs that'll take a year or more for our part. We've been working on the current one for the last ten months or so."

She hated the thought that the whole business could fall apart now. Unless she could get him acquitted in a very public way, there was no future for GreyWebb.

"When the ammunition plant was broken into, were you liable in any way?"

"That remains to be seen. But they did let us in to see what went wrong. It was clear pretty early that the security video had been doctored and that the electricity was down that night."

"Why?"

"Good question. There wasn't a storm, and there were no reported power outages in the area. If equipment malfunctions, the manufacturer is responsible, but if it's tampered with, that's another thing."

"So what kind of security did you install there?"

"I can't get specific," he said, "but in a general sense, I can tell you that we designed multilayered theft-proof systems, from the parking lot and landscaping to the windows and doors, with multileveled biometrics to get into the building. Most of the employees in the building have to scan their ID cards to get in, but in the more secure areas, the scans get more advanced. The highest security rooms, where chemicals and explosives and the ammunitions themselves are stored, even scan vein patterns in the employees, so they're almost impossible to breach."

"Then how do you explain the theft?"

"Either it was an inside job, or someone there let the thieves in."

She walked around, looking at framed pictures of some of their jobs on the wall. "So when the power went down that night, did all the security systems stop functioning?"

"No, most of them are also battery powered as backup. But the power outage might explain why the security footage had an interruption."

Dustin had come a long way. She wished she could go back to fifteen years ago, when he'd run out of money for his last year of college, and tell him that he would build a business from nothing, and it would be successful. "This is impressive, Dustin. Pat would be proud."

He breathed out a laugh. "No, she wouldn't."

"She would. Look what you've done."

"Yeah, I bet she loves that whole prison thing hanging over me. She always knew I had that potential."

"I always knew about your real potential."

He leaned on a counter. "You were the only one."

"My mom liked you."

He smiled. "Yeah, I guess she did. I appreciated that. How is your mom?"

Jamie walked across the room and looked at black-and-white pictures on the wall of Travis and Dustin at work sites. "Mom's doing well. She's a big help with Avery."

"Avery's great, by the way."

She smiled and turned back to him. "Thank you. She likes you."

"I always wondered," he said. "Was Joe a good dad?"

Her smile faltered. "He was . . . Well, she wasn't that old. He was just . . ."

"That would be a no?"

She turned back around. "He had problems," she said. "Don't get started on I-told-you-sos."

"I wouldn't do that," he said. "I'm sorry I asked. It was insensitive."

"No, it's okay." She sat down at one of the computers. "He wanted to be a good dad. He tried. He just couldn't seem to hold it together for long enough stretches."

She knew what he was thinking. He had warned her away from Joe several times when she started dating him. He'd told her Joe used drugs, that he was a different person behind her back. He warned her that she could ruin her life with him. Why hadn't she listened?

When she and Joe got engaged, Dustin signed up for the army. He'd told her there was no connection between those two things, but she had sometimes wondered.

She was quiet as they drove back to the rental.

"What are you thinking about?" he asked.

She smiled. "I'm just processing things."

"My case?"

She drew in a breath. "No. Dustin Webb as an adult."

He gave a faint smile. "I know the feeling. I had to process Jamie Powell as an adult."

She made sure no one was behind them when they turned onto the street where the Airbnb stood. Checking her watch, she said, "I have to get to the office. I have a staff meeting."

Dustin sighed. "I keep feeling like I need to go check on my work site. I have all these people to call and appointments to cancel."

"Don't call anybody," she said. "Don't cancel anything. Just keep your head down."

"I always thought it was innocent until proven guilty."

"Don't believe it. Not in a case where everybody's watching."

He didn't say anything else as they got out of the car. She transferred her bag to her car. "You'll feel better if you're not trolling the Internet reading things about yourself," she said.

"Probably."

"What you can do is bring Travis to my office today so I can interview him. Do you think he can get away?"

"The kids will be in daycare, and Wendy will probably be at the hospital. Maybe he can come."

"It's really important," she said. "Stress to him that your entire future might depend on it. No pressure."

"I'll do my best."

She got into her car and pulled away. She hoped Travis would do what was necessary for Dustin.

31

I realize this is a PR disaster." Jamie sat rigid in the conference room after the staff meeting, fully prepared to fight to keep Dustin's case. When the partners had asked her to stay behind to brief them on it, she'd known things could go badly.

Max wasn't helping. He sat in his chair in that way he had, with his legs crossed at the knees and his torso slumped back. It had never bothered her before, but today it looked smug. "This client was found with boxes of explosives in his trunk right after the bombing."

"First of all," she said, "he didn't have bombs in his car. He had one ingredient, and not much of that."

"That ingredient was a plastic explosive," Max said.

"Please let me finish," Jamie cut in. "I have security camera video from the hospital's parking lot, showing two people loading something into his trunk the night before the bombing. There were dozens of people who could have broken into ChemEx. Employees, contractors, security people . . ."

"The guy was in the Ordnance Corps of the army," Max added.

Jamie's eyes met and held those of her mentor. "I was going to mention that," she said, not disguising the vexation in her voice. She turned back to the other attorneys, who listened with censure in their expressions. But she was determined not to wilt. "He was in the Ordnance Corps, so he does know how to assemble and disassemble bombs. That doesn't make him a likely suspect. It makes him a likely target."

"And he installed the security system at the ammunition plant in question?" John asked.

"Yes. I'm still convinced he's innocent. But even if he wasn't, he has a right to competent counsel."

Sue Brackton, another partner who had also become Jamie's friend over the past two years, leaned forward. "Honestly, I think the PR for the firm is a good thing. It raises our profile."

"But the PR is negative," Max said, moving out of his slouch and leaning both arms on the table.

"Still," Sue said. "Negative PR raises our profile. Especially if we get behind her and she wins the case."

"I will win," Jamie said, "because he didn't do it. I've known this man most of my life."

Paul Lewis closed his file and steepled his hands in front of his face. "We'll have press camped out at the front door."

"We don't usually shy away from the press," Jamie said.

"No, we don't."

"I disagree," Max said. "He isn't our type of client."

Jamie snapped her head at him. "You mean because he isn't the head of a major corporation or the son of a Fortune 500 mogul? This is not a pro bono case," she said, enunciating the words distinctly. "His fee will be covered. And as for his 'type,' his caliber is miles above the inside traders and embezzlers that we often represent."

"I don't know," John said. "Maybe Sue is right. It will get national attention. If Jamie handles this case as well as she's handled her others, it'll come out in our favor."

A hush fell over the room, and finally Max sat straighter. "Looks like I'm outnumbered. Guess I'll go along with it, but, Jamie, you'd better not let us down."

"I won't," Jamie said, closing her file on Dustin and scraping her chair back from the table. "Thank you, everybody. If you'll excuse me, my client should be waiting." But as she left her colleagues in the conference room, a sense of deeper purpose fell over her. She had to win this case. There was no other option.

32

The bodies had been released, and the families had started funeral arrangements. Desiree's parents had set her funeral for tomorrow, and they'd asked Taylor to speak.

"I don't think you should do it," Harper told her as she sat at the table with an untouched salad in front of her. "Look at you. You can't even eat. Have you taken the new medication yet?"

"Not yet."

"Go take it now."

Taylor wished her sister would go home. She went to the kitchen for a cup of water and took the new pill. "There. I took it."

"Seriously, Taylor. How can you do a speaking engagement right now?"

She was getting so tired of this. "It's not a speaking engagement. It's a funeral for my friend."

"It's too much to ask of you!"

Taylor sighed and dropped her face into her hands. Maybe

Harper was right. "I don't even know what I'll say. That I'm sorry I saved myself and left them?"

"It was a bomb, Taylor. How in the world could you have saved anyone?"

When Taylor couldn't answer, Harper tried again. "Please, just try to eat."

Taylor forced herself to take a bite. She picked up the remote and turned on the TV. The news channel she had been watching earlier came up. The chyron at the bottom of the screen made her gasp.

Arrest made in bombing at Ed Loran rally. "They arrested somebody!" she said, turning up the volume. She waited as the current story ended and the broadcast segued into the next one.

"Police say they got an anonymous tip that security contractor Dustin Webb was connected with the bombing. When they pulled him over, they found RDX, a plastic explosive used in the bomb, in the trunk of his car. We reached out to his attorney, Jamie Powell of Lewis, Brackton and Devereaux in Atlanta, but she has not responded."

Taylor choked on her food and started to cough. Tears came to her eyes, and she tried to clear her windpipe. "Did they say Jamie Powell?"

Harper was staring at the TV, too. "That's the woman we talked to."

Taylor cleared her throat. "That woman is the bomber's attorney! Where's her card?" She grabbed her phone and looked for the number. She found it, but her hands were shaking. "I'm calling her." She tapped the number. She didn't expect her to answer, but the attorney picked up on the third ring.

"Jamie Powell."

"This is Taylor Reid." Her voice was raspy, broken, and shaky. "We talked the other day? At the police station? You bought me coffee?"

"Yes," Jamie said. "How are you, Taylor?"

"How would *you* be if you'd just found out you were lied to, so some terrorist's attorney could pump information out of you?" Her pitch rose with each word. "You're representing the guy who murdered my friends!"

Jamie's tone seemed unruffled. "I didn't lie. He's not the killer. I know how it looks to you, but I can promise you, he's the wrong person. I'm trying to find the right killers. My client was set up by them. He's as much a victim as you are."

Hot tears rolled down her cheeks, and Taylor's head began to throb. "I just wanted to let you know that I'm onto you. You're a bloodsucking, lying leech. Don't ever come near me again." She clicked the phone off and threw it across the room.

"Okay, that's it," Harper said. "We've got to get out of this house. Come on. Get your shoes on. We're going to a movie."

"I'm not going to a movie!" Taylor screamed. "I don't want to go anywhere there's a crowd." She screamed it as if Harper had something to do with the bombing, as though her sister was trying to lure her into another murder scene. She knew even as she shrieked it that she was overreacting. She had to get herself together, but she could not quell the rage pulsing through her.

"Then we'll go to a store," Harper said quietly. "We'll get you something to wear to the funeral."

"I don't want to shop." She sat down and sobbed, unable to stop.

Harper brought her a box of Kleenex and let her cry for a few minutes. "I'm upset, too," she said. "I feel betrayed. I shouldn't have let her talk to you."

"I should have realized. When does a lawyer help the police? What did I even tell her?"

"About the truck. Nothing she wasn't going to learn anyway."

Taylor blew her nose, wiped her face, and tried to take a deep, cleansing breath.

"Come on," Harper said. "Get your shoes on."

Taylor was trembling. "I hope that man rots in hell. And his lawyer with him."

Harper went and got Taylor's shoes. "Put them on," she said.

Taylor followed her sister's orders, but the rage wasn't buried. It still rippled through her heart and her pounding head.

33

Travis checked his watch and counted the hours that Crystal had been asleep. She needed her rest, but whenever she slept this soundly, he couldn't help wondering if she would ever wake up. She was losing the battle, but he wouldn't let her stop fighting.

Her hair was soaked with sweat, and her face had a slick sheen. There was a new purple bruise on her upper arm, adding to the ones on her lower arms. Her lips were crusty and cracked, only slightly more pigmented than her pale skin.

He wanted to take off his mask and crawl into bed with her, press his lips against her face, and just hold her. But she was so fragile, and he couldn't feel her cheek through this blasted mask.

He noted a difference in her breathing and sat down beside her. "Crystal?" he asked gently. "You awake, love?"

Her eyes fluttered open, the green of them providing a startling contrast to the death-gray pallor of her skin. Still, a suggestion of a smile curled her lips infinitesimally upward. "I am now," she said.

He took her limp hand and laced his fingers through hers. "I have to leave for a while this morning, but I'm worried about you. You've been asleep a long time."

"Tired," she said. "How could I be so tired?"

"You've been working very hard."

"I've been lying here like a log." She reached up and touched his face, the part that wasn't covered, and he took her hand and held it against his cheek. "You didn't sleep last night, did you?"

"Of course I did," he said.

"You haven't even changed clothes. Where are you going like that?"

"I have to meet Dustin at his lawyer's. Your mom is coming to stay with you."

"You should shower and change."

He checked his watch. He didn't have the time or energy to do either.

She closed her eyes. For a moment, Travis thought he'd lost her to sleep again.

"Hey, Grey," she whispered after a moment, not opening her eyes.

"Yeah, love?"

"When can I see the boys?"

"Not yet, babe. Your resistance is too low. They're little petri dishes . . ." His voice trailed off, but he didn't have to finish. They both knew what that would mean. But he couldn't brook the sadness in her eyes. "We'll FaceTime later."

"You can dress them in little biohazard suits. They'd love it. Tell them they're astronauts."

"The doctor doesn't think it's a good idea."

"I just want to hold them. Feel their hair. Look into their sweet little eyes."

He leaned over and pressed a kiss on her cheek through his mask.

"We'll do it soon. We just have to get through this rough patch."

She got tears in her eyes, and he wished he could take them away. This was a cruel disease. He wished he could defy it and sneak the kids in. But he knew better.

There was a knock on the door and Wendy stuck her head inside. Crystal tried to sit up. "Come in, Mom."

Her mother stepped inside, wearing the prescribed mask, hair covering, and gown over her clothes. She seemed to assess her daughter's condition as she came toward her. "How you doing, sweetie?"

"Good. Slept well."

"Awesome." Wendy looked at Travis. "You go on. I've got this."

"I'm going." He bent over his wife and pressed another kiss on her cheek through his mask, wishing he could pull it down. Then, addressing her mother, he said, "Call me if . . . if you need me, okay?"

Her mother nodded grimly, then rallied and pulled two papers out of the bag she'd brought. She brandished them for Crystal. "Miles and Mason made these for you."

Crystal managed to sit up slightly and, delighted, slapped her hand over her mouth. "Fingerpaintings?" The word was spoken with more energy than Travis had heard in her voice all morning. "You let them fingerpaint!"

"They're naturals," Wendy said. "The paint is made of pudding, by the way."

"Which explains the mouth print on Mason's."

"That's a kiss," Wendy informed her matter-of-factly. "Especially for you." She laughed. "You should have seen the mess!"

Knowing Crystal was in good hands, Travis slipped out of the room to meet Dustin.

34

"Can I get you some coffee?"

Dustin looked up at Jamie's assistant, Lila. "No thanks, I'm good."

She left him sitting in Jamie's office, and he looked around at the place where Jamie spent much of her time. It looked like her, with its warm touches and pictures of Avery. She had come a long way.

Somehow that made him feel worse.

Her association with him, especially now, couldn't be good for her. It might ruin her reputation and make her as hated as he was.

He pulled out his phone, googled his name, and scrolled through all the horrible things being written about him. This morning, on the way here, he had made the mistake of driving by his house to see whether the press was there. He had seen so many reporters and cameramen on the street that he'd turned off a block before his house.

What had this person done to him, this enemy who had planted evidence in his trunk? How would he ever overcome it?

He looked up when he heard her voice, talking to Lila before coming in. She got her messages and walked in. "Sorry I'm running late. I was with the partners, so I couldn't leave."

"Were they giving you a hard time about me?"

"Not at all. They're glad I took your case. Did any of the media bother you after I left?"

"My phone's been vibrating constantly, but I'm not taking any calls."

"Good. So where's Travis? Is he coming?"

"Yes, he's running late," he said.

She sat down at her desk and locked her gaze with his. Just the sight of her eyes made him feel a little better. It always did.

"Dustin, I've been thinking since we went to your office, running everything through my mind. Things about you and Travis."

"Yeah?"

"I want to suggest a possibility that I know hasn't even crossed your mind. And you aren't going to like it. But as your lawyer, I have to consider everything."

"Let's hear it."

She took a deep breath. He could see that she was choosing her words very carefully. "Travis. He knew how to break through the security system, he had the blueprint of the building—"

"No." He stared at her, unable to believe she would suggest such a thing. "Travis did not set me up."

"I'm just saying that we can't rule anything out. He knew when you were going to be at the hospital and he knew when you left. He may be the only one who did."

"He never left when I was there. He couldn't have gone out to smuggle something into my car. Besides, others knew. Nurses, doctors . . ."

"He's the only one who knew what you knew about ChemEx. What if he was working with the people who did this?"

"It's not possible." Dustin got up, paced across the room, and turned back to her. "I've known Travis for years. You know when someone is capable of something like that. Besides, you met the man. He's a basket case over his wife. You think he took the time to plan a theft of an ammunition plant, make bombs, and commit a major act of terrorism in his spare time?"

She came around her desk and looked up at him. "Again, I'm just brainstorming. In order to help you, I have to figure out everyone else who could have done it. And I'm not suggesting he did all of it. Just like the DA is not suggesting you did."

"He can't suggest that, because I can confirm my alibis."

"So can Travis, probably. We'll see."

"Travis did not steal those explosives!" Dustin's voice was so loud that she closed her door. "He's as much a victim of circumstance as I am! And he would never do that to me. Frame me like that, make me go to jail . . ."

She sat back down. "Sometimes friends can let you down."

Dustin had to make her understand. He dropped into his chair, set his elbows on his knees. "I'm not claiming Travis is a saint," he said more quietly. "But he's no more a thief than I am. You know the way you believe in me, Jamie? The way you knew without asking that I was innocent? Well, that's how I feel about Travis."

"I understand," she said. "But it strikes me that he hasn't been all that helpful. He's not going out of his way to be interviewed so I can help you."

"He is going out of his way, right now. He'll be here any minute."

"I hope so. I know he's stressed out about Crystal, but if someone came to question me about you when you were in a position like this, I would be there answering every question they had to help clear you. I wouldn't put it off and make excuses."

"That's not what he's doing."

"Okay. If I'm wrong, I'll be the first to admit it. If he shows up, I'm going to question him hard, Dustin. I have to."

He hated that. It wasn't right. "Just remember he's not at his best."

"I will. But it strikes me that you look sadder about my suggestion that he did it than you do about the allegations against you."

"I'm just—"

Lila opened the door. "Mr. Grey is here."

"Okay." Jamie looked at Dustin, and he drew in a deep breath and tried to clear his head.

"Send him in," she said.

Travis walked in still wearing the clothes he'd had on yesterday, and his hair looked like he'd forgotten to brush it. "Sorry I'm late," he said. "I ran into the doctor on the way out of Crystal's room, and I had to talk to him."

Dustin stood up and gave him a hug. "Did he have anything good to say?"

Travis looked distracted. "Not really. We can talk about it later."

Jamie was glad he didn't want to delve into it now. As tragic as Crystal's situation was, Dustin's was tragic, too, and she didn't want them getting off task. "Thank you for coming in," she said as he took the chair next to Dustin. "It's helpful for me to work in the office so I can have a couple of paralegals and my assistant sit in on our meeting."

"The doctor didn't have any new revelations, did he?" Dustin cut in.

Travis glanced at his friend. "She's okay right now. Her mom is with her, and she was in good spirits, mostly."

"Good," Jamie said, seizing that. "I needed you here this morning so we could go over what your activities have been for the last couple of weeks. I've gotten Dustin's, and I know yours will probably come up, too."

"My activities?" Travis asked. "Why mine?"

"Because you're Dustin's partner. It's inevitable that you'll be part of this equation."

He sat stiffer. "Do I need a lawyer, too?"

"Maybe," she said truthfully.

"Well, I'd want you if I need one."

She looked down at her legal pad. "I appreciate that. I'm not entirely sure that would be in Dustin's best interest, but we don't have to worry about it right now. Just be thinking about someone else in case it turns out you need one."

"In my best interest?" Dustin asked. "It would be in my best interest for you to represent Travis."

"No," Travis said. "Listen to her."

"I am listening, but if you need a lawyer—"

Travis's phone rang, and he glanced down at it. "I'm sorry. I have to take this. It's Wendy." He picked it up. "Hello? Yeah, Wendy, what's going on?"

Jamie met Dustin's worried eyes. Was this The Call? The one they'd feared?

Travis's face twisted and a vein popped out on his forehead as tears pushed to his eyes. Jamie could hear Wendy's voice. She sounded upset.

"Oh, no. No, it's okay. I'm coming. I'll be right there."

Travis tapped the phone off and got to his feet. "I have to go. Crystal's . . ." He stopped, swallowed, tried again. "She's got a really bad nosebleed, and her fever has spiked. Her platelet count is so low that they can't get it to stop."

Dustin sprang out of his chair. "I'll drive you."

"No, I'm fine. I want you to stay here and finish this with Jamie. You've got to stop thinking about me."

"But, Travis—"

"I mean it," Travis said, as if Dustin's gesture of sympathy angered him. "I'll call you later."

"If there's anything I can do, man. Anything at all—"

"I know."

Jamie stood up. "Travis, when things calm down, could you send me a copy of your calendars for the last few months?"

Dustin looked irritated. "Jamie, he can't think of that right now."

"I'll do it," Travis said. "Just . . . I don't know when I can. I have to go."

Travis went out the door and disappeared out of sight, and finally Dustin turned back to Jamie and closed the door behind him.

"A nosebleed," he repeated. "When she gets those, sometimes they last for days. They give her transfusions. It can be really serious."

Jamie didn't know what to say. "She's in good hands, Dustin."

He nodded and sat back down. "Yeah, I guess."

"I'm sure they'll let you know if she gets worse."

"Yeah." He rubbed his jaw and studied her. "Jamie, he's not faking this. He was here, all set to answer your questions. He's not being evasive."

"I know. I could hear Wendy's voice on the phone. She sounded pretty upset."

"Yeah." Dustin stared into space, as if desperately trying to decide what to do next. "I just don't want you to think that he's dodging questions. He's not. She's really, really sick."

"I know, Dustin. Let's try to shift our focus to you. I'm going to get my paralegal in here, and we're going to go over your schedule for the last few weeks."

"Sure. I have everything on my phone calendar."

Jamie called one of her paralegals, and as she waited, she wondered if she could get Dustin's head back in the game.

35

If he hadn't been able to tell from Crystal's continuing nose-bleed that her condition was getting worse, Travis would have known it from the worry in the doctor's usually hopeful face that afternoon when Dr. Grafton led him into the hall. The oncologist had struggled with them through this long battle of disease, remission, and more disease. Now he tapped his pencil on his chin, then scratched the eraser against his forehead that was pleated with the burden of his profession. "Travis, it's not good news," he said. "Her platelet count is down to zero. She has a fever of 106."

Travis rubbed his stubbled jaw. "She could have seizures or brain damage."

"We're trying to get it down. But I have to warn you. She may not have much longer."

Travis felt something snap in his chest. "So you're giving up on her? Just quitting?"

"No, of course not. We're still fighting. But I have to be honest with you."

He covered his eyes and sucked in the sob rising to his throat. "What's going to happen? Is she going to suffer more?"

"She does have pain, and we're helping her with that. Most likely, she'll fall asleep and be in a state of unconsciousness for some time. You might hear a rattle or deep snore."

"The death rattle?" he muttered.

"That will mean she's in transition."

Travis shook his head and took a few steps away, then turned back. "You think that's going to happen? Like today? Tomorrow?"

"I can't say when. But soon."

"She's just sleeping," he said. "She'll wake up. She's not there yet."

"Meanwhile, we're taking her off the new course of treatment. It's not working well for her."

Travis slumped against the wall. "If you take her off the treatment, what will you do instead?"

"Go back to what we were doing before."

"But she was going downhill. This had so much promise. You said it could be a game-changer. That she might get worse before she gets better."

"Promyelocytic leukemia is aggressive, and her body is too weak to fight the rapid disease progression. She's rejecting platelets as fast as we transfuse her."

"I'll get more people to give blood."

"Her mother gave yesterday. We can't take more from her until at least tomorrow."

Travis wiped the tears under his eyes. "So what do we do?"

Dr. Grafton looked down at the printout of the test results

he held, as if studying them again might shed one more ray of light on her illness. "We keep transfusing her with platelets. If we can bombard the bloodstream with enough of them, sometimes we can neutralize the antibodies."

"I gave blood yesterday, too. What else can I do? There must be something. I can't just sit here and watch her slip into a coma!"

"Keep talking to her. Sometimes, just when you think you've lost them, they come back. Crystal's strong. She's still got some fight in her."

"Yeah, she's the strongest person I know. She wants to see the kids. That might help her."

"It could hurt her more than it will help. She can't fight infection. We're trying to keep her from going into septic shock."

"I get it," he said. "There's no good answer."

"Do whatever it takes to appeal to her strength," Dr. Grafton said. He squeezed Travis's shoulder and forced him to meet his clear, thoughtful eyes. "Just know that I'm not giving up."

That was little comfort. "Thank you, Doctor."

He waited for a moment until the doctor had gone, then returned to the sterile area at the entrance to Crystal's room, slipped a gown back over his clothes, stepped into the paper boots that went over his shoes, and put on the cap and mask that would make it less likely he would transport germs into the room. Then, stepping through the door, he went to her bedside.

"Wake up, Crystal," he said in a wobbly voice. She was sleeping hard as blood saturated the packing they had changed just half an hour ago. "Please God, wake her up."

There was no response, but he kept standing beside her, watching her breathing patterns, her peaceful slumber. But she wasn't at peace yet, he told himself. She was in misery. Her lips were bruising blue, and her nose—packed with gauze—was bruised and purple, the color extending to the circles beneath both eyes. *Pull her back*, he told himself, but something deep inside him, some growing sense of compassion, questioned him ruthlessly. *What are you bringing her back for? More pain? More agony? More failure? Hasn't she earned a chance to rest?*

He thought of Mason and Miles. She couldn't go yet. She hadn't said goodbye. She hadn't made her peace with leaving them.

He thought of the elation they'd felt in this very hospital just over two years ago, when they'd held those two little pink squirming boys, fussing about their treacherous journey through birth as they breathed their first breaths of air. Joy had been diapered and swaddled that day, and motherhood had completed Crystal. He had never seen her so happy.

It was brutal to take that from her now.

He lowered himself to the bed beside her, collapsing from the weight of his emotion, and bowed his head as tears plopped onto her gown. He wondered if they contained germs that could do her harm and hurriedly wiped at his eyes.

"Crystal, please wake up," he said in a louder voice. "Please! I'm not ready to say goodbye yet! I won't do it!"

When there was still no response, he stood and leaned over her again, feeling a fury like none he'd ever experienced. "Crystal, you're just letting yourself slip away. I'm not ready yet. Please, just wake up!"

In the quiet that followed, he could have sworn he heard a heavy sigh wheezing from her throat and a distinct change in her breathing. *Is she coming back?* he wondered, taking her hand and holding it to his mouth, every fiber of his being pleading for her to make the effort.

"Come on, baby, you can do it," he said. "Just fight it. You've never been a quitter. Don't quit on me now."

He saw her lips move infinitesimally, and she squeezed his hand.

It wasn't much, but it was enough to tell him she was still there. She wasn't gone yet.

36

It was late afternoon when Dustin finally left Jamie's office and headed toward the hospital to check on Crystal. Several times during the day, he'd called the nurses' desk to try to get information on her condition. "Critical" was the latest report.

He reached the hospital and pulled into a space beside Travis's truck. He got onto the elevator with a man and a little girl of no more than four, holding a Get Well Soon balloon. Dustin smiled at her.

"I got a balloon for my mom," she announced.

"She'll love it," Dustin said.

The elevator stopped on the second floor, and they got out. The little girl looked over her shoulder at him and waved, and he waved back. As the doors closed, sadness swept over him. He said a silent prayer that the child's mother would be okay.

A fleeting thought of Avery, smiling as she interrogated him, skittered through his mind. She was a doll, so much like Jamie.

How could Joe have valued getting high more than his wife and daughter? Didn't he realize what he had?

He had never liked Joe when Jamie dated him in high school. He'd heard too much about him and had seen him at parties. He was always the one who had a stash of weed or pills. When Dustin warned Jamie about him, she insisted he'd changed. He was a great guy, according to her.

She was always interested in Dustin's opinions, and he expressed them without reservation. But she still dated Joe. And when they got engaged . . .

He got off the elevator on Crystal's floor and went to her room hoping to find Travis. Instead, he found the door open and the bed empty. An alarm rang out in his heart, and he turned around, searching the halls for someone—anyone—who looked as if they might know what was going on.

A nurse came out of a room across the hall, and he touched her arm. "Crystal Grey. Where is she?"

She glanced toward Crystal's empty room. "Oh, she's been moved to a laminar air-flow room."

Dustin took a few seconds to catch his breath. A laminar air-flow room—where no germs could penetrate the sterile walls, where only the sickest patients were isolated and treated. "I guess her husband's with her, huh?"

"Yes, and her mother, I think."

"She's going to pull through, right?"

She glanced away. "We just have to wait and see."

Dustin closed his eyes, and the nurse added, "But she has the very best doctors. Really, they're doing everything they can for her."

He nodded and looked in the direction of the special rooms,

knowing he couldn't go in. He wasn't family, no matter how much he felt as if he were. "Could you tell her husband that Dustin is here when you get a chance?"

"Of course," the nurse said. "I'll give him the message right now, but he might be a while."

"Oh." Dustin let out a deep sigh, then looked back up the hall. "Never mind. He's got a lot on his mind. I wanted to go down and give some blood, anyway."

"That's good," she said.

She went to the nurses' station, and Dustin went back to the elevator and waited for the doors to open. He should have come earlier.

He got off the elevator on the main floor and cut across the lobby to the room he'd frequented so often to give blood. The thought of what Travis was going through made him shudder.

Years ago, when their greatest worry had been getting through basic training and then their deployment to Afghanistan, they'd half expected to be killed in battle or maimed due to an IED. Once they were back home, they thought the danger was over, never dreaming they'd have to face even greater disasters just living their normal lives.

When he was finished donating blood, his phone vibrated. He glanced to see which news outlet was trying to reach him now, but it was a client, asking him how he could get in touch with Travis. He had an emergency situation.

Dustin returned the call. "Jeff, this is Dustin Webb. Travis is tied up right now with a family emergency, but I can help you."

He braced himself, expecting the caller, the security director at one of their local builds, to say he didn't want to speak to an alleged terrorist, but the man seemed oblivious to what was going on. "Yeah, Dustin, we had a power outage and our mainframe crashed, and now our security system isn't accepting any of our passcodes."

"I can take care of that," Dustin said. "I'll be right over."

After he hung up, he realized he would have to go by the office to get into his database of passcodes, or else go back to the Airbnb to get his computer. But maybe Travis's was in his truck.

He texted Travis.

Hate to bother you right now. But I'm downstairs. Just got emergency call from Twin Tech. I don't have computer with me. Is yours here?

He waited a minute, then Travis texted back.

Yeah, it's in my truck. You have my key?

Yeah, I'll get it. Is Crystal okay?

No. Still bleeding. Fever too high. Getting septic.

Dustin's stomach sank. This was bad.

He wouldn't let himself dwell on that right now. He went out to Travis's truck and unlocked the door with the key he kept on his keychain, since he often drove the truck himself to transport equipment. He slipped into Travis's passenger seat.

He looked around the cab of the truck for the computer and found it under the seat. He pulled it out and looked for the charger in case he needed it. Travis had a computer bag on the back floorboard, so he retrieved that and looked inside.

He found the charger and grabbed it, but a paper in there caught his eye.

It was a xeroxed copy of a diagram of canisters, with the letters "RDX" written at the top. He pulled out the paper and studied it. The lines drawn between the cannisters connected them all and continued to the side, to a single point where Travis had written "Detonator."

He felt a kick in his gut.

Take it easy. It's not what it seems.

He sat there for a moment, studying the drawing, trying to make sense of it. There was an explanation. There had to be.

He put the paper back into the bag and took the computer and charger to his car. A growing knot of fear rose to his throat as he started the engine. He pulled out of the parking lot in a fog, wishing he could just drive for days until all of this was behind him.

37

Jamie left the office after receiving a text from Dustin saying that Crystal was in dire need of blood. Giving blood was something she could do.

As she drove, her phone vibrated, and she answered on bluetooth. It was Max, from work.

"I came by your office," he told her, "but you'd left."

"I'm heading to the hospital," she said.

"Jamie, I know what the partners said today, but I wanted to appeal to you personally. This isn't going to be good for our firm. We lost the Stolzer account this afternoon."

She didn't have time for this. "They weren't even our clients. They were only considering us."

"Well, they've ruled us out now that all this has happened."

"Max, I'm not dropping the case."

"Has it ever occurred to you that you're probably not the best one to represent him anyway? Dzhokhar Tsarnaev had an attorney. Call someone like him."

"Tsarnaev was guilty. My client is not. And he has faith in me. I know I can do this."

Max started into his lecture as she came to a red light. She stopped and glanced at the car in the next lane. The driver was staring at her.

She squinted through the glare of her window, but couldn't see clearly.

"Jamie, I don't think you're taking the mood of the country into account."

The light turned green, and Jamie started to move forward, then stepped on her brake to see if the other car continued on. But that car hesitated, too. Jamie went ahead, and the other car pulled into her lane behind her.

Was she being followed?

"This is serious, Jamie. Are you listening?"

She looked into her rearview mirror and tried to see the driver's face. It was a woman, but she couldn't quite see her features.

"Jamie, are you there?"

"Max, I need to call you back. I have to go."

"Jamie!"

She clicked off the phone as she reached the hospital parking lot. She turned in, and the woman followed her.

She found a parking space close to the door she would go in. The woman in the other car had turned up another row of the parking lot. Jamie sat still and watched her in her mirrors.

The car slowed as it came around to Jamie's row. As she passed Jamie's car, Jamie caught sight of her face. It was Taylor Reid.

Jamie jumped out of her car and walked through the parking lot toward the girl's car, but Taylor accelerated and drove out of sight.

Why was Taylor following her? Did she want to give her another piece of her mind?

Jamie reined herself in. Maybe Taylor hadn't been following her at all. She could have been coming to visit another survivor of the bombing. She could just be at the wrong building. It could all be a coincidence.

But why had Taylor driven away when she knew Jamie saw her?

Was she following Jamie, hoping to get a glimpse of Dustin? Another layer of uneasiness fell over her as she hurried inside.

38

Jamie called her mother as she went through the maze of the hospital corridors, looking for the blood donation lab. "Mom, are you busy?"

"Just finishing up some work. What's up?"

"Dustin's friend in the hospital is having a hard time, and she desperately needs blood. He said they're looking for donors. Do you think any of your women's group members might be willing to help?"

"I'll call them," her mom said. "And I'll sure come."

"Really?"

"Anything for Dustin."

Jamie saw Wendy on the phone in the hall just ahead of her, under the sign that pointed to blood donations. "Wendy!" she said, hurrying toward her.

Wendy got off the phone and hugged her. "Hey, honey."

"I'm here to give blood, and I called my mother, and she's getting some of her friends to come and give, too."

"Oh, God bless her!" Wendy said. "That would be such a help. I'm waiting for some others to get here, too. I'll take you in and introduce you."

Jamie followed her toward the room. "Is Dustin still here?"

"No," she said. "I haven't seen him in a while."

Wendy pointed her to a nurse who was already drawing blood from some others. Wendy hastily introduced the couple as Travis and Crystal's friends. Jamie took the table next to the woman.

Wendy hurried back out. A friendly nurse approached Jamie. "I'm so glad so many people are coming for her," the nurse said as she started Jamie's IV. "That patient is having a hard time, it sounds like."

Jamie looked away as the needle found her vein. "Tell me something," she said. "Why is a nosebleed so critical in a leukemia patient?"

"Because she can hemorrhage to death." Jamie watched her hang the bag and connect the tubing. The nurse checked the bag to make sure the blood was flowing the way it should, then resumed her explanation. "Platelets are her problem."

"So how do transfusions help? Is it just to replace what she's lost?"

"She needs platelets so her blood will start clotting again. She's had problems before with her body rejecting the new platelets, though."

Jamie closed her eyes and imagined how futile the whole ordeal must be to Travis and Wendy, and even to Dustin. "How awful."

"It can be overwhelming. But these families keep doing everything in their power, and maybe there'll be one thing that will work. I've seen it happen over and over. Prayer works, too. Do you pray?"

Jamie leaned her head back on the pillow as her blood filled the tubing. "Yeah."

"That's stronger than any medicine," the nurse said as she walked away. "Call me if you need me."

Jamie closed her eyes and thought about her answer to whether she prayed. She did pray throughout the day, quick hit-and-run prayers as needed. But she knew those weren't the kinds of prayers that moved mountains or helped dying people heal.

Where had she lost that?

Maybe it was after Joe died, when she had gone from feeling numb, to outraged, to guilty, then numb again. She had blamed God for not protecting Joe from himself, and for not guarding her family. For a while, she hadn't prayed at all. After all the prayers she'd prayed for Joe's addiction problems, prayers that had never been answered, she had been overwhelmed with the unspoken sense that prayer didn't matter.

After that first year of widowhood and single motherhood, she had eased back into praying, but she had never returned to the deep, intimate talks with God, or the yearning to hear his still, quiet voice.

But now there were Dustin's tragic circumstances and Crystal's urgent needs. Where else could she go for help on either of those things? She needed some quiet alone time with God.

"Did Wendy say your name is Jamie?" Wendy's friend asked her, cutting into her thoughts.

She looked at the woman Wendy had introduced as Emma. "That's right. How long have you known Crystal and Travis?"

"Two or three years."

"Do you know Dustin, too?"

"Yeah, we're all friends," the woman said, lowering her voice. "I couldn't believe what I saw on TV last night. Dustin would never do that."

"No, he wouldn't."

"I was stunned when I saw it. It's unbelievable that this is all happening at the same time."

"I'm the attorney representing Dustin."

"You are?" Emma sat straighter. "Is he going to get out of this?"

"We're working on it," Jamie said. "When's the last time you saw Dustin?"

"I've seen him up here a couple of times in the last week. He comes whenever he can. He's been trying to keep their business going. And there are times when Travis asks us not to come."

Jamie shifted on her table. "Does Dustin have any enemies you can think of?"

"Not one," Emma said with certainty. "He doesn't make enemies. He's a good guy."

"I know," Jamie said. "I've known him since I was a kid."

"Do you think he was set up?"

She didn't want to go into the evidence she'd found. "It looks like it."

"It has to be the person who bombed the rally, right?"

While Jamie considered how to answer that, the nurse came to the man on the other side of Emma and removed his IV. "You're all finished. I'll get you some juice."

Emma looked over at him. "Babe, Jamie is Dustin's attorney."

He slid his legs over the side of the table. "He's innocent."

"I know." Jamie asked them as many questions as she could manage without appearing to interrogate them, but other than a few random names of other friends who'd visited the hospital, she didn't get much that would help Dustin.

She only hoped that her blood platelets would do more good for Crystal.

39

When Jamie brought Avery home that evening, Dustin's car was parked at the Airbnb. She had picked up a pizza on the way, and when they got inside, she knocked on his bedroom door to offer him some.

He opened the door but didn't come out. "I've already eaten," he said. "But thanks."

Even though Dude bounded out of the room to greet her and Avery, Dustin stayed where he was. She stood there for a moment, wondering if he was upset about Crystal or his plight, or the combination of everything. She wanted to help, but she didn't know how.

Avery had turned the TV on to *Sofia the First* and was watching as she shared her food with Dude. "Where's Dustin?" she asked.

"In his room. He's already eaten."

"He seems nice," Avery said. "I like him."

"You have good judgment."

Avery smiled. "When can we go home?"

"I don't know, sweetie. But it's not so bad being here, is it?"

"No, it's nice, and I love playing with Dude. But I want to play with my friends, too. And I need my own stuff."

"I get it. This is all inconvenient. But it's just temporary."

"And it's for a good reason," Avery said.

"Yes, it's for a very good reason."

Avery's attention turned to the TV, and Jamie tried to eat. Dustin's state of mind weighed heavily on her. Had she offended him today when she suggested that Travis could be a possible suspect? With all the other offensive things happening in regard to him, she couldn't see how that would have shut him down.

She thought of taking him something to drink, but he clearly wanted to be left alone.

She spent the evening upstairs with Avery, and when her daughter was asleep, Jamie went quietly downstairs. Dustin was still in his room. She went to his door and knocked lightly.

He opened the door and looked out at her. He hadn't changed clothes from when he'd been in her office today, so at least she hadn't gotten him out of bed.

"Are you okay?" she asked. "I've been worried about you."

"I'm fine," he said.

"I know Crystal's not doing well. I went to the hospital and gave blood."

"Thanks for that."

"My mom and her posse are giving, too."

"That's great. Thank her for me."

He didn't want to talk, but she couldn't seem to stop. "I met some of your friends when I was giving blood. They think a lot of you. I think you'll be in good shape with character witnesses if this does have to go to trial."

He looked at the floor without answering, and she wondered what was bothering him the most—the fact that she'd discussed him with his friends, or the idea of it going to trial. "I'll go to bed now. I just wanted to say good night. There's still some pizza in the fridge if you want some."

"Thanks."

Glad he couldn't hear the insane narration in her head, she went up to her room and resolved not to see him again until tomorrow.

Avery was already asleep in Jamie's bed, so she went into the other upstairs bedroom and sat on the bed. It was time to pray—not just drive-by prayers, but a real, in-your-face talk with God. She lay on the bed facedown and whispered aloud how sorry she was that it had been so long since she'd last talked to her creator like this. As she grew closer to the throne of God, an old sense of homesickness came over her. She had missed him.

Tears flooded her eyes, and she whispered her love and her desire to get back in touch with him. Then, in a rush of need, she poured out her fears and supplications for Dustin and begged for God's intervention. Then she pled for mercy and healing for Crystal and peace and preparation for her family and friends, if it was God's will for her life here to end.

An hour passed before she felt God's warmth comforting her. He had heard her, and he wouldn't leave her prayers unanswered. He never really had, she realized. He had answered her, had taken care of her and Avery, had seen them through the dark times. He hadn't forced Joe into compliance no matter how much she had wanted him to. God didn't work that way, and as hard as that was to accept, she had known that all along.

His ways were mysterious and sometimes painful. They didn't always make his children happy. But one thing was for sure. God used everything. He always had a purpose.

She dried her face and went into the hall. It still sounded quiet downstairs, so apparently Dustin hadn't come out of his room. She went back into the bedroom where her daughter slept and crawled under the covers with her.

With the knowledge that God was listening, she allowed herself to drift to sleep.

40

"You didn't sleep last night, did you?"

Taylor, sitting on the couch with her computer on her lap, turned her weary gaze to her sister. "Why does that sound like an accusation?"

"Because it is. I checked the sleep medication the doctor gave you, and you haven't used it. When's the last time you slept?"

Taylor sighed. "You really should go back to your apartment. I don't need a babysitter."

"Well, clearly you do! I promised Mom and Dad that I wouldn't leave you until I was sure you were okay. Did you at least eat?"

"Yes, I ate."

"What did you eat?"

"I went out before you even woke up and got something at Burger King."

Harper sat down on the coffee table in front of her sister and stared at her over the laptop. "That's another thing. You were out so much yesterday, but you didn't go to work and you didn't buy anything for the funerals. What were you doing?"

"I ran errands. I do have a life, you know. I never had to check in with you before."

"Are you at least taking the new medication?"

"Yes. I took it this morning. Trust me, I know I need it."

Harper left her alone then, and Taylor knew she was probably in the bathroom checking the number of pills in the bottle to see if she had missed a dose. That was fine. She had actually taken it. She had a racing pulse to prove it, and her palms itched, and every now and then she broke out in a cold sweat. She couldn't see any benefit to the medication yet. Her intrusive, repetitive thoughts had multiplied and were more frequent, but she supposed they were harmless.

She locked back in on her computer screen and studied Dustin Webb's face. She had used her credit card to sign up for a service that gave her every public record about him that it could find. That included criminal records, but nothing had been added to that part of Dustin's report since some minor things in high school and college. She'd been studying every detail of it, cross-checking it with other information she'd found about him on the Internet.

Yesterday she had driven by his house and his business, hoping to find him at either place. There were media out in front of his house, so she couldn't go to the door. His office parking lot was empty.

She had no idea what she would do when she found him. Confront him and tell him what a reprehensible, bloodletting psychopath he was? Or go into a rage and attack him?

She was five-five, and he was six feet tall and outweighed

her by about sixty pounds. And a man like him would probably be armed. Maybe she should be, too.

She printed out the file of data she had on him, then went into her bedroom to get it from the printer. She changed out of the yoga pants she'd had on since yesterday and put on some jeans and a shirt that would make Harper think she'd tried.

She could hear her sister in the shower, so Taylor quickly grabbed her things. She should leave before Harper got out, then text her that she was shopping for something for the funeral. Maybe Harper would actually go to work and leave Taylor alone for the day.

She had a lot to do, and she had to do it alone.

41

Dustin didn't come out of his room until Jamie had left to take Avery to school. Before leaving, she texted, asking him to come to her office again this morning. He told her he would, but he dreaded looking her in the eye. She had always been able to tell when he was keeping something from her, and what he'd found in Travis's computer bag yesterday was huge.

He just wasn't sure what it meant. Did it mean that Travis had made the bombs? Had he planted explosives in Dustin's car and tipped off the police? Had he blown up Trudeau Hall?

No. Impossible. There had to be a simple explanation. Maybe Travis was just thinking through the bombing, trying to figure out how a truck bomb could have done so much damage. Dustin had done some speculating himself about that.

But he hadn't drawn out such a detailed diagram.

Travis had. That thought swirled through Dustin's mind. Should he confront his best friend?

Crystal's condition still weighed on him. He couldn't take

Travis's attention away from her right now. Things were too dire.

Should he tell Jamie? Didn't she need to know that her gut feelings about Travis might be warranted? But if Dustin's instincts about Travis were right, that would take Jamie down a rabbit hole that would lead nowhere. He couldn't assume anything before he talked to Travis. He had to keep this to himself for now.

Jamie could see that Dustin hadn't slept much last night, despite the fact that he hadn't come out of his room even to eat. He had arrived at her office when he'd said he would, but he was brooding and distracted. Something was wrong.

"I got a list of the employees at ChemEx, showing everyone who has access to the security systems. It's a big list." She handed him the printout. "Do you know anybody listed here?"

He looked over it without much enthusiasm. "Some of them."

"Can you mark the ones you know?"

He circled some names, then handed the paper back to her.

"Is there anyone on the list you talked to in the weeks leading up to the theft and your arrest?"

"No. I hadn't seen those people in a year or more."

"Except for Travis."

"Yeah, except for Travis." His words came out quieter, almost as though he were pulling them back even as he spoke them.

"I keep wondering why the perpetrators didn't set him up. If they knew you were at the hospital, they must have known he was. Why wouldn't they have planted the RDX in his car instead of yours?"

"Just lucky, I guess."

She wasn't amused, and she knew he wasn't trying to be funny. "Another thing. Why wouldn't they set up any of the current employees? You're a step removed from all this, since you're not really involved with the plant anymore. It would have made more sense to pick one of these people."

"None of this makes sense," he said.

She stared at him across the conference room table. He seemed listless, as if he wasn't even trying. Yesterday he had at least offered ideas and possibilities, and had been forthcoming about everything they had discussed. Today she couldn't get anything substantial out of him.

"Who knew you were going to the hospital that night?"

"Didn't we already go over this?"

"Yes, but I thought maybe you thought of someone since yesterday."

He sighed and shook his head. "I didn't tell anybody, but it wasn't like I was disguised. People saw me."

"But specifically, did any of these people on the list know?"

"I told you, I haven't talked to any of them in a year."

"Are you on any online groups for people in the security industry?"

"No. I'm not a joiner."

She knew that about him. "It makes sense that Travis might have told some of your clients his wife was in the hospital. Someone who would have guessed you'd be there."

He got up and went to look out the window, thinking. "I guess that's possible. We were working two jobs. I was the lead on one, and he was lead on the other. You get to know the contractors and architects pretty well. He probably did tell some of them. But all this . . . It's implausible. That he would mention that Crystal's in the hospital, and then that they would assume I'm there, and then somehow get into my car without leaving a scratch and plant explosives?"

"I know it's unlikely. I'm just trying to find connections. What about Travis's friends or family? Or Wendy's? Did she have friends or family who might have come to check on Crystal and saw you there?"

"I haven't met any. And the friends of ours who saw me there would never do something like this."

She made him write them down. He wrote the names of two couples. "Did anyone else call the hospital to check on Crystal? Anyone who might have asked if you were there?"

"I don't know who called! I'm not their family. I didn't get those calls."

He was clearly irritated, and she felt as if she was badgering him. She got up and went to her door. "I'm going to get some coffee. Do you want some?"

"Yeah, that would be good."

She went to the break room and got two cups. What was going on? Why was he resisting her so?

She brought the coffee and packs of cream and sugar and set them in front of him. She waited as he took a long sip.

"Dustin, something's changed since yesterday. You're a lot more defensive. You're irritated that I'm asking you these questions. Last night you avoided us completely. What's going on? Did something happen?"

He hesitated for a few seconds too long, and she could see that she'd hit the nail on the head. "No. I'm just tired and sick of all this. I never thought I'd be in a situation like this."

She knew he was evading. Yesterday when he'd left her office, he had gone to the hospital. Had Travis said something that he didn't want to tell her? Or had it been later, when he went to handle the emergency for his client? Had someone confronted him?

Why wouldn't he tell her?

She studied him for a moment, noting the way he avoided looking at her. "Dustin, you could be indicted any day now, and it won't be for the original charges. They'll officially connect you to the bombing this time. You'll have to go back to jail, probably without bond. While you're free, we can't leave a single stone unturned. Time is running out."

"I'm well aware that I could be spending the rest of my life in jail. And so is everybody else who watches the news."

"We can reverse this," she said. "I just need all the information."

"I'm doing my best, Jamie."

But she wasn't satisfied. His eyes, his choice of words, his body language all told her he was keeping something from her. She resolved to keep working on him. She wasn't going to give up that easily.

42

There was blood on her arm. Sitting in her car in the Walmart parking lot, Taylor realized she had scratched an itchy rash until it was raw.

Where had the rash come from? She hadn't noticed the red bumps before, but now she pulled up her pants leg to another itchy spot and saw that it, too, was mottled with red, raised bumps.

Could it be a reaction to the medication she'd just started? She would have to look it up later and maybe call her doctor. She dug through her purse for the small bottle of hand sanitizer she carried and dotted some over the broken skin.

Her phone rang, startling her, and she checked it. Her sister had discovered she was gone. She didn't want to talk to her. Taylor switched it to silent and got out of the car.

A couple across the parking lot were looking at her, and she crossed her arms as she walked, fear tightening her chest. A woman stood just outside the door, as if waiting for her. Taylor felt herself sweating as she walked past her.

The room seemed to spin as she stepped into the cool building, and she stood there a moment, taking it in until the spinning stopped. She didn't feel well. Maybe she should go home.

But no, she had to do this. She tried to clear her thoughts and headed toward the back of the store. There were too many people here, and they seemed oblivious. Didn't they know about the explosion? Didn't they realize it could happen here?

Her phone vibrated as she walked through the store. She glanced down again. Still her sister. She ignored it. Then a text popped up on the screen.

Where are you? Why won't you answer?

She sighed and texted back. Her hands trembled, so she misspelled it, but she deleted and tried again.

At Walmart. Can't talk on phone from inside.

She hoped her sister bought that. She'd heard it was hard to get cell calls inside a big box store, but she had taken calls from here many times.

Why did you just leave? Are you okay?

Taylor didn't even want to answer that. She wasn't okay. How could she be? Dustin Webb was walking around free to do it again. How could anyone be okay?

She saw a mother and child shopping for a bike, and the kid was bouncing up and down and trying to get it out of its slot in the bike section. She wanted to ask the mom why she would bring her child here, in public, where anyone could ram a truck into the side of the building and set off a mushroom cloud.

She kept her jaw clenched and went to the area where she'd seen guns being sold before. Now it only had sports and camping equipment.

She saw a clerk and walked toward him.

"Can I help you?" he asked.

"Yeah," she said. "I want to buy a gun."

He shook his head. "We don't sell them here anymore. But there's a gun store right up the road."

She felt like an idiot, and as she walked toward the doors, her intrusive thoughts assaulted her again. *They hate me here.* That came from out of the blue, she knew. No one hated her. But on her way out, she saw two more people staring at her. Watching her. They knew what she was trying to do. But she couldn't let them stop her.

She must have scratched at her arm as she walked back to her car, because by the time she was behind the wheel, she had blood on her fingertips. She sanitized again. Why hadn't she bought some itch medication?

The thought left as quickly as it had come. The gun. She had to get the gun. She pulled out, going north, and found the store about a block from Walmart.

She checked the small parking lot. There was no one hanging around, looking for her. She went inside, and the bald, chubby man behind the counter greeted her. "Can I help you, ma'am?"

She glanced beyond him. There was no one else here. "I need to buy a handgun," she said.

"Do you know what kind you're interested in?"

She scratched her arm again. "I'm not sure."

"Do you want it to fit in your purse, or does it matter?"

"Yeah, maybe. But I want it to be powerful."

He unlocked the counter and pulled out one. "This is popular with women, for self-defense. It's small and easy to carry."

She took the gun in her hand and slipped her finger through

the trigger guard. "When I was a kid, my dad took us to the shooting range sometimes. I used to like firing a .44 Magnum."

"Oh, so something bigger." He pulled one of those out, and she took it in her hand. "It has a kick," he said.

"I don't care." She would gladly let it knock her down. She just didn't want to miss.

As she held the gun in her hand, her gaze strayed to the shotguns and rifles on the wall behind him. That was what she needed. Something she could shoot from a distance. But who was she kidding? She didn't have the skills to be a sniper.

"I'll take this one," she said. "Do I have to apply for the license here?"

"Yeah," he said. "There's a sixty-day waiting period to get a license in Georgia. You can buy it today, but you can't legally carry it until sixty days is up."

She hesitated, then realized no one would know unless she used it. If she decided to do that, it wouldn't matter anyway. She filled out the necessary forms, then bought .44 Magnum cartridges and allowed the sales clerk to escort her from the store.

She sat in her car for a minute after he went back in. Now what? She had to find Dustin Webb. If the police didn't care enough to keep him locked up, she would take matters into her own hands.

43

Dustin knew he had wasted the time with Jamie today, but he'd been counting the hours until he could get out of there. When she finally gave up on him, he went to his car and headed where he'd been wanting to go all day. He had to get to his office and see if he could find anything else in Travis's things.

The phone was ringing when he got inside. He waited for it to go to voicemail, but it immediately began ringing again. He went to the phone at his desk and unplugged it from the wall. Then he went to Travis's desk and did the same.

He stayed at Travis's desk and opened his drawers, taking a mental inventory of everything he found there. Nothing seemed unusual.

He grabbed Travis's wastebasket and dumped it out. There wasn't much, since neither of them had spent much time in the office this week. Nothing stood out. He went through each of the trash cans in the building, then looked through boxes and file cabinets.

Finally he sat down at Travis's desktop computer and scrolled through his emails. Nothing there caught his attention. He closed the email and checked all the files that had been saved in the last month. They were all work-related.

He returned to his desk and sat staring for a moment. If he worked backward from the bombing, was it possible that Travis could have carried out these crimes? There was no way he had gone out to rent a U-Haul truck the day before the bombing, much less taken the time to fill it with explosives. He hadn't left the hospital that whole day and night. Crystal was too fragile.

Assembling the explosives into a bomb before loading it into a truck would have taken days. For the driver to have gotten away before the bomb went off, he would have had to have a detonator. That took wiring and work. It was virtually impossible for Travis to have spent any time doing that, even before Crystal wound up in the hospital.

But Travis was involved. Why else would he have had that diagram? He had known when Dustin was going to be at the hospital. He even had access to his car key. Was he working with someone else? If so, who?

He wanted to give his friend the benefit of the doubt and not report anything so flimsy as a piece of paper with a sketch that could have been the result of Travis speculating after the bombing. It could be as simple as that.

So why didn't that explanation give him any peace? He vowed to keep digging until he got to an answer that satisfied him.

44

Jamie spent the rest of the day researching each of the people on the list of those who had access to ChemEx, but none of the information she gathered shed light on the case. She pulled into her mother's driveway to pick up Avery and glanced next door, where Dustin used to live. Pat's house hadn't changed much, even though so much time had passed. She heard water spraying in the backyard, and over the fence she saw the top of Pat's straw hat.

She decided to talk to Pat before going into her mother's house. She went to the gate and knocked, then opened it partially. "Miss Pat, it's Jamie."

Pat looked up from scrubbing out the planters that held the potted flowers she had tended for years with much more love than she'd ever offered Dustin. "Jamie! How are you doing?"

Jamie hugged her. Pat grabbed a towel and dried her hands. "Come in, honey. We'll have some coffee."

"I can't," Jamie said. "I just came to pick up Avery. I heard you back here, so I wanted to come over for a minute and talk to you about Dustin."

Pat stiffened and went to turn off the water. "I really have nothing to say on that subject, Jamie."

Jamie sighed and sat down at the picnic table where she and Dustin had sat so many times. She recalled the few times she had eaten here with them for barbecues, when between each bite, Dustin had suffered Pat's scathing, critical orders. "Sit up straight, Dustin," or "Don't gulp your food," or "Put your napkin in your lap," or "Get your elbows off the table." Jamie had always been self-conscious when eating in front of the woman, even though Pat's tongue-lashings seemed directed only at Dustin.

"I know you've heard about Dustin's charges," she said.

"Yes, the police interviewed me. Then I heard it on the news. Imagine my pride."

"He didn't do this. I have ample proof."

Her smile was tight and strained. "Dustin always could convince you of anything."

Lightning flashed in Jamie's brain. "And you were always quick to believe the worst about him."

Pat turned back to the planters and continued scrubbing. "I gave him a roof over his head, I fed him, and I bought him clothes to wear. I shouldn't be faulted for not being able to control him. There wasn't one thing I was ever able to do about it." She twisted to look Jamie. "You know, I never had one minute of trouble from my own children. That ought to tell you something."

Again, Jamie tried to keep her voice even. "It does tell me something. It tells me that your own children knew they were loved and appreciated. Dustin's parents died when he was six, and he was in and out of foster care until he came to you. He didn't have the luxuries your kids had."

"You don't think I accounted for that? I did. But he was in trouble every time I turned around. He never came home on time; he sneaked out of the house after everyone had gone to bed; he skipped school at least once a week. I never asked to raise him!" Pat blurted. "But all those years of raising my children to be exemplary went out the window the first time Dustin humiliated our family."

Tears stung Jamie's eyes, and she realized she'd made a mistake in coming here. She stood up. "I feel sorry for you," she said in a cracked voice.

"Me?" Pat asked.

"Yes, you. Because you'll never have the chance to know what a good man Dustin is. You cheated yourself out of finding that out."

"I did the best I could," Pat bit out.

"What you did was make him an outcast in your home. Did it ever occur to you that Dustin got into so much trouble because of that? That it was easier for him to think you didn't like him because he was a troublemaker? That maybe he couldn't bear the idea that, in your eyes, he was unworthy of your love?"

"You tell that to the judge when you get to court," Pat said. "See how your psychoanalysis of him stands up against an exploding bomb and dozens of dead bodies." She banged her fist on the table, shaking her whole body. "I won't take responsibility for the kind of person he is! I won't do it!"

"Well, you won't have to!" Jamie said, and before she had to hear another word, she left Pat's yard. She wouldn't bring Pat up to Dustin again.

45

Dustin was no closer to finding answers to his questions about Travis, despite his efforts to get to the bottom of it today.

When Jamie got home with Avery, she brought Chinese food and spread the boxes out on the counter. She seemed quiet and distant, and Dustin wondered if it was a response to his mood.

Avery took up the slack. "Be sure to check my backpack," she told Jamie. "I brought some good art home. And a note that I'm an awesome kid."

Dustin smiled.

"You did?" Jamie glanced at her. "Seriously?"

"No, not seriously," Avery said. "But I deserved one."

"I bet you did," Jamie said. "You're definitely an awesome kid."

"I got in the talent show."

"You did? Why didn't you call me?"

"Everybody got in." Avery shrugged. "But it's still fun."

"So what's your talent? Singing?"

"No!" Avery said, as though that idea was ludicrous.

"Dancing?"

"Absolutely not."

"Then what?"

"I don't know," Avery said. "I'm still trying to think what my best talent is. I have a lot to choose from."

"That's right. You do."

"Like, I could draw or tell a joke."

Dustin couldn't help meeting Jamie's grinning eyes.

"Well, you have a lot to think about."

"Jordan Harris is gonna do gymnastics. Mom, can I take gymnastics?"

"We can talk about it. It's kind of late to think all that through tonight."

Avery got quiet for a moment, and Dustin wondered if she was imagining herself doing triple flips in the air.

"You know what I wish?" she asked suddenly. "I wish I had a big brother."

Jamie got up and took her plate to the sink. "Where did that come from?"

Avery shrugged. "Amberlyn has a big brother, and one time he beat up a boy who tripped her in the cafeteria."

Dustin chuckled softly. "How did we go from a talent show to Amberlyn's big brother?"

"He takes gymnastics, too."

"Oh," Dustin said, as if that made perfect sense.

"Eat," Jamie said. "We have homework."

Dustin watched Jamie load her dish into the dishwasher. She seemed fatigued and distracted, as if she'd been as immersed in this puzzle as he had. But she was lacking one of the pieces.

He thought again of sharing it with her, but this wasn't the time. Not yet.

When Avery begged him to let Dude sleep with her, Dustin made sure it was okay with Jamie and let him go. When Avery and Jamie went upstairs to do homework, taking Dude with them, that dark cloud of Travis's duplicity fell over him again. He wouldn't be able to sleep tonight. He would wait until they were asleep and slip out. He had things to do. He wanted to get to the bottom of this tonight.

When the lights upstairs went out, Dustin left the house and walked out to his rental car. He started it, hoping the sound wouldn't wake them.

He drove for fifteen minutes to the long, sparsely inhabited street where GreyWebb's storage units were. They'd rented them two years before when they'd needed more storage space.

He unlocked the first door, then went into the hallway of the air-conditioned, multiunit building. The doors to the individual units were lined up down the hall, all in a temperature-controlled environment. He went to their first unit and slid up the door. Turning on the light, he stepped inside.

The equipment they were going to install on their current job was stacked where he had put it when it came in a couple of months ago. He wandered among the boxes, looking for anything that shouldn't be here.

Everything looked as he expected.

He stepped back out, relocked it, and went next door to the other unit. There were a few TV monitors and some other equipment left from their last project. Behind those, at the rear of the unit, he saw an unmarked box. He didn't remember putting it there. He opened the top—and sucked in a breath.

The box was full of detonator caps.

They were the kind of detonators that fit on canisters of explosives like the ones found in his car. Heart pounding, he looked around for anything else. Travis had set up two sawhorses with a piece of plywood on top. What had he done there?

There was a trash can in the back corner that hadn't been emptied in some time. Dustin dug through the trash and found some wadded papers. He smoothed one out. It was a sketch that looked like an earlier draft of the diagram Dustin had seen yesterday. He smoothed another one—it was a more intricate diagram explaining how to connect all the canisters to one detonation point that could be controlled by a phone.

Dizziness spun his thoughts. He squatted, trying to calm his mind. He sat there for a moment, staring at the diagram, as a million brutal thoughts stampeded through his head. Travis was involved. He *had* played a part in the bombing at Trudeau Hall. There was no way around it.

His best friend had set him up. Travis was deliberately sending him to prison.

But Crystal . . .

For a moment, Dustin considered getting rid of it all, burning the diagram, cleaning up the evidence. But he thought better of it. He took a picture of the diagram and more photos of what he'd found, then dropped the wadded page back into the trash can where he'd found it.

Leaving things as he'd found them, he locked the unit and left the building. He sat in his car for a moment, trying to think. He had to do something, but what? Go to the police? Call Jamie?

But what would that mean for Travis? Would they swarm

the hospital to arrest him in front of Crystal? The thought sickened him.

He made a U-turn and headed in the opposite direction.

He rolled down his windows and let the wind blow through his hair as he sped through town, heading for the hospital where his best friend sat like a mourning husband rather than a deceitful jackal who was leading a second life. Dustin's eyes stung, and he didn't know or care if it was from the gritty wind or the even grittier truth scratching at his soul.

All he knew was that it was time to bring this to an end.

46

The hospital corridor was quiet at midnight, except for a nurse outside a room typing on a laptop computer that sat on a rolling stand. At the nurses' station, Dustin saw another nurse glued to her computer. He straightened his cloth mask to cover his face so he wouldn't attract anyone's attention—that suspected terrorist whose face had been all over the news—and slipped past them, unnoticed.

He went to the isolation room with Crystal's name on the handwritten sign next to the door. He knocked quietly, then opened the door and looked inside. There was a plastic curtain inside the room, cordoning off Crystal from the germs that might be brought in.

He stepped back and closed the door. He couldn't go in there. Trying to decide what to do, Dustin started back up the dimly lit hall.

"Dustin?"

He turned around and saw Travis coming out of the room,

taking off his mask. He was still wearing the paper gown over his clothes and the shoe coverings.

"What are you doing here so late?"

The sight of him rang like an alarm in Dustin's ears. He restrained his urge to lunge at him. His breath was shallow as he stepped toward Travis. "We're going outside," he said. "We have to talk."

"Outside?" Travis swallowed and looked at his watch. "It's midnight. Why do you want to go outside?"

Dustin lowered his voice and stepped toward him. "Because if I deal with you right here, it might disturb the patients."

Travis's eyes widened. "Okay, okay."

"Outside," Dustin said again. "Now."

Travis started toward the door to a courtyard where patients went to smoke, even though it wasn't officially allowed within a block of the hospital. No one was out here now. He opened the door for Dustin, and Dustin stepped out into the cool night.

"What happened, Dustin? What's going on?"

The false innocence in Travis's voice snapped the last restraints of Dustin's rage. Every muscle in his body went rigid, and his hands closed into fists. "How could you do this to me?" he asked through his teeth.

Travis's eyes widened as though he was truly blindsided. "What are you talking about, Dustin?"

Dustin lunged at him then and shoved him against the stone wall. "You set me up!" he said. "Do you know what you've done?"

Travis pushed him off. "I don't know what you're talking about. I'm going back in to my wife."

When Travis reached for the door, Dustin swung, his fist

smashing across Travis's jaw. Travis came right back at him, his own knuckles cracking into Dustin's cheekbone.

Dustin felt no pain. His lips curled with his words. "I went to the storage unit. I saw the detonator caps. I found your diagram!"

Now it was Travis's rage that seemed to change the air. He took a step toward Dustin, and for a moment Dustin wondered if Travis felt trapped. Would he try to fight his way out?

Instead, Travis's expression morphed from that of a caged animal to that of an anguished child. "It's not what you think," he said through gritted teeth. "I never knew things were gonna turn out the way they did."

Dustin stood frozen. "People were murdered! Some of the survivors are in this hospital. Their families are suffering."

"I know about suffering," Travis threw back. "I did it all for Crystal!"

"For *Crystal*?" The words were so absurd, so out of context, that Dustin couldn't process them. "Don't put this on her. She doesn't deserve that."

"Don't you think I know that?" Travis asked. He raised his hand to cover his eyes as tears seized him. "I never meant for it to get so out of hand. Let me explain."

Explain? How could he explain this? Feeling like the wind had been kicked out of him, Dustin dropped into a chair a few feet away from Travis. "I'm listening," he said.

Travis went to the table and pulled out another chair. "Insurance wouldn't cover Crystal's treatment."

"What does that have to do with this?"

Travis took a fortifying breath, as if trying to steady his voice. "A couple of weeks ago, a guy approached me. I don't even know his name. He offered me enough money to cover all of

Crystal's treatment, if I'd find a way to get some explosives out of ChemEx."

Dustin gaped at him. "You can't be that stupid."

"He said they were doing some mining on their own property."

"Mining? For what?"

"I didn't ask. I just thought it was harmless. It was easy money, and I needed it. You have to understand, Dustin. I was desperate. She was dying, and her medication wasn't working, and we were at the end of the road except for this one experimental treatment. I really believed that if I had enough money, I could save her."

An airplane cut slowly across the sky overhead, and Dustin watched it, letting that explanation sink in. He got up, went to the balcony rail, and looked down at the parking lot. "Why didn't you come to me? Why didn't you once ask me for help? I would have given you a loan, or gone to the bank, sold my house. We had the credit line. You could have used it."

"It wasn't enough. We're talking hundreds of thousands of dollars, Dustin."

"I don't care," Dustin said, turning around. "You don't finance medical treatment by selling bombs to terrorists. And you don't point the police toward your friend!"

"I know that now!" Travis cried, standing up and starting toward Dustin. "When I heard about the bombings, I realized how stupid I'd been. But it was too late."

"Did you put the explosives in my car?"

"No."

"Did you tell your partners where I'd be and let them do it?"

Travis covered his face again and sucked in a sharp sob, like a little boy who'd been caught in a shameful act. "I was scared,

Dustin," he said in a high-pitched voice. "I didn't steal the explosives, but I got the guy into the facility and doctored the security video. I didn't think the amount he took would be missed. But then it was on the news. ChemEx had reported the theft, and when they questioned us, I knew they might have me on the list of suspects. I couldn't go to jail and let Crystal find out what I'd done. It would have killed her for sure."

"So you called and told the police it was me?"

"No, they did that. I wasn't going to let you go down for it. I just wanted a little more time."

Dustin could make no sense out of that. It didn't fit any pattern he'd known about Travis. There had been no hint of bad blood in their friendship. Dustin rubbed his face and let out a loud groan. "This is insane. I don't believe that you didn't touch the bomb. I saw the diagram. You made the detonator for them."

"No, I didn't make it. I just showed them how to."

Dustin looked back down at the parking lot, wishing he could dive over the railing and end it all. But he wouldn't let Travis do that to him.

Travis came up behind him. "This sounds horrible, I know. But you're not in my shoes, Dustin. The guy said if they were caught, they would take me down with them. But I thought of a way to get the heat off me. When you were at the hospital, I remembered that you had a backup car key in your office desk drawer. I got it, then when you were here at the hospital, I called the guy and gave it to him, and told him to put some of the RDX in your trunk."

Dustin stared at him before speaking. "When I realized it must have been you, I told myself no, you would never do that.

There had to be some good reason you had that diagram. But there isn't! You did this to me!"

"Just listen." Travis sucked in a breath and went on. "They put the boxes in your car, and I think what happened is, the next day, they tipped off the police. Believe me, I never would have done this if I'd known they were going to commit a terrorist act. And I would have confessed before you had to take the heat."

"But I am taking the heat! I was arrested. They put me in jail! I'm being accused! And don't give me that I think what happened stuff. You set it up. You probably did it yourself."

Travis sat back down and crumpled up. He looked different than Dustin had ever seen him. Cowardly, deceitful, stupid . . .

But suddenly a thought occurred to Dustin. "Wait. You have this guy's phone number?"

Travis looked up. "It was a burner phone. I tried calling it again after the bombing, but it was turned off. I'm sure they've gotten rid of it, especially if they used it to call the police."

"Give me the number anyway."

Travis found the number in his Recent Calls and showed it to Dustin. Dustin put it in his phone. "Travis, you're the only one who can identify this person. You have to talk to the police."

"Not yet!" Travis said. "You have my word I will before you go back to jail."

"Your word means nothing!" Dustin bit out.

"I just wanted a little more time," he said again. He tipped his head to the side, his face a pitiful distortion of pain and weary acceptance. "She's dying, Dustin. Don't you see that I can't leave her right now?" His lips trembled as he spoke. "Other than my wife, you're the best friend I have in this whole world. Give me just a little more time and then I'll turn myself in. It'll all be over."

Dustin's mouth twitched as he looked at the honest misery in his friend's face. "Do you have any idea what you're asking me? Just by knowing this I could be considered an accomplice." Dustin realized how absurd that was. He was already being accused of a terrorist attack.

"I've never asked you for anything before," Travis said, taking Dustin's shoulders, "and I know you have every right to turn me in right now, this second."

Dustin shoved him back. "Get your hands off me. You should have gone to the police yourself, the minute you knew there was a bombing."

Travis nodded grimly. "I realize that. I should have. But I didn't. It was all about Crystal."

Dustin shook his head and turned away, tormenting, torturous thoughts flailing through his mind. "You have to help them find these guys."

"I will," Travis said. "But she's still bleeding, Dustin. She's had four transfusions. She's septic. The color is draining from her face, and every time she dozes off I think it's for the last time."

As much contempt as Dustin had for Travis right now, he had that much love for Crystal and those two little boys. Travis was a hero to them, a knight in shining armor, always there to make things better. He didn't want to turn her image of her husband into that of a monster who'd been complicit in so many deaths.

"Please, Dustin. We've been friends for so many years."

"That's what I was just thinking." Not able to stomach the conversation any longer, Dustin left Travis there and took the stairs down to the first floor. Before getting in his car, Dustin opened the trunk, just to make sure it was empty. He looked in the back seat. Nothing.

Fatigue and helplessness weighed him down as he drove back to the house.

Pulling into the driveway, he saw that the light was on in the kitchen. Had she noticed he was gone? He closed the door quietly so he wouldn't set off Dude's barking if he was awake.

Dread filled him as he walked slowly into the house.

She was sitting on the couch in a circle of lamplight, wearing sweatpants and a T-shirt. "Dustin?"

He tried to lighten his voice. "What are you doing up so late?"

"I heard your car when you left. Where did you go?"

He cleared his throat. "To the hospital. I'm sorry I woke you up."

Her face changed when she saw the swelling bruise under his left eye. She stood up. "What happened to you?"

"Nothing. Just—"

"You went out in the middle of the night and look like you've been in a fight."

"I just wanted to check on Crystal."

She stepped toward him and touched the bruise. The tenderness almost made him lose the tenuous hold he had on his emotions. "I want to trust you, Dustin," she whispered. "I need to trust you. What are you hiding from me?"

Dustin let out a long rush of breath, then sank onto the couch and covered his face. "Sit down," he said. "Put your lawyer hat on. We have to talk."

47

I knew something wasn't right. I knew Travis was ducking the questions." Jamie paced across the living room, her mind racing with the steps she would have to take. She had to stay calm. She had to think like an attorney, with strategy and caution.

Dustin was wrecked. She had never seen him so disheartened, though she'd seen him deal with injustice before.

"I have to call the police, the DA."

"Now? In the middle of the night?"

"Yes," she said. "We don't have a choice. If we drag our feet, you're complicit." She sat down next to him on the couch and touched his back. "I know this is hard for you. But you haven't done anything wrong. If you keep this information from the police, then you will have broken the law."

"I know. We have to tell them. But Crystal . . . I just keep trying to imagine how it will play out. Will they go straight to the hospital to arrest him? Will she see them put handcuffs on him? Will the shock of it all push her over the edge?"

"Dustin, is there any possibility that Crystal isn't as close to death as we think? That Travis could be using her for cover?"

"No. I've talked to the nursing staff and her mother. She's in critical condition. They've put her in a laminar air-flow room. She's bleeding and septic."

"Okay, then we have to deal with that. But the fact is, Travis put her in this position, not you. He caused this."

He rubbed his eyes. "It's not about him anymore. It's about my friendship with her."

"Do you think if Crystal knew what was going on, that she would expect you to take the heat?"

"I don't know."

"Well, if she did, then she's not your friend." She went to the counter where her phone was charging and unplugged it. "I'm calling them now, Dustin. We're going to set up an interview."

He nodded. "I'm ready."

It was one in the morning when Jamie called the DA. "I'm so sorry for waking you up, Louis, but my client has new information about the theft at ChemEx and possibly the bombing at Trudeau Hall."

She waited as the DA got Detective Borden on the call with them, then she told them what Dustin had told her.

They were going to be up all night.

Dustin went into his bedroom as Jamie talked on the phone. A sense of deep, impending doom weighed him down. This was pretty quickly shaping up to be one of the worst nights of his life.

If only she could delay his interview with the DA and the detective until later in the morning, just to buy Crystal a little more time.

The thought shocked him. What was he doing? Was he hoping Crystal would die sooner so she wouldn't have to see what a monstrous thing her husband had done? Or was he simply rooting for her to live, in which case she would have to see it all play out?

He opened his computer, trying to think past this phone call and the interview he would be forced to sit through, in which he would have to tell the police that his best friend was involved in all those deaths. But who else was involved, besides Travis? Who would have paid Travis for his help in stealing explosives? Who would have blown up the Ed Loran rally?

He created a spreadsheet on his computer, with three columns headed Personal Enemies, International Terrorists Targeting an American Crowd, and Political Presidential Rivals.

He almost deleted the third one, since Loran didn't seem to be enough of a threat to the other candidates to make him into a target of assassination. Still, he couldn't rule it out. Loran was a Libertarian. Either political party could want him out of the presidential race, so the bombing could just as likely have been carried out by Democrats as by Republicans. He wrote both in that column, then tried to think of special interest groups that might have a beef with Loran. None of them seemed so passionate that they'd kill him.

He moved to the "Personal" column, trying to remember what little he knew about Loran's background. He had been CEO of Cell Three Therapeutics, a biotech company that manufactured pharmaceuticals and medical supplies.

Could it be a rival company that wanted to retaliate for something? A disgruntled employee? A union group? An environmental group?

He moved to the "Terrorist" column and typed in "ISIS." They were the ones responsible for most of the foreign terrorist attacks in the US, and they didn't need a specific reason, other than a crowd. But ISIS usually took credit when they successfully carried out an attack. It also didn't fit their usual MO. ISIS terrorists often died in their own terrorist attacks. Whoever this was had gotten away before the bomb was detonated.

He heard Jamie's low voice in the kitchen trying to work out a time for the interview.

Dustin moved on. What about the guy who had approached Travis? He should have asked Travis more questions. How had the guy contacted him? Where had he met him? How had the money been exchanged?

Jamie got off the phone and came to his bedroom door. "Okay, that's done."

He closed his computer and followed her to the living room. "Are they going to arrest him?"

"Not yet. They're going to call me back with a time for your interview."

"Is it going to be soon—like tonight—or in the morning?"

"I'm guessing soon," Jamie said.

"What about Avery?"

"If they want us to come in, I'll have to drop her by my mom's." She put on a pot of coffee. "How do you feel?"

"I don't know," he said. "I guess I'm glad that they know, so I'm not an accomplice. But I don't look forward to the questioning. I wish I knew more."

"I was thinking. Before they swarm your office with a search warrant, maybe you could get some information from your security video there. You have cameras inside and out, don't you?"

"Yes, of course."

"If the guy who approached Travis met him there, wouldn't it be on video?"

Dustin opened his computer. "Might be. Travis didn't tell me anything about where he met him."

He navigated to the app that showed GreyWebb's security system. The first camera view that came up looked down on the main room. He and Travis had worked so hard to build this, but now everything had changed. How could any of their work continue? One of them was going to prison, and even if by some miracle it didn't turn out that way, their friendship wouldn't survive this.

He opened the archives.

"What day was he approached?" Jamie asked.

"I don't know. But I'll go back to a week or so before the ChemEx break-in." He found the security video of their building for that week and fast-forwarded to times Travis was in the office. He carefully observed everyone who came and went during that time.

They normally didn't see clients at their office, so there weren't that many visitors. He fast-forwarded to each person who'd arrived, but he knew and could account for all of them.

Jamie sat down next to him and started typing.

"What are you doing?"

"I'm writing your statement, just as you told me. You can revise it and reword it when I'm done."

He viewed the video of the next few days, stopping at each arriving visitor. Finally, in the video from a week before the theft, he found someone he didn't know. It was a man who was possibly in his early twenties, looked about six feet tall, and had dark hair under a baseball cap and brown glasses. Dustin checked the video feed from the parking lot camera and saw that the man drove a white unmarked van. He walked with a slight limp.

"This guy."

Jamie stopped typing and looked at his screen.

"I don't know him, and it's around the right time."

He backed up the video and played it again as Jamie watched. Dustin found the best angle of the man and snapped a picture of the video with his phone since that was the quickest way to capture the image as a still.

"Were you in the office then?"

"No, I was at a job." He fast-forwarded as the man and Travis talked. "They talked for thirty minutes."

"He has a white van," she said. "Could be the same one that pulled up behind your car at the hospital when they put the boxes in your trunk. Try to see the tag."

He tried to zoom in on the tag, but the man backed all the way out of the parking lot without turning around, and Dustin couldn't get it.

"Okay, so what time was that whole visit?"

He read it out to her, and she wrote it down. "Okay, see if he comes back."

Dustin fast-forwarded through each day's video after that. "Here he is, days later."

Jamie leaned in to see. "What's he carrying?"

"A bag."

"What could he have brought to Travis?"

"Cash," Dustin said. "Either that, or he wired the money to Travis."

They never saw what was in the bag, but this time he was there for over an hour.

"Where were you that day?"

Dustin checked the calendar on his phone. "I was at a meeting for contractors bidding on a new project. Travis knew I'd be there most of the afternoon."

"The theft at ChemEx was just a couple days later."

"His face is more visible. No hat."

"Get some screenshots."

Dustin did, but also snapped pictures of the screen with his phone.

"Do you know how to do a reverse image search?"

"You bet I do." Dustin's adrenaline was pumping now, chasing away the fatigue. As Jamie poured their coffee, he did the reverse image search and uploaded one of the pictures of the man's face.

Jamie brought him the coffee and sat down next to him as the computer buffered.

A list of website articles loaded, all containing pictures of the same man. "That's him."

"Who is he?"

He clicked on one of them. "Samuel Bates, from Gainesville, Georgia."

"Screenshot him and send it to me. I'm putting him in the statement." She went back to typing furiously as Dustin took the screenshots and phone snapshots. He wished they had a printer here.

"See what you can find out about this guy."

He googled Samuel Bates. There were a couple of obituaries

of his parents and one of a little sister over the last few years. "He has two brothers—Jack Bates and Anthony Bates."

He googled them, but didn't find anything more than those obituaries.

Jamie's phone chimed, and she answered it quickly. "Hey, Louis."

Dustin could hear the DA's voice, but he couldn't hear what he was saying.

He went back to the obituaries of the Bateses' parents. They had both died the same year. In the final paragraph of both obits, the family had written, "The family blames Cell Three Therapeutics's toxic waste, which caused three hundred cases of cancer in the Raven community, including fifty-seven children."

He touched Jamie's arm. She kept talking to Louis, but she glanced at the screen. Dustin pointed to the reference to Cell Three. It was Ed Loran's company. Jamie's eyes flashed.

"Okay, we'll be there. See you soon." She hung up and read the Bateses' statement. "You did it. You found the motive."

His heart pounded as he searched for Samuel Bates's address. When he found it, he snapped that on his phone, too. Jamie went back to her computer. "We have to be there at three thirty. That's almost an hour and a half. I have to get Avery up. But I'm going to finish this first."

He gave her Bates's address and went to the bedroom to change clothes as she typed, putting all the information they knew into his written statement.

48

It was eight in the morning by the time Detective Borden and his partner seemed to be winding down with Dustin and Jamie. Exhaustion was setting in deep in Dustin's bones, but he couldn't let himself get lethargic now.

"It's time to drop the charges against my client, Detectives," Jamie was saying. "He's given you all the information he has, and it's clear he had no part in these crimes."

"Can't do it," Borden said.

"Why not? You don't have a case against him."

"We have his word on these things, and that's all. We haven't confirmed any of it."

"We confirmed it. We practically took you to the door of the man who committed the theft and the bombing. How can you still think Dustin was involved? And Travis Grey . . . You have the evidence at the storage unit. The security video of Bates coming to talk to him. He wasn't talking to Dustin! You have the video of that same van in the hospital parking lot, and the transfer of boxes into Dustin's car. You can't ignore these things!"

"We're working on all of this as we speak. I have people checking out these claims right now. But the charges still stand."

Jamie was about to lose it, but Dustin watched her pull herself back in. "Are you at least going to talk to Travis today? Confirm any of this with him? Check the storage unit? Dustin gave you the key."

"We can't give you a play-by-play of our investigation, Ms. Powell."

"I don't have to tell you how serious this is. The Bates brothers could strike again. You can't assume that Loran was their only target. Judging by the volume of explosives stolen from ChemEx, they still have material left over. They could do this again."

"We're well aware."

When they finally let them go, Dustin followed Jamie out to her SUV. "So . . . do you think they believe anything at all that we told them?"

"I don't know."

"Do you think they're going to take Travis in today?"

She sighed. "I think so. But we have no control over this. Where is your storage unit?"

He told her the name and address. "We can't go over there."

"We're not going in. I just want to know if they're there."

He was quiet as Jamie drove through town. When the storage unit sign came into view, Jamie slowed.

"Thank God. They're here."

Dustin sat straighter as he took in the sight of the police cars and the crime scene tape around the building. "They listened."

She nodded. "Travis may be arrested today after all. We might be all right."

Dustin tried to relax, but the thought that the cops may have swarmed the hospital, too, made his stomach churn.

49

The night had stretched too long for Taylor as she lay awake, scenarios of her coming face-to-face with Dustin Webb playing out like waking dreams in her mind. Before dawn, she got up and made coffee, careful not to wake her sister.

Desiree's funeral was today, and Taylor still didn't know what she was going to say. Why had she agreed to this? She got her laptop and tried typing a few sentences to open with. But her heart wasn't in it.

They would all be staring at her, thinking that she had saved herself. They would all be judging her, hating her. Anything she said would sound inauthentic . . . just words that meant nothing.

She scratched her arm over the bandage she had put on it last night. Now her leg was bloody where it had been itching. And there were other places on her body where a rash was forming. It was as if the guilt festering in her body was pushing its way out. The very idea of her standing in front of Desiree's parents when she could have saved their daughter made her sick.

She forced herself to type some more. There were stories about Desiree she could tell, anecdotes about funny things she'd done, kindnesses she'd bestowed on others, things she cared about.

But it was still all meaningless.

"You're up early."

She looked up at Harper. "Yeah. I had to work on my thoughts for the funeral."

"Good. I was wondering when you'd get around to that." Harper poured herself a cup of coffee. "Did you find anything to wear?"

"No. I'll have to make do with something I have." Taylor thought of when she and Desiree had gone to Gulf Shores together for a sorority dance. Desiree had found their blind dates on a dating app, but the two guys who showed up were close to their parents' ages, despite the photos on the app.

"Here, take your medicine."

Taylor took the pill and washed it down, then kept typing. They had denied being Taylor and Desiree and had managed to ditch the men.

No, that story wasn't right. It was stupid. People would be sitting there, wondering how she could tell a funny story when she'd let her friends die.

She finally gave up on the speech and forced herself to shower. By the time she got out, her ears were ringing, and her head was beginning to hurt. She took some Tylenol and got dressed. She didn't have a black skirt, and her raw, rashy leg showed beneath all of her other skirts. She opted for black slacks and a white blouse, with a short, waist-length blazer. She looked like she was going to a marketing conference for work, instead of a funeral to bury her best friend. But she had nothing better to wear.

That ringing in her ears was still there when she met Harper in the living room. It was probably just nerves. Her pulse was racing, and she imagined her blood pressure had shot up. It would all be over soon. She just had to get through it.

"Are you sweating?" Harper asked her as they got their things to go.

"Yeah. It's hot."

"I'm not hot. Are you okay?"

She shrugged. "Freaking out a little. I'll be okay."

"You know you don't have to do this."

"I owe them this. It's the very least I can do."

Taylor was quiet as Harper drove her to the church. When they went in, several of Taylor's friends grabbed her and hugged her tearfully. She slipped away from each of them, not willing to accept the comfort they offered or share in their pain.

Harper sat with her near the front of the crowd, in the seat the family had reserved for her. The visitation went on at the front, before the funeral started, and she watched with dull eyes as Desiree's parents greeted the visitors next to the closed casket. Behind them, the people in the pews talked quietly, and there was some laughter a few rows back.

"How can people laugh at a funeral?" Taylor muttered.

"I don't know. Deep depression is a hard place to stay for a long period of time. People need a break in it."

"No, they just don't get it," she said. "They don't understand what happened."

Harper looked at her. "Are you sure you're okay?"

"Stop asking me that," Taylor said. "No, I'm not okay. I'm not going to be."

"I can tell her parents that you'd rather not do this."

"I'm doing it," she said again. The ringing in her ears got louder, as if someone had turned up the volume, and she wanted to get up and run out of here, and leave her sister and all these laughing people behind her. Surely there was something more important she could be doing. Something that actually helped.

The family took their seats when the music began, and Taylor felt dizzy as the funeral started. She was so hot that her body felt muggy and damp under her clothes. She wanted to take her jacket off, but she needed to keep it on.

The preacher stepped to the podium and started to speak, but the ringing in Taylor's ears muffled his words. Her turn would come after he was finished, and after Desiree's little sister read a passage from the Bible.

Panic pounded through her, and she wiped the sweat on her forehead. Her bangs were wet. She glanced behind her and tried to gauge how fast she could get to the door. It would create drama if she got up and ran out. She didn't want to do that.

An itch started on her ribs, and she scratched through her clothes. From the corner of her eye, she noticed someone across the aisle watching her.

They hate me. They were all watching her, waiting to see if she would snap. Why had she come here?

"You're up," Harper whispered. "Go."

Taylor looked up at the podium. She had completely missed Desiree's sister reading the verses. She forced herself to her feet. The ringing blared in her ears.

She went up the steps to the church stage and stood behind the podium. She didn't look out into the crowd. She couldn't.

"I've known Desiree since our freshman year of college. We were pledging the same sorority . . ."

Sorority? Really? She didn't want to talk about their sorority. Tears filled her eyes. Her mind raced for the right thing to say.

"We had dates one time to a dance in Gulf Shores . . ." No, that was wrong, too. She ventured a look at Desiree's family on the front row. Her mother had tears on her face, and she looked hopefully up at her, as if she expected comfort.

"I left her." The words were out of her mouth before she could pull them back. "Both of them. I was with them when it happened, and . . . the reason they probably kept the casket closed is that they couldn't find—" Desiree's father stiffened and looked at the pastor, seated on the stage behind Taylor. She cleared her throat. "I didn't even see her. I didn't look back. It was just smoke and screaming and . . . I didn't go back for them. I didn't even think about them."

Suddenly, Harper was next to her, and the preacher was on the other side, and they were walking her off the stage. She wanted to finish, but what would she say? It was mortifying. Harper got her back to her seat, but Taylor pulled away from her and kept walking, faster and faster, until she was running from the building. She got to her car and pulled away before anyone could come after her.

She had ruined the funeral. She probably wouldn't even be invited to Mara's. How could she have been so unprepared? How could she have said those things?

She had to make it up to them.

She drove until she was far enough from the church, until she was on the same side of town as Dustin Webb's business. She would park in front and wait to see if she could spot him. It was the only way she could make it right.

50

Dustin lay on the bed next to Dude for a while after Jamie left to go back to her office, but sleep wouldn't come. Visions of Travis being arrested and taken from his dying wife played over and over in his mind. There was nothing he could do to prevent it.

Were they searching the GreyWebb office yet? Had they confiscated their computers? Restless and wanting to know how seriously the police had taken his interview, he drove to his office. Thankfully, there were no media here, and the parking lot was empty.

He parked in front of the door, but before getting out, he saw the new locks that had been drilled into the door. So the police had been here and had locked him out.

He sat there for a minute, trying to decide what to do. Had they also gotten warrants for the Bates brothers? Were they searching their houses, too? Maybe this meant the Bateses' scheme was beginning to crumble.

From down the street, Taylor saw Dustin pulling into the office parking lot. Her heart hammered at this opportunity. She thought of driving over there right now, going into that building, and ending this, once and for all.

But she hesitated, and hated herself for it. She was a coward. She was selfish. She was self-centered. She had saved herself and left her friends behind. Now she couldn't even do this.

But if the police were watching him, and they likely were, they would see her entering the building. They would learn that she had a gun, and they would conclude that she intended to kill him. She would be arrested immediately. How would that solve anything?

She sat there waiting for the combat to resolve in her brain, knowing that her friends' murderer was just yards away.

Dustin flipped through the notes and pictures on his phone and found Samuel Bates's address in Gainesville. He could drive up there, since he had nothing else to do today. He could see if the police had acted on his tip, and if they hadn't, maybe he could find more information to give them.

His fatigue did nothing to slow his racing thoughts as he drove north to Gainesville.

He had to see who this man was, figure out where he worked, who his friends were, who might have been involved in this thing he was being accused of.

The hour-long drive did nothing to calm him. Instead, with each mile he drove, he felt his chest tightening more, and anxiety over what was happening to his friend rising. He needed to pray for Travis, for Crystal, for the police . . . He pulled into a Walmart parking lot and rested his head against the steering wheel. "Lord, everything going on today is horrendous. Layers of devastation. Crystal is already fighting the battle of her life, and now this."

His face was wet. He wiped it on his sleeve. How could any of this end well?

"The Bates brothers may still be free. Please . . . don't let there be any more bombs. You're the only one who can control this."

Cars parked near him, and people got out and walked into the store. Life was going on as if everything were normal, even though dozens of funerals were happening in Atlanta this week. It seemed wrong, somehow. Didn't these people know that evil lurked near here? That there were people building bombs?

He pulled himself together and got back onto the highway. He followed the signs to Gainesville, even though he didn't know what he would do when he got there.

Taylor kept her distance behind Dustin, following him off the Gainesville exit ramp. When he pulled into a Walmart parking lot but didn't get out of his car, she parked some distance away, watching him, her hand inside her purse, clutching her gun. Did he know she was following him? Should she act now?

It wasn't a good place to confront him. She couldn't do it with security cameras everywhere and people coming and going. She was relieved when he pulled back into traffic the same way he had been going.

She followed him again. Maybe he hadn't seen her, after all. Her ears were still ringing, and her head was beginning to hurt. She had bandages on both legs and her arm now, and new rashes had popped up, itching her to distraction. Her hands trembled and her thoughts raced.

Could she do this? If he went to a place that wasn't so monitored, could she really get out of her car and shoot him?

He had murdered Desiree and Mara and Ed Loran and dozens of others. He deserved this. It could be the only way she could live with herself.

51

Dustin's GPS took him to Samuel Bates's apartment complex. He'd half expected a pocked parking lot and appliances rusting on the grass, but instead it was a well-landscaped area with expensive cars parked outside. He found Bates's apartment on the second floor of the K building. He parked across the parking lot from Bates's door, waiting for someone to come out. He'd decided the best he could do was take a picture of Bates and of the tag on the white van or any other vehicle that might be his.

He looked around the parking lot for the van he had seen in the security video. There it was, sitting in one of the spaces in front of Bates's apartment. Dustin got out of the car and snapped a picture on his phone of the tag and the van.

As he slid back into his car, he saw a gray sedan pull into the lot. The woman driving wore a baseball cap and sunglasses. He watched her pull into a parking space. She didn't get out. Was she just going to sit there, like him?

A sudden shudder went down his back as he realized she was

watching him. Was she with the media? Had she followed him from Atlanta? Or worse, was she a cop, assigned to tail him? Of course—and now they'd documented his visit here. What would they think about his reason for coming?

His phone rang. It was Jamie. He picked it up. "Hey."

"I have some updates," she said. "They're still searching the storage units."

"Still? What's taking so long? The stuff is right there."

"You said there were a lot of boxes and equipment. My guess is that they're going through all of it."

Dustin checked Samuel Bates's door again. "I went by my office, and they've put new locks on the door."

"That's probably good news. But Travis still hasn't been arrested."

He struggled with the conflicting feelings that irritated him. At least Travis still had that time with Crystal. But did that mean the police weren't buying his story? Had they decided the detonator caps and the diagram were Dustin's?

"What do you think? Are they going to arrest him?"

"If I were them," she said, "I would have people up there watching him. Plain-clothed detectives in the waiting rooms and other hospital rooms, hanging out in the hallway. He's not going anywhere. But I'm not them, and I can't exactly explain why they're moving so slowly on all this."

He wished he could go to the hospital and check it out, but after his fight with Travis last night, how could he?

"You okay?"

"Yeah, fine."

"Have you managed to sleep any?"

He didn't want to tell her he wasn't even home, that he had

gone to Gainesville to see if the police had done anything about the Bates brothers. She would go nuclear if she knew he was sitting outside the bomber's apartment. "Maybe a little."

"Good. I'll call you back if I find out anything else."

He hung up and checked the woman's car again. She was still sitting there. He thought of walking over to her and telling her that the guy she really wanted was right up there, in that apartment, and that this was his van.

He started his car again and looked up at the apartment one more time. Just then, the door opened, and Samuel Bates walked out. There were two other guys with him.

Dustin set his phone on video, and as the men came down the stairs, he zoomed in and taped them. They didn't look his way before getting into the van. Dustin had to leave now. If he stayed, they would know he was watching them. He pulled out of the parking lot and checked his rearview mirror. The woman wasn't following him.

He turned onto the busy street and into the parking lot of a convenience store, then did a tight U-turn and watched the Bates van pull out of the apartment complex.

He followed them when they turned the other direction. They drove through town to a building that looked like a converted car repair garage. An old, faded sign said "Bates Plumbing." The three got out and went inside. Samuel was limping slightly, just as he had been on the security video.

Was this where they'd made the bombs?

He took pictures of the building, the signs, and the other two cars parked there, making sure he got their tag numbers.

As he turned to head home, he looked for the gray sedan. The woman didn't seem to be following him.

Maybe he was just paranoid. She could have been there waiting for a friend, or sitting in her car talking on the phone before going into her apartment. Maybe his imagination had gotten the best of him.

52

Taylor had been completely focused on Dustin as she sat in the parking lot at the apartment complex. She had considered walking to his car and shooting him through the window, but something had told her to wait until he got out of the car. He never did.

When he'd pulled out, she had started her car to follow him, but the three men who'd just come out of an upstairs apartment caught her eye. She had seen two of them before.

That feeling she'd had after the bombing flooded her again, drenching her in sweat, her heart racing to keep up with her thoughts. She couldn't catch her breath and felt dizzy and confused.

Where had she seen them before?

As they pulled out of the parking lot, she stayed where she was and tried to think. Something to do with that day.

Then it came to her. She dug through her purse, ignoring the gun, and pulled out her phone. There had been a dozen calls from her sister, but she ignored them and went to her photos, her hands trembling.

She flipped through the pictures she had taken after her escape from Trudeau Hall and found the video she'd taken from her car's dashboard as she'd waited for her friends that night.

She slid the bar through it, making the images move in jerky fast-forward motion, until she found the one she was looking for.

There! She turned the video on and watched as two guys dressed in Ed Loran T-shirts jogged up the sidewalk and got into the car in front of her.

Was Dustin Webb connected with them? When she looked up again, their van was out of sight, and so was Webb's car. She had lost them.

It was them, she thought. Those men. They had something to do with the bombing, too. From the depths of her soul, she knew it.

With new purpose, she headed back to Atlanta, trying to lay out the logical steps she'd need to take to make sure they were all caught.

53

In Crystal's room, Travis stroked his rubber-gloved fingers along her cheek and looked into the hazy-sick glaze of her eyes, searching for the woman who had once exuded such vibrant life.

"Tired," she whispered. "Need to rest."

A tear rolled down his cheek, and he smeared it away. "Okay, love. Go ahead and rest."

"Love you . . . Don't be angry."

He almost didn't hear the endearment, her whisper was delivered on such a thin wisp of breath, but when he realized what she'd said, an alarm went off in his heart. "Why would I be angry?"

"Tired," she whispered again. "So tired." Her eyes closed as she drifted into a shallow sleep, and he held his breath, trying not to suck in the sob lingering in his throat. Was she telling him that she was too tired to fight? Was that why he would be angry? Because she was ready to let go?

He bowed his head as tears stung his raw eyes, and he fought the urge to shake her and force her to wake up. Sleep was a powerful drug, one that she needed right now. But death was even more powerful, and like a narcotic that promised peace and numbness, it was calling to her.

Its voice was stronger than his.

But after death, what would happen? He'd avoided that question his whole life, even when Dustin would bring it up. He didn't believe in God, so why would he believe in an afterlife?

But now that question hung above him like the certainty that death was coming for her.

What if there was a God? What if her death was only a temporary state, and he could see her again one day, and his children could see their mom?

Wanting it didn't make it true. But the arbitrary nature of his beliefs, all based on his belief in the accidental soup that made humans into beings that could cure diseases and travel off the planet, seemed less and less likely now without some greater force to guide them. His truth seemed wobbly, even though he'd used it to justify what he'd done to Dustin. How could it stand when people were dead and so many families were going through what he was feeling with Crystal?

He didn't like those truths. But not liking them didn't make them untrue.

Knowing that she would be asleep for a while and that he was too weak to keep his emotions quietly contained, he stood and started out of the room, discarding his sterile clothing with vicious rips and wads once he was past the walls that were supposed to protect Crystal from contamination.

He looked up and saw Wendy standing in the hallway, watching him with sad eyes. "She's just sleeping," he said. "You can go on in."

She reached up, hugged him, and pressed a motherly kiss on his cheek. That prompted more tears. Wendy wiped them off his face.

"You go take a break. Get something to eat."

Travis nodded. He wasn't hungry, and he didn't want to venture far from this floor, which felt like a sanctuary. That was another wobbly truth. It wasn't a sanctuary. If Dustin had gone to the police about Travis's part in the bombing, they wouldn't care if he was in the cafeteria or in the cancer center. It was just a matter of time.

54

Dustin's room in the Airbnb grew darker as the sun set, but he didn't turn on the light. Instead, he sat motionless in the chair in his room, staring pensively at the video he'd taken years earlier as it played on his computer screen.

Crystal Grey ran across the television screen, sweaty and wearing a T-shirt and jogging shorts. "Get that camera off of me, Dustin Webb. I don't want to have to kill you."

Dustin fast-forwarded to the next scene with Crystal. He smiled as her nine-month-pregnant belly—so big it made his own stomach hurt—dominated the screen.

Travis was on his knees in front of the camera, which was balanced on the tripod, and Dustin chuckled lightly as he watched himself step into the picture. Mischievously, Travis lifted Crystal's maternity shirt, exposing her bare stomach.

"I'd rather not have my gut exposed for posterity, thank you," she told her husband, pulling her shirt back down.

But Travis had a plan. "Just let me draw a little face on it."

"That's my skin, you lunatic."

"They're nontoxic, washable markers. I checked."

She finally gave in and let her husband sketch two eyes, two enormous ears, a nose over her navel, and a huge, buck-toothed mouth on her belly.

Dustin heard himself laughing, and Crystal's laughter turned into uncontrollable hysterics, until tears ran down her face. "If I go into labor with this on my stomach, someone is going to die."

He was glad he'd gotten that on camera.

It was the last time they'd been together before their lives had changed, when Miles and Mason had come into the world.

The tape progressed to the scene of the two tiny babies just hours after their birth, and Crystal lying in her hospital gown, completely exhausted but euphoric with pride over the perfection of those two little boys.

"Uncle Dustin, you realize you're looking at the first set of co-presidents in the United States."

On tape, Dustin leaned over and shook one of their tiny fists. "Nice to meet you, Mr. President."

Funny how things changed. What was to become of those babies now, with their mother dying and their father facing a prison sentence? Though it was completely irrational, he felt responsible.

He heard the front door open and close, then a knock on his bedroom door. Carrying the computer with him, he went to answer it.

Jamie stood there, her face sober and her eyes direct. "I left Avery with Mom in case something happens tonight."

"Like what?"

"Like another interview? More questioning?"

Dude scratched on the back door, and Dustin set the computer on the coffee table and went to let him in. The dog bounded to greet Jamie ferociously, then went to his water bowl. Dustin's computer was still playing his home movies. He paused it, but Jamie said, "Don't. I want to see."

He clicked Play again. Jamie sat down on the edge of the couch and studied the face of his bright, happy friend on the screen, heard her quick wit and her even quicker laugh. "Is that Crystal?" she asked.

Dustin nodded. "Yeah, that's her."

"She's beautiful."

It was after the babies had come home, and Crystal was bemoaning the fact that she looked her worst.

"I don't think you've ever looked more beautiful." Travis pulled the camera back and showed the two little babies in her arms.

"She looks so healthy there. So strong."

"She is strong," Dustin said. "She's fought for a long time. She was never going to surrender to this easily." He looked at Jamie. "Have they arrested Travis yet?"

She sighed. "No. They still have to convince the DA and judge of probable cause, investigate more, and make sure they have a solid case."

"If they don't think there's probable cause, then that means they don't believe me. They still think I'm the culprit."

"Don't think that," she said. "It's not that simple."

He looked back at the video on his screen. "At least Crystal doesn't have to know yet."

"Yeah. Maybe it's a God thing. Not for Travis, but for her."

The reminder that God was still watching over Crystal filled his heart with gratitude. The situation could change at any moment, but each minute counted. He hoped Crystal could pass into eternity without ever having to know what her husband had done.

55

Crystal's death came so peacefully that Travis wasn't aware of it until the nurse who'd been watching her monitor stepped into the room and met his eyes with silent, soul-deep sorrow.

Days ago, Crystal had made him and Wendy promise that they wouldn't allow resuscitation if she died. "I don't want to be dragged back once I cross that threshold," she'd said.

Travis hadn't been able to stop his tears. "But, Crystal, we need you here. We don't want to let you go."

"Let me rest," she whispered. "This has been so hard. But you're in God's hands, and so are the boys. I've had to give them up to him. Now it's your turn to give me up to him."

He had ultimately made the promise. Now he regretted it, and in truth, he hadn't given her up yet. She was being ripped away from him. He'd had no real choice. But he hadn't yet let go.

He looked up at the nurse, his eyes denying what his heart couldn't accept. The nurse wiped a tear from her eye, and suddenly his heart absorbed the truth. She was gone.

"No," he whispered, a sob catching in his throat. "I thought she was sleeping."

"She was," the nurse said. "She went quietly." He looked up through his tears and saw Crystal's mother standing outside the room, still pulling on a sterile gown, preparing to come in. But when Wendy saw Travis's eyes through the glass, her face distorted into a miserable twist of despair. Letting the gown fall to the floor, she pushed into the room, her eyes focusing on the only child she had ever had. "God, please," she whispered.

Travis went to her, his arms reaching out to receive comfort more than to give it. But Wendy had little to give. "So many things I meant to say," she whispered. "I thought there was still time."

They wept together, wordless pain in anguished groans. Wendy pulled away from him and went to the daughter she had outlived, kissed her, and wept on her chest. After a while, she straightened her daughter's blankets, like a mother tucking her child in for the night.

When Wendy prayed, Travis just watched. "Thank you, Jesus," Wendy whispered as she wept. "Oh, thank you."

When it seemed she had stopped praying, he wiped his face. "How could you . . . thank him?"

She managed a sad smile despite her tears. "Look how gently she passed. He took her out of her suffering. She's well now."

Travis looked down at her. His wife's face was more relaxed and peaceful than she had looked in months. Those pain-wrought furrows were no longer etched between her eyebrows. The lines on her forehead had been erased.

He tried to imagine that she was waking up in heaven, realizing that the pain was gone, knowing that disease was no longer eating away at her body. She was free and light, and her darkness and sorrow had been lifted. There was only light and joy.

Please let it be true. Please don't let it just be a wishful heart.

They wept together until the nurses and orderlies, with their sympathetic eyes and somber faces, came to take Crystal's body away.

Travis couldn't handle it. He slipped out of the room and through the exit door at the end of the hall and into the stairwell. He trotted down the staircases until he was on the first floor. Before he left the building, he checked through the vertical window. There was no one looking this way, so he stepped out and went to his truck.

He had expected that, by now, Dustin would have turned him in. Was it possible he hadn't? The police hadn't been to the hospital at all, as far as he could tell. Crystal hadn't had to learn what he'd done. He broke into tears again as he drove, and he wanted to hug his boys and protect them from the news.

Instead, he drove in a different direction.

56

Taylor had raced back to Atlanta at eighty miles an hour, every instinct in her body telling her to get to the police station to tell them about the two men she'd seen in Gainesville and their connection to her video.

When she found Detective Borden in the office, she was stunned by his attitude. He came out to her looking irritated, as if he had too much to do to waste time with her again. "I have ten minutes," he said.

"Ten minutes is enough. I have to show you something," she said in a rush as he led her to an interview room.

As he closed the door to the room, he looked her over. "You're sweating," he said.

She ignored him and found the video on her phone. "I was following Dustin Webb today, and he went—"

"You what?" He was still standing, as if he wasn't going to give her the benefit of a sit-down talk. "Why were you following him?"

"That doesn't matter. What matters is—"

"Yes, it does. You shouldn't be following him."

She sprang up. "Listen to me! He went to these apartments in Gainesville."

"Gainesville?" Borden asked. "Did he talk to anyone?"

"No, he stayed in his car. But while I was watching him, these guys came out of the apartment he seemed to be watching. And I recognized two of them. Look, I have them on video from that day of the bombing. They were parked in front of me."

He was paying closer attention now. He sat down, took the phone, and watched the video of the two guys trotting up the sidewalk and getting into the car.

"I don't see anything unusual here," he told her. "Some guys just coming to their car like you did and like everyone else parked on that street did."

Was he dense? She was getting impatient. "No, you don't get it. Why would Dustin Webb be waiting for them if they were just 'some guys'? But if they were involved in the bombing—"

"Wait a minute." He stood and opened the door, leaned outside, and said something to someone. Then he stepped into the hallway and closed the door behind him. She could hear his muffled voice through the door.

Finally Borden and another man came back inside. "Thanks for coming in. We know who these men are. We'll take it from here," Borden said.

The other guy had his hands on his hips. "Don't follow anyone else. You're interfering with an investigation and putting yourself in needless danger."

"Everybody's in needless danger, because you let him out! I can't eat and can't sleep, and I can't trust you to protect us, so I followed him. Somebody had to."

The two detectives thought she was crazy. She could see that in their eyes.

"Did Webb talk to these men?" the second detective asked.

"No. They came out, and he left the parking lot before they did. They went opposite directions. At least, I'm pretty sure they did. I got distracted because I knew I recognized them, and I couldn't think how. Then I remembered the video. You really know who they are?"

Borden leaned forward and spoke to her like a guard in a mental ward. "Taylor, you're not on the police force. You're interfering with an investigation. Now, if you don't stop this, I'm going to have to arrest you."

"If there's another bombing while he's running free, that's on you. I'll tell everybody that I tried to give you information and you wouldn't listen."

"We are listening," Detective Borden said. "We're working on the case, day and night. We have people following all of our viable leads. We know you have a stake in this. A lot of people do. But I'm telling you that you can walk out of here right now and go home, or we can arrest you for interfering with an investigation. You can't do our job, but you might ruin what we're working toward."

She felt the courage seeping out of her. "Are you even going to check? Get their names, their backgrounds, see where they were that night? If they know Dustin Webb? Don't you even want my video?"

"I've already air-dropped it to my phone." He handed the phone back to her.

She stood straighter. "Please tell me who they are."

"Thanks for coming in."

"Wait. Are they involved with the bombings?"

Borden and the man went to the door, opened it, and motioned for her to walk out. "We'll call you if we have any more questions."

The ringing in her ears went up an octave. Her head felt like it had been struck by lightning. She grabbed her purse from the back of her chair and slipped the strap over her shoulder. She left the interview room and stormed out of the department.

Even though they knew who the men were, they still thought she was crazy. The truth was, she felt crazy. She was going off the deep end. It was the anger, the maddening regret, the crushing guilt. But all of that could be resolved if she could just see the people responsible for her friends' deaths pay for what they'd done.

But these men she'd just talked to couldn't be trusted to make them pay. She would still have to do it herself.

57

Dustin was back at the Airbnb with Jamie when Wendy called. When he saw her name on his phone, his stomach sank. He touched Accept and said, "Wendy, hey."

The stopped-up hollowness in Wendy's voice was apparent the moment she spoke. "Hey, sweetie. Has Travis called you yet?"

He put it on speakerphone so Jamie could hear. "No, I haven't talked to him today."

She let out a hard sigh. "Crystal left us."

Though he'd expected the news, it came like a sledge-hammer in the center of his heart. He covered his mouth and tried to speak, but words wouldn't come.

Jamie already had tears in her eyes. "Wendy, this is Jamie. How are you doing?"

"I'm okay," she said, though Dustin knew she wasn't.

Dustin found his voice. "How is Travis?"

She didn't answer for a moment, then said, "I don't know where he is."

Jamie sucked in a breath. "What? He's not there?"

"No. He was here with her when she passed, but while they were moving her, he just left. I know he's upset."

Dustin looked at Jamie. She was already reaching for her phone.

"Did he say where he was going?"

"No. I thought he'd be here with me. Calling people and taking care of things. I guess he just shut down."

Dustin tried to comfort her the best he could, but when he got off the phone, he heard Jamie talking to the police. He sat there a moment, his face in his hands. She was gone, his sweet friend who had meant so much in his life. He hated it for Travis, for the boys, for all of them. But where had Travis gone?

Travis had vowed to turn himself in the moment she died. Maybe he was headed to the police station. Maybe he just hadn't been able to bring himself to tell Wendy what he had done.

Jamie got off the phone and looked down at him. "He didn't go to turn himself in."

Dustin wiped his face. "Has he had enough time? Maybe he's on his way."

"Why weren't the police at the hospital, waiting to arrest him? How could they just let him walk away?"

Dustin got up. "He could still do the right thing."

"He's not going to do the right thing, Dustin!" she cried. "You think he's this honorable person who puts his family first, and he's not. He committed an awful crime that led to a heinous mass murder. You really think he's going to walk in there and say, 'Hey, I'm your guy'? He's not going to!"

Dustin just stared into space.

"Dustin, I know you care a lot about him, and I know you're

upset about Crystal, too. But what he did to you was unconscionable. I'm sorry if I don't believe his wife's death is going to give him a sudden surge of integrity."

Dustin stood up. His body felt heavier as he moved. "I'll go find him."

"You won't find him. He's probably left town."

He shook his head. "He wouldn't do that." Dustin started to the door with one clear purpose in mind. "He'll turn himself in."

He hurried out to his car. He had to find Travis before this whole thing got worse. As angry as he was at his friend, he had to save him from himself.

58

It was disturbing how little things changed after someone died. As Dustin searched for Travis, the sun still shone and birds still sang. The breeze still whispered through the leaves. People still ate and went to work, appointments were kept, and the nurses and doctors on the fourth floor probably went on with business as usual.

But Crystal was gone.

A strange emptiness yawned inside Dustin, as if some vital part of himself were missing. His friendship with Crystal had been the first real friendship he'd had with a woman after Jamie.

Dustin looked for Travis at home, but his truck wasn't there. The babysitter's car was still in the driveway.

He headed to the office, praying he would find him there. He wouldn't be able to get in, but maybe he could intercept him. But there were no cars in the GreyWebb parking lot. He pulled in and sat there a moment, trying to think. Where else would he go? Would he jump on a plane and skip town? No, not without his boys.

Maybe he went to the funeral home to take care of Crystal's arrangements before he turned himself in. He checked his GPS for the funeral home Travis would probably choose and headed there.

Travis's truck wasn't there, but he could have switched his truck for Crystal's car to throw off anyone looking for him. But her car wasn't there either. Dustin got out and went to the door, but it was locked. Closed.

He got back into his car and tried to think. His phone chimed, and he looked at the message. It was from Wendy.

Try the lake.

The lake was one of Travis's favorite places, the place where the two of them had often fished before the boys were born, the place where his children loved to play.

As he drove south, he thought of last night, when he and Travis had come to blows. His friend had betrayed him. He was still betraying him. He had set him up and stood by while Dustin sat in jail. He had lied until he was caught. Then he lied again.

Still, Dustin hadn't given up on him. The last few weeks couldn't be allowed to define their years-long friendship. Travis had been under so much stress, searching desperately for a way to save the mother of his twins. What would Dustin have done if he'd been in the same position?

He didn't think he would have facilitated the theft of explosives that could be used for a terrorist attack.

Travis didn't have the same value system that Dustin had. Though he'd seen the changes in Dustin, he hadn't joined him on his faith journey. He didn't have the Spirit's nudging when he came to forks in the road. He didn't have the Bible's guidance. He didn't feel the need to ask what God would want from him.

But maybe Dustin was just looking for ways to let his friend off the hook. Travis had done something that couldn't be excused. If he was trying to hide from the authorities, or if he was considering taking his own life . . . then Travis wasn't the man Dustin thought him to be. Still, Dustin needed to find him.

He had no idea if he was searching to save Travis, or himself.

It took Dustin forty minutes to reach the lake, where Travis had brought him and Jamie mere days ago. When he reached the clearing where they always parked their cars, he breathed a deep sigh of relief. There was Travis's truck. But Travis was nowhere to be seen.

Dustin walked through the playground to the water's edge. He didn't see Travis in either direction. The blinding sun cut across the water, making it hard to see to his right, where Travis usually fished.

Birds sang in the trees overhead, and the wind whipped the leaves, as if there might be rain coming. A few clouds moved across the sky. Dustin started up the hill, walking along the bank toward a curve up ahead that he couldn't see beyond.

The heat was sweltering, and the humidity was oppressive. He wiped his forehead, then his hand swept under his eye, where the bruise from last night was still tender.

He went around the tip of the peninsula, heading toward a spot where the water was deep and usually full of fish.

Then he saw him. Travis was sitting on the ground, his arms hugging his knees and his face tucked into his arms. Dustin slowly walked toward him without saying a word.

Travis heard his footsteps and looked up, his eyes wet, red, and swollen. Seeing Dustin, his face twisted in even more anguish, and he choked out a sob.

Dustin sat down on the grass beside him. For a long time, he let Travis weep. When Travis seemed to be spent, Dustin spoke.

"Do you remember that day we brought Crystal with us to fish out here? Remember how excited she was when she caught her first fish?"

Travis wiped his eyes. "Yeah. She almost fell in the water, jumping up and down."

"Remember she wanted her picture taken with it? It must have been four inches long, but you would have thought it was a monster bass."

"Yeah. Then when I told her she'd have to clean it, she threw it back in."

They laughed, a soft sound of relief and surrender, but the laughter died on a sad note.

"I wish I'd brought her out here again before we checked her into the hospital this time," Travis said. "Time just moves so fast."

Dustin tore a blade of grass out of the ground.

"All that stupid stuff I did was for nothing. No matter how much money they paid me, it couldn't keep her alive." His wounded eyes met Dustin's. "But every day with her was precious."

"I know it was." Dustin got up and stood looking out at the water. "God gave you the time with her. I don't know how it happened." He turned back to him. "I did go to the police. I had to tell them what I knew, otherwise I would have been an accomplice."

Travis's jaw popped, as if he didn't know how to take Dustin exposing him. Dustin felt a surge of guilt, even though he knew it was irrational. He picked up a rock, tossed it into the water, watched it plop. The water rippled in concentric circles, which faded and disappeared. They were still for a moment, and Dustin wondered if Travis was blaming him for not covering for him. Dustin kept his eyes fixed on the water, his spirits as low as the rock that had sunk to the lake's murky floor. "I didn't want any of this for you," he said.

Travis wiped his face and nodded. "I know."

"But if you don't turn yourself in and confess, they're going to think you had something to do with planting the bomb and targeting the people who were killed. If there's another bomb . . ."

"But my kids . . ." He shook his head. "It's so unfair to them."

"You chose it, Travis!" Dustin said. "Yes, it's unfair. It's horrible for them. Losing their mom and now their dad." Anger climbed into his throat, and he set his hands on his hips and took a few steps away, then turned back. "Why couldn't you look down the road and see what this whole thing would cause? The implications for the twins? For me? For yourself?"

"All I could see down the road was losing Crystal."

"So tell me. Are you just going to sit out here? Are you still not going to do the right thing, even now? Are you going to let me go down for this?"

"I just want to bury her."

Something deep in Dustin's chest snapped as he realized Travis was asking for another few days. "They're not going to give you that. They're going to arrest you."

"I won't let them find me."

Dustin gaped at him. "You're being stupid again, Travis.

What's wrong with you? Even if you manage to hide from them until the funeral, they'll arrest you there, in front of everyone—the kids, Wendy, everybody. You don't get to call the shots here! How would you even hide? You'll be a wanted man."

"I know that," Travis said. "What do you think has been going through my mind?"

Dustin stood looking at him, that debilitating disappointment in his friend rising up in his heart again. Travis was about to make the wrong choice, once again.

"Those men," Dustin said. "I know who they are now. Samuel Bates and his two brothers. They had a vendetta against Ed Loran because of toxic waste that his company caused. It killed their little sister, both parents. They sued, but lost the suit." Dustin pulled his phone out and showed him the picture of Samuel Bates. "This is the guy, right?"

Travis stood and looked at it. "Yeah, that's him."

"The police know about him. I told them. If you turn yourself in now and cooperate, you'll probably just be charged with theft. If you wait and more people die, then you'll be charged with multiple counts of murder. Can you really live with that? What if more people die?"

"I can't live with any of this!" Travis shouted. "But I have to put my boys first."

"You're not putting your boys first. You're putting yourself first. I don't get it, Travis—how could you have any part in a terrorism plot and still refuse to do what's necessary?"

"Look at me!" The shrieking, female voice came out of nowhere, and they both swung around. A girl stood at the edge of the woods drenched in sweat, with a wild look of hatred on her face. She held a gun pointed at Dustin.

He put his hands up and took a slow step toward her. "Put the gun down."

Suddenly the gun fired, its thunder crashing across the water.

59

The kick of the gun knocked her back, and the lightning crack of the gun firing deafened her. Then sound returned, a distant, muffled sound of voices yelling, as her ears rang.

She aimed again and shouted for them to get down on their knees, arms up, and she tried to steady her hands to shoot again.

Sweat dripped into her eyes from her wet bangs, and her head was splitting with migraine pain. Her vision was blurred, and for a moment, she wasn't sure which man was which. Had they switched places? They moved to their knees in jerky motions, like some 1920s film in slow motion, and for a moment the world around her spun. She couldn't faint. She couldn't faint. She had to finish this.

She had been waiting on the street near Dustin's office when he'd come there some time ago. He had pulled into the parking lot again but hadn't gone into the building, and she had followed him when he drove away. She had almost lost him near the lake, but once she got past the cars that had come between them, she saw him turning onto the road leading to the lake.

He was already out of his car when she reached it. There was another truck parked there. He was meeting someone. Maybe another of the bombers. What if it was one of the men she'd seen at the apartment in Gainesville? What if they were plotting another attack?

She got her gun out from under the seat and checked the cartridge. She got quietly out of the car and closed the door gently so it wouldn't alert them. The heat and humidity assaulted her, making her feel sick. Her head had never hurt like this, and she was soaked with sweat even though she'd been in her air-conditioned car. But she couldn't let that stop her. The police hadn't acted yet, so she had to. There was no one else.

She walked past the playground and over to the trees, then skirted over a ridge that made a peninsula. There was a trodden path in front of the trees, so she followed it, holding the gun down with both hands.

If she could overhear them plotting, maybe she could record it for the police. She stepped into the trees and turned on her phone's video camera. She shoved it into her pocket, camera forward. Then she followed the path until she heard low voices. Again, she stepped into the trees, taking every step carefully, quietly, through the brush and limbs, until she saw the two men beside the water.

She came up behind them, clutching her gun. It was time, she thought. She could take care of them now. She could end this whole thing in two pulls of the trigger.

But her hands were wet, shaking, and weak, so she hesitated.

She couldn't hear them for the ringing in her ears. She stepped closer.

"Can you really live with that?" Webb was saying. "What if more people die?"

"I can't live with any of this!" the other guy shouted. "But I have to put my boys first."

"You're not putting your boys first. You're putting yourself first. I don't get it, Travis—how could you have any part in a terrorism plot and still refuse to do what's necessary?"

She dragged in a deep breath. *More people could die?* Taylor felt the tremor coming over her, weakening her fingers, reminding her of that explosion and her desperate escape while Mara and Desiree bled or burned to death behind her.

She couldn't let it happen again. Rage exploded within her. "Look at me!"

As they turned and Webb stepped toward her, she lifted the gun and fired, its deafening blast knocking her back.

She raised the gun again, forcing herself to maintain a firm grip, and shouted, "Get down on the ground! Now! Hands above your head."

The other guy knelt with his hands up, but Webb kept standing. "Hold on," he said, talking in a gentle voice as he would to a panicked animal he was trying to calm. "There's no need for a gun. Just put it down. Tell us what you want."

"I want justice!" she cried. "I want my friends to be alive. I want you in prison."

"Who are you?"

"Get down!" she shouted again, aiming for his forehead.

He knelt.

"I know what you did," she said to Dustin Webb, "and I

know who you did it with." She took a step back as dizziness threatened to knock her over, but she steadied herself. "There can't be any more bombs, any more death. I can't let that happen. I didn't help my friends, but I can do this. I can make sure you never do it again." She ran out of breath and gasped for air, but the air was so heavy, so thick, and her head seemed to float. She clutched the gun tighter.

Dustin could tell by the way she held the gun and the slurred passage of her words that she wasn't in control. The bullet had hit the dirt next to his foot. The next one might not miss.

"Were you there? At the rally?" Dustin asked.

"Yes! You murdered twenty-five people! How are you allowed to go free? How could they set bond and give you the chance to do it again?"

She steadied the gun, and Dustin thought it was over. She was going to kill him, right here. This was how it would end.

"He didn't kill anybody!" Travis's words echoed above the sound of the wind. "I set him up! It was me. It wasn't him."

Dustin kept his eyes on the girl.

"I didn't plant the bombs," Travis went on, "but I helped the bombers get access to the explosives."

The girl was pale, as if all the blood had drained from her face, and she swayed on her feet.

"Dustin had nothing to do with it," Travis said. "Don't kill him. Kill me."

Dustin looked at Travis with dread. Was this turning into a form of suicide, now that Crystal was dead? Had this been his plan all along?

"Don't kill either of us," Dustin shouted. "I know you're grieving and you've been horribly traumatized, but killing us won't solve any of it. It'll just traumatize you more."

"You don't know anything about me," she bit out.

"I know you're not the kind of person to do this. You cared about your friends, and you're sick over what you saw. You're impatient for a resolution. But this won't bring it." He swallowed and tried to slow his racing thoughts. "I think I saw you the other day in Gainesville. You were following me, weren't you?"

She didn't answer—just kept the gun on him.

"Those men coming out of the apartment, who got into the white van, they're the ones."

"If you weren't involved, how would you know?" she cried.

"Because I met with one of them," Travis said. "I took money from him. I needed it for my wife's cancer treatments. I would have done anything to save her, but it didn't. She died today." Travis's face twisted and reddened. Tears ran down his face. "If you want to take me to the police yourself, you can," he said. "I'll go with you. I'll tell them everything. Just let Dustin go."

She was confused now. "I don't trust you."

"Then tie us up and call the police," Travis said. "You can sit here with us until they come. I have stuff in my trunk. Plastic ties, I think. You can tie us up."

Dustin could see that the gears in her brain were turning as she tried to work it out. Finally she drew in a breath and said, "Get up."

They both got to their feet, hands still raised. "That way," she said, and they took a few steps back the way they had come. Dustin glanced over his shoulder and saw her close behind them, just out of reach, but with that gun aimed at the center of his back. Despite what Travis had said, Dustin was clearly still the culprit in her mind.

They rounded the peninsula and headed toward the playground where their cars were parked. As they neared his truck, Travis pointed toward the big toolbox that spanned the width of the truck bed. "They're in there."

"Open it," she said. "Don't touch anything else."

He opened the lid and raised his hands again. There was a clear bag with white plastic ties that they used for securing equipment.

"Step back," she said, and they moved away from the truck.

She kept the gun on them and reached for the bag of ties. She opened it with her teeth, then sticking the bag under her arm, she got out a couple of ties.

She looked at Dustin. "Get on your knees." As Dustin lowered to the ground, she stepped closer to Travis. "You, put these on him. Hands behind his back. Now."

Travis stepped toward her and reached for the ties, but instead of taking them, he swung and knocked her to the ground, then ripped the gun from her hands.

Dustin scrambled up. The girl screamed and fought Travis for the gun, but it didn't take him long to break free. He backed away and lifted the gun, pointing it toward the girl. His finger slid over the trigger.

"Stop!" Dustin threw himself between the gun and the girl, knocking Travis back. The gun went off again.

60

Jamie tried to focus on digging deeper into Samuel Bates and his brothers. But she couldn't concentrate.

Crystal's death and Travis's disappearance had left a gnawing in the pit of her stomach.

Did Dustin know what he was walking into if he found Travis? What if Travis was so distraught about Crystal's death and his own plight that he took his own life without ever telling the police of his part in the bombing? What if he left Dustin to take the heat? Could she prove Dustin's innocence, given the damning evidence in his storage units? Without Travis's confession, a jury might conclude that Dustin had made up the details after Travis was dead, when Travis couldn't defend himself.

Beyond that, she dreaded the thought of what Dustin was putting himself through right now, if he found his best friend dead, or if he had to watch him destroy himself.

She grabbed her bag, threw her computer into it, and rushed out. Lila stopped her. "Are you leaving?"

"Yeah," she said. "I don't know when I'll be back, but I'll call you."

"If the DA calls, I'll forward the call to your cell phone."

Jamie hurried to the elevator, punched the Down button, and trotted out to her car. She got behind the wheel and called Dustin, but he didn't answer. She started her car, then texted him.

Dustin, if you find him, don't approach him. You don't know his state of mind.

But she knew Dustin well enough to know that he wouldn't listen.

She didn't have Wendy's number, so she sat in a parking lot, pulled out her computer, and did a quick search. She found Wendy's cell number and her address. Quickly, she dialed the number and pulled out of the parking lot.

No one was answering their phone today. She supposed that Wendy would be screening her calls, trying to avoid all the people offering condolences while she made the arrangements to bury her child. When Wendy's cheerful voicemail greeting came on, recorded days before the tragedy had happened, Jamie couldn't bring herself to leave a message.

She clicked the phone off. She would go to Wendy's house instead. But when she got there, she found only the babysitter with the two boys. Wendy hadn't come home yet, the babysitter told her.

Jamie had never had to deal with a loved one who died in the hospital, but maybe Wendy had to wait until the medical examiner took the body. Her heart went out to her. What a brutal, lonely time it must be for her if Travis had left her to do this alone.

She headed to the hospital, then hurried to the elevator and rode to the fourth floor. Just as she had suspected, Wendy sat in the waiting room, staring vacantly into space.

"Wendy," she said.

Wendy looked up at her. "Jamie." She stood and hugged her.

"I'm so sorry about Crystal," she said.

"Yeah. Thank you. You didn't have to come, sweetie."

Jamie felt guilty that she hadn't come for the purpose Wendy thought. "Is Travis here?" she asked.

"No, honey. I told Dustin a little while ago that I thought he was probably out at the lake, thinking things through. He hasn't come back."

The lake, where they'd taken the kids to play on the playground! "I have to go talk to them," she said. Wendy didn't ask questions. Why would she? She still had no idea what her son-in-law had done.

She headed back to her car. Her phone rang as she got in. She saw Louis Dole's name come up. He was returning her call. She swiped it on. "Louis."

"Yeah, Jamie. I'm at the police station and I don't have much time."

"I was calling about Travis Grey," she said. "His wife died today and he's dragging his feet about turning himself in. If you want to arrest him, I think you'll have to do it now."

"We're getting a team together as we speak," he said.

Relief blew through Jamie like a brisk wind. "I think he's at Lake Phillips. It's off the 95 exit, then a few miles south. There's a big playground there. I've been there once before."

"Can you meet us somewhere and lead us?" he asked.

"Tell me where to meet you."

Dustin would be furious, but she couldn't let him be victimized by Travis again. Travis was desperate and despondent, and the prospects for his future were bleak. If he'd been heartless enough to implicate Dustin before, how much more likely was it now when his arrest was imminent?

She drove as fast as she could to the church parking lot where they were meeting. The SUV full of SWAT team members in protective gear was already there, along with some patrol cars and an unmarked car. She dreaded the thought that Dustin could get caught in the crossfire.

Detective Borden came to her car when she pulled into the lot. "DA Dole said that you're going to lead us to where Travis Grey is."

"That's right," she said, "and Dustin Webb is with him. Please, I don't want Dustin caught in the gunfire. Travis lost his wife today, and his state of mind is unstable. I don't want anyone to get hurt."

"You take us to the turnoff, then you stay put. Got that?"

"Yes," she said. "Just promise me you won't hurt my client."

"We never intend to hurt anybody," Borden said.

He got back into his unmarked car. Two patrol cars followed Jamie out of the lot, with the SWAT van close behind. She drove faster than the speed limit. When she reached the turn into the clearing, she turned on her blinker, slowed, and pulled onto the grass next to the lot, giving them clear access. The two patrol cars, the unmarked car, and the SWAT truck turned in.

As soon as she'd turned off her ignition, she heard a gunshot. They were already shooting? Why?

She got out and ran up the dirt road to the police cars, but the officers were still in their vehicles, and she couldn't see beyond them. The door to the patrol car flew open. "Get down!" the driver told her. "It's coming from them."

61

The round whizzed past Dustin's ear as he grabbed the girl and pulled her down next to him. She screamed, but she wasn't hit. He scrambled to his knees and got between her and Travis.

"That's enough, buddy," Dustin said in a breathless voice. "Put the gun down."

"Move!" Travis shouted. Sweat ran down his face, and his eyes had taken on a feral look.

"Travis, don't do this!" Dustin got his feet under him and kept the girl blocked. "Are you trying to kill us both?"

"If I have to," Travis said.

Dustin didn't believe him. "It's not going to bring her back. It won't get you out of this."

Travis had both hands on the gun, the barrel pointed at Dustin's chest. "I didn't want any of this to happen! I'm not this guy!"

Dustin heard the girl wheezing behind him, as if she couldn't catch her breath. He reached back and touched her arm, keeping her behind him.

"I know you're not that guy," Dustin said. "Come on, man. I'm on your side. And this girl, she didn't do anything. She's lost people, too."

"There's no hope. My boys are the ones paying for all this. They'll never be the same. A dead mother, a father in prison. It would be better if they buried me, too." He turned the gun toward his own head.

"Travis, no!"

"Freeze! Drop the gun!"

Dustin sprang forward and knocked Travis's arm back. Cops in SWAT gear came out of the woods from everywhere, surrounding them.

"Drop it!"

For a moment, Dustin thought Travis might pull the gun back to his head, or make a run for it, forcing the police to shoot him. Instead, he seemed to freeze.

The despair that came over Travis's face as the police descended on him pierced Dustin to his core. They knocked him to the ground and yelled for Dustin to get down, too. He fell to his face as they strapped his hands together.

The girl was wheezing harder, and before the police got to her, she took a few steps, then collapsed in a heap.

62

Jamie ran up the dirt road toward the lake where she'd heard the gunshot. The police had both Travis and Dustin on the ground. She ran toward Dustin, but two of the armed officers held her off. "Stay back!"

She saw Dustin get to his feet. He wasn't bleeding. He was okay. She started to cry.

Travis seemed fine, too, but beyond them, a cluster of police crouched over a third person. She heard a siren growing closer, and an ambulance pulled in. EMTs rushed toward them.

"She's going into anaphylactic shock," she heard someone call out.

She? She couldn't imagine who it was until they loaded her onto a gurney with an oxygen mask over her face. It was Taylor Reid.

"Was she shot?" she asked Detective Borden when he came toward her.

"No. What are you doing in here? I told you to stay back."

"Why do you have Dustin restrained?" she demanded.

"He had a gun. We're taking him to the police station."

"I'll meet you there," she said. She started back to her car, then turned around. "Is the girl going to be all right?"

"They gave her adrenaline, and they're taking her to the hospital."

"Is she conscious?" she asked.

"Yeah, they said she came to."

"Can I talk to her for a minute? I can call her sister if I can get her number."

He shrugged, then waved her toward the ambulance. "Go ahead."

When Jamie got to the ambulance, the EMTs were getting an IV started in Taylor's arm. She lay on the gurney, her skin covered with red blotches and bandages. Her chest rose and fell rapidly with the struggle to breathe.

"Taylor, it's me. Jamie Powell. I'll call your sister if you can give me the number."

Taylor looked weak as she pulled her phone out of her pocket and handed it to Jamie.

It was still taping. She'd had it on video. She had probably recorded the whole scene with Travis and Dustin as it had played out. Jamie turned it off and navigated to the contacts. She called Harper and told her to meet Jamie at the hospital.

She assured Taylor that Harper would be there, then opened up the video. She called out to the detective.

He came back to her as if ready to arrest her just to get her out of the way. "What!"

"Taylor was videotaping the whole thing. It's a sixteen-minute video."

He took Taylor's phone and played the video. Jamie watched over his shoulder. They saw the trees as Taylor moved through the woods, heard the sound of men's voices talking distantly. Then Dustin and Travis came into sight. Neither was armed.

Detective Borden turned up the volume as Dustin begged Travis to turn himself in. Then they heard Taylor screaming, "Look at me!"

Then came the gunshot, and the trek to the truck to get the plastic ties. They watched Travis knock the gun out of her hand, grab it, and turn it on her.

They watched Dustin throw himself between them, protecting the girl.

The detective took the phone to his car, and Jamie knew this was almost over. The video showed clearly who the guilty party was in this tragic case. Dustin would be exonerated.

As the ambulance pulled onto the dirt road, lights flashing, Jamie went back to her car. She waited until the police cars with Dustin and Travis pulled out of the clearing, then followed them to the police station.

63

The press had gotten word of the arrest, and as Jamie pulled into the police station parking lot, she turned on the radio and scanned until she found some local news. ". . . the bombing at Trudeau Hall that killed twenty-five, including presidential candidate Ed Loran. When the three men—Samuel Bates, Jack Bates, and Anthony Bates—were taken into custody, the police found more explosives like the ones used at Trudeau Hall, as well as evidence that their next target was to be a townhall meeting for the re-election of Mayor Frank Japarti of Raven."

Jamie leaned back hard on her seat and burst into tears. She thanked God for the action the police had taken. It should be an open-and-shut case with the explosives in their possession.

She turned up the TV as the reporter went on. "The Bates brothers, we're told, were part of a class-action lawsuit against Cell Three Therapeutics, at which Ed Loran was the CEO. Their allegation was that the toxic waste from the company had caused cancer across the community, resulting in the deaths of their eight-year-old sister and both parents, as well as many others in the small community."

Jamie wiped her eyes and got out of the car. If Dustin didn't go free after this, then there was no justice. She tried to look professional as she muscled her way through the media and hurried to the front door of the police station.

She pushed inside and headed to the sergeant's desk. "I'm Jamie Powell, and I'd like to know the status of my client who was just brought in—Dustin Webb."

"Take a seat, Ms. Powell. We're all a little busy right now. I'll call the detective, and we'll get you back there before they interview him."

She didn't sit down. Her heart was pounding as she stood in the waiting area. This interview couldn't come soon enough.

64

Taylor was breathing better by the time she got to the hospital, but her heart still raced, and the world around her still spun. As they wheeled her down the hospital corridor, she heard Harper beside her.

"I'm her sister. What's wrong with her?"

"Anaphylactic shock," one of the EMTs said.

The words made it through the ringing in her ears. "What?" Taylor asked, trying to sit up. The movement of the gurney made her fall back down.

"What caused it?" Harper asked.

"We're not sure. Is she on any medications?"

They had asked Taylor something like that in the ambulance—Have you taken any medication or eaten anything?—but her mind had been racing too much to settle on a response.

"Yes," Harper said. "She started a new medication for OCD a couple of days ago."

They reached a room and wheeled her gurney in. "Have you noticed any reactions before this?" a nurse asked.

"No, I haven't noticed anything," Harper said. "She's taken it every day."

Taylor pulled off the oxygen mask. "Rash," she said. "I've had a rash." She showed them the rashes on her legs and arms.

"Is that why the bandages?" one of the EMTs asked.

"Yes. I was scratching myself raw."

"You didn't tell me that!" Harper said. She looked at the EMT. "She's a survivor of Trudeau Hall. She's been erratic, depressed, and anxious, and obsessed with the bombing and Dustin Webb, the killer."

"He wasn't the killer." Taylor took a deep breath of oxygen from the mask again, then pulled it away. "He saved my life."

Harper looked distraught. "Now she isn't making sense."

"Yes, I am. I was with him."

She was making her sister cry, which distressed Taylor, too, but she needed to explain. But she couldn't seem to find the breath.

"Where did you find her?" Harper asked the ambulance driver.

"She was at the location where they made the arrests."

Taylor pulled the mask off again. "Of Dustin Webb and that other guy. I almost killed them."

"Taylor!"

"He saved my life," she said again. "I wasn't thinking right. My thoughts were mixed up, and my ears are still ringing . . . head hurts . . ."

"You should be feeling better soon," a nurse said.

Taylor put the mask back over her mouth and lay still as they moved her IV bag and clasped the oximeter on her finger.

While the EMTs gave the nurses the rundown on what they'd done, Taylor focused on her sister's withering look. "I'm sorry."

"Taylor, you could have died. Why would you do such a dangerous thing?"

Taylor was too tired to go through it again.

"Why didn't you tell me what that medicine was doing to you? You were supposed to call the doctor if you had any adverse reactions."

"I didn't connect it."

"You were too distracted." Harper stopped a nurse coming into the room. "Can you call her psychiatrist who prescribed this medication?"

"Yes, we'll do that right away."

Harper was crying now, as if she'd caused the reaction herself. "I was supposed to be watching out for you."

Taylor tried to sit up but fell back. She reached for Harper's hand. "You did watch out for me. It wasn't your fault. I did what I thought I had to do."

Harper came into her arms, and Taylor hugged her tightly. "I'm okay now," Taylor said. "I'm here. I'm gonna be okay."

Harper wiped the tears from her face, and as she moved away, Taylor noticed the TV near the top of the wall across from her. She found the remote attached to her bed. She clicked it on, and it came up on a local station.

The sisters listened to the local news as the nurse injected more medication into Taylor's IV, and elation surged within her as she heard about the arrests of the Bates brothers and the man who had almost killed her—Travis Grey.

Justice was being served, with or without her. Her muddy

thoughts and the unwise actions she'd taken because of them hadn't hampered the investigation. Maybe it had even helped.

As the medicine entered her system, the ringing in her ears subsided, and she felt her breathing coming more easily. Her mind grew lethargic, but that was better than her frantic, racing thoughts.

She was going to be all right. The nightmare was almost over.

65

When the police let Jamie into Dustin's interview room, she didn't care who might be watching through the two-way glass. She threw her arms around his neck, and he held her, too, the two of them clinging together as if time would whisk them apart if they gave it the slightest chance.

But time didn't do that. Instead, the charges against Dustin were dropped, and he was allowed to walk free. Jamie held herself together until they were in her car, but the moment they were inside, she crumbled. As she succumbed to her tears, Dustin pulled her into his arms again.

He kissed her neck as he held her, then he pressed his forehead against hers and stroked the tears from her face. She knew before he moved his chin that he was going to kiss her, and she leaned into it and met him.

It was as though she fell headlong off a cliff, but it was a cliff she'd been running toward. She was ready for the drop.

When the kiss ended, he held her face against his. "I missed you all those years."

She pulled back and looked at him. "Why didn't you ever call?"

He closed his eyes. "You were with Joe, and it was brutal watching you fall for him. I had warned you, but you weren't listening. And some part of me thought he was better for you than I was, anyway."

"You knew better than that. You warned me about the drugs."

"But you ignored it, so I told myself it was just a phase. He was from a good family, and he would have money and stability, and I couldn't even finance my last year of college."

"That wasn't your fault."

"I was a mess when I joined the army."

"I wanted to hear all about it. But you cut me off, and I grieved." She pulled back to her own seat and took a tissue out of her purse. "When Joe died, I really needed you. But you didn't call."

"I didn't call because I didn't want to need you. But I did."

She looked at him. "That doesn't make any sense, Dustin. We were friends."

"We were more than that," he whispered. "And I've spent my whole life thinking I didn't deserve any of what you were to me."

She took his hand and brought it to her lips. "You did, though. And I did, too. It's time to admit that."

He kissed her again, and that sensation returned. She wondered if she would always feel this way, that free-falling-into-comfort feeling that seemed so nostalgic, even though it hadn't happened until today. "I'm glad God brought us back together," she said.

He smiled. "I do kind of wish he had chosen another way to do it. But I'll take grace anywhere I can get it."

As the two of them drove away from the police station, Jamie let reality sink in. The ordeal was over. But the rest of her life had just begun.

66

The night before Crystal's funeral seemed to tick on forever. Dustin lay awake in his own bed, wishing he could feel the relief of freedom, but instead he felt deep sorrow over his friend's death.

When dawn finally put the darkness out of its misery, he got up and showered, then dressed for the funeral. Wendy had called last night to tell him that Travis wouldn't be allowed to attend Crystal's service, but they were allowing him to witness it through a Zoom call.

Though Wendy had sounded strong, Dustin knew she was on the verge of collapse. "I don't know if I can do this," she said. "I never planned to bury my baby."

Dustin had no idea what to say. "I know."

"Can you help me at the visitation before the funeral? Since Travis isn't going to be there, I need to know there's someone to prop me up."

"Of course," he said. "And I can keep the kids corralled."

"No, I'm getting a babysitter," she said. "I don't know how to explain any of this to them. They're too young to understand. I don't know if it's the right thing, but I've been praying about it, and this is what I've come to."

"Then I'm sure it's the right choice."

She got quiet, and he heard her soft crying over the line. "How will I get through this, Dustin?"

He sighed, wishing he had the answers. "I don't know, but when I was in jail, I got through the night by going over and over the Twenty-Third Psalm. 'He makes me lie down in green pastures; He leads me beside quiet waters. He restores my soul.' It gave me a little peace as I pictured the green pastures and calm waters. And it made me feel better to know there was restoration ahead."

Wendy was quiet for a moment. "I sure hope you and Jamie get together," she said. "You deserve a good woman in your life."

Dustin smiled at the intuition Wendy had about the two of them, and he knew the restoration of his soul would be tied to his relationship with Jamie. "I think we are together," he said.

"That makes me feel better," she said. "You're a good man, Dustin Webb."

Despite the press conference the DA had given yesterday, announcing that Dustin had no part in the crimes his partner had committed, or in the mass murders committed by men he'd never met, all his company's work for the rest of the year had already been canceled, work his business depended on. The tarnish would be hard to erase.

His mood was somber as he approached the funeral home, set back from the road in a grove of pines. The building seemed like a peaceful sanctuary from the rat race of everyday life. As he pulled into the parking lot, the sight of the place struck his heart in an old, tender spot he hadn't expected to feel. He had forgotten that he'd been here once before. Years ago, when his parents died.

He pulled the car into a parking space, cut off the engine, and stared straight ahead at the doors through which he'd gone so many years ago. He'd held back his tears that day, trying his six-year-old best to buck up and be a man. He remembered that his rigid exterior hadn't even crumbled when he'd seen his parents lying in their coffins, patched up and painted to hide the injuries of the car accident that had taken their lives . . . injuries that were never given the chance to heal.

It wasn't until the coffins were closed that he'd lost control, and he remembered running out of the room and hiding in the bathroom, where he cried his heart out.

When he came out, the crowd was gone and the funeral procession had left him. No one had noticed he wasn't there.

It was then that Dustin realized he was on his own. That feeling had driven him through the rest of his growing-up years.

He heaved a deep sigh and started up the steps to the funeral home. Unable to go in just yet, he walked around the building to the trees skirting it. He sat down on a bench for a moment, staring through the trees as another, stronger memory of his mom tugged at his heart.

He still remembered her scent, and the soft feel of her lips on his cheek as she tucked him in at night. He remembered, too, the love his father had shown him when he went from wrestling on the floor with him to hugging him tight enough to squeeze the breath out of him. They had taught him and nurtured him carefully, as if they knew instinctively that those years would have to last Dustin the rest of his life.

He had never again experienced that kind of love, that unconditional acceptance. At least, not until he'd met the girl next door. Jamie had always made him feel he belonged. Even in her youth, she had pointed him toward the true belonging that his soul longed for—his belonging in the family of God. He hadn't embraced faith until a few years after he left town, but her example had hit its mark.

Now he closed his eyes and prayed for his friend Travis, who faced years in prison, the loss of his wife, and estrangement from his children. Travis, who'd been such a friend to him until his wife got desperately ill. He prayed for Wendy as she would, today, bury her daughter and take over parenting her grandkids. He thanked God for Crystal's life and all the humor and joy she had brought to Dustin.

When he finally felt strong enough to be of use to Wendy, he went to the doors. Wendy was waiting for him just inside the quiet front lobby.

"I decided to close the casket," she said, bursting into tears as she spoke. "I knew I couldn't stand there with people looking in at her and . . ."

Dustin hugged her and she went quiet. When she let him go, he pulled out a handkerchief and handed it to her.

"Did I make the right decision?"

"You did if it's right for you."

She wiped her eyes carefully. "Look at me, falling apart, when you've been in jail and had your whole life turned upside down."

"I'm fine," he said. "This day isn't about me. It's about your family."

"You're part of the family," she said, taking his hand and leading him to the room where the coffin waited. The moment

Dustin saw it, he was glad it wasn't open. Crystal had been so thin when she died, and he wanted to remember her with life in her eyes and a smile on her face, as she was in the picture Wendy had placed beside it.

Because Crystal was so young and had made so many friends over the years she'd lived in Atlanta, when ten o'clock came, more than two hundred people turned out to speak to Wendy and stay for Crystal's funeral.

When the funeral was over and the crowd formed in the fellowship hall of Wendy's church, Dustin felt a tug at his sleeve. It was Jamie, who hugged him and whispered, "Are you all right?"

"Yeah, I'm okay."

She looked into his eyes apprehensively. "There's someone here who wants to talk to you."

"Okay," he said.

She nodded toward a woman standing near the door. His aunt Pat.

Dustin's heart caught and stumbled. Dread froze him as he waited for his aunt to cross the room.

"Aunt Pat." He bent over and forced himself to hug her. "It's been a long time. You look good."

"And so do you," Aunt Pat said. "I wanted to come because Jamie said you'd be here."

"Well, I appreciate it."

"I heard you'd been vindicated," she said. "I was glad."

He saw the beginning of tears in Aunt Pat's eyes, and he frowned in confusion. "Well . . . thank you."

"I'm sorry about . . . all of this. The other day Jamie came to see me, and she accused me of slighting you all these years, of always thinking the worst."

Dustin shook his head and held out a hand to stem the rest of her words and make the moment easier. "Don't worry about it. I gave you plenty of trouble when I was a kid. You had every right—"

"No," she cut in. "You were different from my own kids, just like your mother was different from me. I should have given you more of a chance. I should have had a little more faith."

"It doesn't matter now."

He was going to thank her again for coming and back away, but she took his hand and lowered her voice. "You did well after you left us, didn't you, Dustin? The army, the medals, the business that was growing and becoming respected—"

"I'm probably closing the business," Dustin said, as if offering her another prize to hold on to.

"But that's what I wanted to talk to you about," Aunt Pat said, fixing him with eyes becoming more alive. "You built your business from scratch into something to be proud of. It shouldn't be snatched from you like that. You may not be aware of this," she said, "but my Michael is the president of his bank in Marietta."

He withdrew his hand, dreading the comparison to the successful firstborn son, ten years older than Dustin, and wondered if she was about to launch into a rundown of the successes of each of his cousins.

"He's building a new location, and they need a security contractor," she said, her eyebrows arching.

"That's nice," he said. "I always knew he'd be successful. I can probably point him to someone—"

"No," she cut in. "He wants you to design it."

Dustin frowned and stared at her for a moment, not sure

he understood. "Come on, Aunt Pat. Please don't play games with me."

"It's true," she said. "He called me this morning. He told me that he had planned to hire you before you were arrested, and now that you're vindicated, he's ready to get a quote."

Surprised and confused, Dustin looked over his shoulder for Jamie. She was caught in another conversation. He turned back to his aunt. "But . . . isn't he worried about the publicity? His reputation? The liability?"

"Well, he isn't hiring Travis Grey," Aunt Pat said. "Maybe it wouldn't hurt to change the name of your business. But he's hiring you. Dustin, this might be just what you need to get you back on your feet. If the president of a bank would employ you, maybe others will."

"But why?" he asked. "Why would he do that?"

"Because he knows you and he trusts you." Aunt Pat straightened her blazer and dusted lint off it, as if to distract from the moisture in her eyes. "If Michael had still been at home when you moved in with us, maybe he would have kept us from being so hard on you. He always liked you, Dustin."

Dustin felt a lump lodge in his throat, and he gulped. "Tell him . . . tell him I'll call him this afternoon. And thank you. I really appreciate it."

He hugged her, and she patted his back awkwardly. This time when he said goodbye to her, he saw a certain measure of respect in her eyes, as if the events of the past few days had changed her view of him, and she no longer saw him as the troubled boy who would bring her family down. Now she saw him as he really was. Just another human being, struggling to make it in a chaotic world.

Wendy invited Jamie to sit in the family section with Dustin at the burial. Dustin drew from her strength as she sat with her arm hooked through his, and when he lost his hold on his emotions, she wept with him. As her presence comforted him, he realized he couldn't picture himself returning to life without her. She was a gift he hadn't let himself ask for. But God was good and provided what he needed.

Hours after the burial, Dustin took Jamie, Avery, and Dude back to the cemetery to collect all the pots of flowers people had left at the site. Wendy had asked him to get them so she could plant a memorial garden in memory of Crystal. He loaded them all into his trunk, leaving the cut flowers over the grave.

"Are you all right?" Jamie asked him.

"Yeah," he said. "I was just thinking . . . There's something I wanted to show you."

"Okay."

"Come with me."

Farther up the hill, he stepped between markers until he found the ones he was looking for. "My mother and father," he said in a raspy voice.

Jamie put her hand over her heart. "Dustin!" she said, "I didn't know they were buried here." She bent and read the headstones and ran her fingers over the engraved script. "I thought that happened out of town somewhere. I didn't realize they were right here."

He nodded and slid his hands into his jeans pockets.

"Do you still remember their burial?"

"I wasn't here," he said.

She looked up at him. "They didn't let you come to the funeral?"

"No, they let me. I just didn't quite make it to the burial. There was some confusion about which relative I was with. My grandfather brought me here later, before I went into foster care."

Tears sprang to her eyes, but he was glad she didn't tell him how awful that was. He didn't need that sympathy now.

"I wish I'd known them," she said.

"I wish they'd known you. Maybe God gave them a glimpse."

"A glimpse of me?" she asked.

"Sure, why not?" He took her hand in his, brought it to his lips, and kissed it. "He would want them to know that I finally ended up with the one he'd chosen."

Those tears in her eyes spilled over now, and she touched his face and pressed a kiss on his lips.

As they walked back to his car, Dustin saw Avery sitting on the grass with Dude, who was belly-up, letting her pat his stomach. She was giggling and chattering to him, and their happiness lifted above the clouds of the graveyard. It was contagious and exponential, and he didn't want it to end.

When they'd all loaded into the car, Dustin looked up the hill to the section of the graveyard where his parents' shells lay. He couldn't help thinking of that day when he would introduce Jamie to his parents face-to-face, before the generous, grace-filled, luminescent face of the God who loved him and led him where he belonged.

AUTHOR NOTE

I'm writing this in the fall of 2020, a year that was marked by pandemic, lockdowns, racial unrest, businesses closing, jobs lost, wildfires, hurricanes, rioting and looting, and an American election that was contentious, to say the least. Hatred has risen to an all-time high, intolerance has become trendy, and every topic of conversation somehow leads to division. Fear has dominated almost every area of life, and a sense of hopelessness is smothering even God's people.

Look how far some of us have drifted from the promises of God and the teachings of Jesus. Some of us who know better have forgotten who we are, whose we are, and what we're made to do. I came into this year after several life events that had weakened me spiritually, so I was already vulnerable to these blows. I knew what was happening to me as the year unfolded, so when I saw it happening to everyone else, I recognized it. That doesn't mean I was immune to it. I, like many of you, fell prey to anger and indignation, sorrow and loneliness, bitterness and discouragement.

But God hasn't abandoned us, and His promises haven't changed. He is still sovereign, and the miracles and mercies of the past remain today. One of my favorite Bible teachers is Kay Arthur of Precept Ministries (precept.org), and recently, when I was ruminating on the state of the world and my own spiritual condition, I remembered one of her Bible studies in which she talked about the enemy's playbook. It reminded me of what has happened to us this year. When I tried to find it again, I discovered this blog that spelled it all out: https://isaiah544.blogspot.com/2008/06/satans-five-deadly-ds.html

Kay Arthur talks of "Satan's Five Deadly D's," which are the weapons the enemy uses against us, taking us through the stages of our drifting away from what we know. Once we start that spiral, it's very easy for him to attack us. "Your adversary, the devil, prowls about like a roaring lion, seeking someone to devour" (1 Peter 5:8).

He hits us with these, one at a time, and once we hit these markers, we're primed for the next stage. The stages are Disappointment, Discouragement, Dejection, Despair, and Demoralization. It's important to use our tools and weapons early in that spiral, to keep from falling to the next level. The Apostle Paul tells us to take our thoughts captive (2 Corinthians 10:5), and "to fix our eyes on Jesus, the Author and Perfecter of faith, who for the joy set before Him endured the cross, despising the shame, and has sat down at the right hand of the throne of God. For consider Him who has endured such hostility by sinners against Himself, so that you will not grow weary and lose heart" (Hebrews 12:2).

But in case those arrows do get to us anyway, we're given the full armor of God, "so that you will be able to resist in the evil day, and having done everything, to stand firm." We are to wear righteousness, truth, and faith like protective shields, and peace like they're our shoes. We're to guard our heads with our precious gift of salvation and wield the Word of God as if it's a sword (Ephesians 6:13–17). When we're debating and trying to win arguments, we're often not using righteousness, truth, faith, or peace, and we're certainly not drawing people to God's Word or His salvation.

If we can intervene in our own lives and turn back from falling into the enemy's hands, then we can return to what we know and remember how to be kind, how to treat others as we want to be treated . . . We can remember that God warned us of these trials; we can hold on to the fact that this is not all there is; we can care about the condition of others' souls. We can see people not as opponents, but as dearly loved creations of God, who were important enough for Jesus to die for. We will stop trying to win arguments and start trying to win souls. We will stop fighting against our loved ones, our friends and acquaintances, and even people we don't know, and fight, instead, against the true enemies coming against us, enemies who are not made of flesh and blood.

I sincerely hope that by the time you read this, things will be smoother, but I'm guessing it may not be. But take heart, because God is in charge and more interested in building our character than He is in building our reputations. He's more interested in building His Church than he is in helping us to win battles that don't matter in the overall war. He has different plans for us than we have for ourselves, but He knows better than we do. We can trust Him, even when things get dark. Christ can see through that darkness, so let the Light of the World guide your steps, your heart, and your mouth. He won't guide you wrong.

Terri Blackstock

ACKNOWLEDGMENTS

I have wanted to be a writer since I was at least twelve years old, and somehow I've managed to do just that professionally for the last three and a half decades, twenty-eight years of which I've been married to Ken Blackstock.

As much as I love living on my imagination, it just wouldn't have been possible all these years without the support and empowerment from my husband, Ken.

Ken has kept me motivated through a years-long chronic pain condition, continuously reminding me that my writing isn't just a hobby. It's a purpose, and he will do whatever is necessary to help me fulfill it for as long as I want.

Thank you, Ken, for giving me wings, wind, and a tether that keep me from hurling myself into space. Thank you for being the unique and beloved man that you are, for always putting others first, and for being a wonderful father, grandfather, and my best friend. Thank you for hearing God when he nudged us together.

I literally couldn't do it without you.

DISCUSSION QUESTIONS

1. What impact did the events in Dustin's childhood have on who he became?
2. How did Dustin's friendship with Jamie as a child change his life?
3. The death of Jamie's husband changed her relationship with God. Have you ever had a time in your life when you felt disillusioned with God?
4. How did Jamie influence Dustin even when they weren't speaking?
5. Were there signs that all was not well in Dustin's friendship with Travis?
6. How did Dustin's reaction to the truth illuminate his character?
7. Taylor's spiral was fueled by grief, trauma, and mental

illness. Was there anything more her sister could have done to help her?

8. Discuss Travis's dilemma and the choices he made.
9. What was the theme of *Aftermath*?
10. How did God work in this story?

DON'T MISS TERRI'S *USA TODAY* BESTSELLING SERIES, IF I RUN!

"Boiling with secrets, nail-biting suspense, and exquisitely developed characters, [*If I Run*] is a story that grabs hold and never lets go."

—Colleen Coble, *USA TODAY* bestselling author of the Hope Beach and Lavender Tides series

Available in print, e-book, and audio!

One father was murdered.
Another was convicted of his death.
All because their children fell in love.

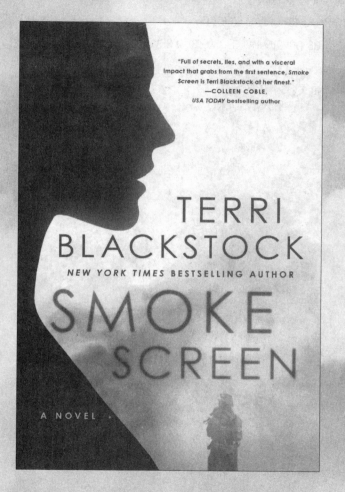

"Full of secrets, lies, and with a visceral
impact that grabs from the first sentence, *Smoke
Screen* is Terri Blackstock at her finest."
—COLLEEN COBLE,
USA TODAY bestselling author

TERRI
BLACKSTOCK
NEW YORK TIMES BESTSELLING AUTHOR
SMOKE
SCREEN

A NOVEL

Available in print, e-book, and audio!

THOMAS NELSON
Since 1798

ABOUT THE AUTHOR

Photo by Deryll Stegall

Terri Blackstock has sold over seven million books worldwide and is a *New York Times* and *USA TODAY* bestselling author. She is the award-winning author of *If I Run*, *If I'm Found*, and *If I Live*, as well as such series as Cape Refuge, Newpointe 911, Intervention, Moonlighters, the Sun Coast Chronicles, and the Restoration series.

terriblackstock.com
Facebook: @tblackstock
Twitter: @terriblackstock